They All Fall Down

Devon Walker

PublishAmerica
Baltimore

First printing

ISBN: 1-4137-0111-6
PUBLISHED BY PUBLISHAMERICA, LLLP
www.publishamerica.com
Baltimore

Printed in the United States of America

For my wife Lindsay who worked as hard on this book as I have, and for my children Eric, Jessica, and Mark.

This book would not be complete without acknowledging the hard work of Patrick Page who saw through the antics of a troubled youth and taught me to love reading and writing.

During the decline of Hitler's Third Reich when Nazi Germany was in its death throws and depleted of manpower, the Nazi leadership called on their youth in a desperate attempt to defend a dying empire.

This is their story.

Chapter 1

04th December, 1944, Memel Bridgehead, remnants of the 4th SS Motorized Battalion, 18th Army, Eastern Front

The bitter cold permeated every part of Keppler's being as he lay on the frozen ground. Beside him lay Georg who faded in and out of sleep despite the biting cold of the Russian front.

'I see you,' he thought to himself as he watched the dark shadows of Russian soldiers lining up in the charred tree line four hundred meters ahead of them. In times past, the Battalion artillery would have dispatched high explosive rounds into the trees and broken up the attack before it even started. Now they were limited to a salvo of twelve rounds during attacks since there was not enough ammunition for proper bombardments.

"They are determined little bastards, aren't they?" Georg mumbled with his eyes still closed.

Keppler looked over to his friend. He wondered when Georg had made his transformation from polished soldier to poor scarecrow. He was much older than Keppler remembered him. His beard was full of ice and his eyelashes were covered in small chunks of frozen breath. In the future when Keppler remembered Georg, he would not think of this aged, frostbitten waif dressed in rags beside him, but rather the youthful, roguish chum from his schooldays.

"They aren't the ones who are hard to fight; it's the cold I can't stand," Keppler mumbled as he rubbed his hands together through worn wool mitts.

"When they come today save the big ones for last so their bodies are closer to our lines. I need a new pair of boots." Georg shifted in the hole slightly and rubbed his booted feet together. "The ones I got last week are too small."

"I think I need to kill a Russian with better gloves." Keppler stopped rubbing his hands together and gripped his rifle. "Let me know if you see a good pair."

Keppler and Georg paused, the cold wind picking a few particles of snow up and depositing them in the shallow firing pit both of the men shared.

"Do you remember that kid from Leningrad who sang tenor?"

"Faintly, what made you think of him?" Georg asked.

"I was just thinking how much he griped about the cold and the way it was ruining his voice," Keppler chuckled.

"Didn't he ask for a transfer to Africa or something like that to preserve his precious singing voice?"

"Yeah but he didn't live long enough to get his rejection letter."

"That's right," Georg said as if remembering it for the first time. "Lucky little bastard."

"Lucky bastard," Keppler repeated.

Both men looked out at the Russian positions and their discussion fell into silence as exhaustion from the cold and endless fighting overwhelmed them.

Keppler lay close enough to Georg that he could feel some of his friend's precious body heat escaping through his worn overcoat. Keppler worked the bolt in his rifle making sure that it was not frozen in place.

"I was thinking," Georg mumbled in a more serious tone, "since death is our only way out of this frozen hell, why do you and I try so hard to stay alive?"

"I think you're a whiner," Keppler joked in response.

Georg looked at Keppler and a slow smile broke across his face. "You're damn right I'm a whiner," Georg said after a moment's pause. "It's the only freedom I have left and I'm going to exercise it to the utmost." Georg started to laugh his wheezy laugh that had earned him several nicknames in their Hitler Youth days. He looked over at Keppler who still had a serious look on his face and winked.

"You take things too seriously, my friend," and at that Keppler too started to chuckle.

Their chuckling was interrupted as a small rock bounced off Keppler's helmet. Both men in the firing hole turned around to see the small beady eyes of their Lieutenant peering above a shattered tree stump to their rear just before he ducked back down out of sight.

"Keppler, is that you making all that damn racket?" the Lieutenant hissed from his hiding place.

Keppler felt no need to answer him. The new officer had only been with their Kompanie for a couple of weeks and in a few more weeks he would be dead just like the rest of them. Keppler realized he did not even know the man's name.

"Keppler, I need you to come with me. You've been transferred to another unit," the Lieutenant continued, his voice carrying up and over the stump. Keppler looked at Georg with a confused look on his face.

"What?" was all Keppler could manage. The ridiculous statement could not be true. "There must be some mistake." Keppler mumbled to Georg who lay beside him silent.

"Hurry up Keppler, before I leave in your place. I don't want to be out here any longer than I need too." The Lieutenant raised his head up a little from behind the tree stump to see if Keppler was coming yet, and his eyebrows scrunched down over his eyes as he saw Keppler laying still and staring back at him.

"I'm not kidding Keppler! Captain Albrecht signed the transfer order himself. You're going to the Western Front. Now hurry the hell up so I can get back to my bunker!" The stern tone attempted by the Lieutenant could not hide the fear in his voice. He was afraid to be so close to the front, outside the protection of his command post.

"What do you think he's trying to get at?"

"I don't think he's joking Keppler, you better go see what's going on."

"I can't just leave you here," Keppler said to Georg. Keppler felt numb all over. "This must be some mistake."

"Then hurry before they realize their mistake," Georg said pushing Keppler on the chest to get him to move out of the hole.

"But we're in this together." Keppler argued, amazed that he was actually struggling to stay in the firing hole. If this was not a joke, it was his chance to get up and walk away from the Eastern Front and he now found himself unable to leave.

"I'd leave you in a second if it meant getting out of here." Georg gave Keppler a harder shove and shot him out of the hole, depositing him onto the frozen ground. Keppler's eyes locked with Georg for a brief moment and he could see the sorrow in his friend's eyes. "Go Johann! Get out of here!" Georg shifted in the firing hole and took up the vacancy where Keppler had been just a moment ago.

Keppler looked back at the pale Lieutenant, waving frantically for him to hurry up. He then looked to Georg who was looking at him again. His friend was smiling.

"I always knew one of us would make it out," Georg said.

"Here," Keppler pulled his last two grenades out of his belt where he had tucked them and handed them to Georg. Georg took the grenades and then grabbed Keppler's hand in his and squeezed it. As Georg pulled his hand away, he turned his back on his friend to face the Russian lines. Keppler wanted to say something, but for a lack of words kept silent as he crawled back towards the Lieutenant's position. Keppler felt like he was watching someone else move towards the rear.

He followed the Lieutenant as the officer scampered through the Kompanie defenses back towards the Captain Albrecht's bunker. The men of the Kompanie all stared at Keppler as he passed by their positions. He could tell by the looks on their faces that they had all heard the news. They looked at him with envy that bordered on homicide; a look that said 'If we can't go, then neither can you.' They were condemned men watching a fellow prisoner receive a pardon.

"I swear Keppler, if you hadn't hurried your ass out of that hole I would have gone in your place." The Lieutenant shook slightly as they entered the command bunker. Keppler had to duck down to enter the short, squat earthen shelter. The musty smell inside was suffocating and caused Keppler's breath to catch in his throat for a moment.

"Ah Keppler," the Captain rose to greet him, "always a pleasure to have you visit." Keppler saluted the Captain who returned the gesture. "Did you know that Keppler here has won the Knight's Cross with Oak Leaves, Swords, and Diamonds Lieutenant?"

"Yes Sir. You've mentioned it several times," the Lieutenant responded as he scurried to the pot-bellied stove in the corner of the bunker where he poured himself some tar-thick coffee.

"And damn well I should! Why the Fuhrer himself pinned it on him! Only twenty-seven people in the entire German army have that medal, and nine of them are dead!" The Captain could see his praise was having little effect on either Keppler or the Lieutenant. He held out the transfer papers to Keppler. "You have received a transfer Keppler and you are to leave immediately for Frankfurt. You have also been promoted to Sergeant, and there will be no ducking the promotion this time."

Keppler felt numb, it was as if he was watching someone else standing in the bunker facing his Captain.

"How can this be Sir?" he finally managed.

"You have some powerful friends."

"I don't have any friends, except for Georg."

"Then you have some powerful associates. Associates that don't want to see you die here in this ill-fated bridgehead."

"But I don't want to go." The Lieutenant dropped his cup of coffee and muttered a low curse.

"You have no choice in the matter. This is a direct order. There is an important military operation being planned for the Western Front and you are needed there to lead less combat experienced soldiers in battle. You will have two weeks to further train and get acquainted with your new truppen." The Captain slapped Keppler on the shoulder. "You are lucky Keppler. The Americans and their allies on the Western Front are not as ruthless as these barbaric Russians."

"Sir, I have a truppen here. Georg is my truppen." Keppler panicked. The thought of leaving this place scared him and he did not know why. All he had thought about each day on the front was how he would get out. Now, the opportunity presented itself and he wanted to stay.

"Georg doesn't need you to stay and hold his hand Keppler. The battle here is over and the Russians have all but won if we fail to seize this opportunity in the West. You are needed there Keppler. Here you are just meat for the grinder. This is no place for one of Germany's greatest heroes to die." The Captain crammed Keppler's transfer into his tunic and the argument was over.

"Get going Keppler! Time is running short. The supply trucks in the rear are waiting to go back to the beaches and you need to be on one of them or you'll never make the ship out of here. The bridgehead here at Memel is on its last legs. There are even rumors spreading that Army Group North has given up all attempts to relieve us and has written the bridgehead off." The Captain looked to the Lieutenant and nodded. The Lieutenant came forward, gently grabbing Keppler by the arm to lead him out of the bunker into the fresh cold air. In a trance, Keppler shuffled along to the supply depot where the Lieutenant deposited him into the back of one of the 3-ton trucks.

"Keppler, can you try to get this in the mail when you get back to Germany?" The Lieutenant handed him a small, crumpled letter, before he turned back down the road towards the command post. The truck lurched. As the driver gunned the 3.9 liter V8 engine, Keppler spilled onto the wooden floorboards of the truck's bed. It sped off towards the beach where the ships waited to take them back to Kiel and to Germany.

'Germany,' Keppler thought, 'how long has it been since I've been home?' He tried to remember his home. He had visited Hamburg in 1943, but it was a shadow of its former self. Allied bombing had ravaged the buildings and the people were not how he remembered them. It seemed like some foreign land, not the place of his birth.

Keppler was suddenly jolted out of his trance by the sound of Soviet artillery smashing into the defenses he had just left. The thumping of his former division's heavy 12cm mortars opened up, sending their 15.8kg rounds into a high arc over the battalion's position. The Russians had started their attack. He opened the flap on the back of the truck, but he could no longer see the Kompanie positions. All he could hear was distant gunfire.

'Goodbye Georg.' Fatigue overcame guilt as Keppler's eyes began to droop. The truck flap fell back into place and Keppler curled up to welcome his first sleep in three days.

Chapter 2

Captain Wilhelm Manser looked at the duty roster on his desk. He wondered about Keppler, the boy he had molded into a national hero. Keppler had been one of his finest students. Keppler's fame had resulted in free drinks from many of Manser's countrymen when they found out he used to be the legendary Johann Keppler's Hitler Youth leader.

Behind him on the wall, a large painting of Hitler stretched up to the ceiling. Manser always imagined the Fuher was actually looking down on him, and Manser knew that Hitler would be filled with pride at what he saw. One day Hitler would know the name Wilhelm Manser.

He only met the Fuher vicariously through the boys he trained to be soldiers. Keppler was not the only one of his pupils to shake Hitler's hand, although he was the most highly decorated. Now Keppler was returning home to him. Leaning forward Manser admired his own reflection in the polished oak of his desktop. The top of Manser's desk, like his boots, was polished to a mirror shine in which the cracks of his teeth were visible. The reflections showed an Arian face, a pure Arian face; he was pre-destined to greatness.

Manser was happy he had the power to deliver Keppler from certain death in the Memel bridgehead. It was one of the benefits of his newly appointed command in the 12th SS Panzer Division. He could request certain personalities and Colonel Faust was most pleased in Manser's request for Keppler. As the Colonel said, Keppler's death on the Eastern Front would benefit no one. Manser could not have agreed more. He needed someone like Keppler to catapult his own career to greatness.

Manser had assumed a command in the 12th SS Panzer Division only a few months ago. Many of the soldiers he commanded simply changed their uniforms from Hitler Youth to SS, and followed him over. He had won permission to keep all of his boys with him, even though some of them were 'alarmingly young' as Colonel Faust had put it. That was no matter to Manser. All he cared about was getting his due. He had been in command for over ten years, and he had not been properly recognized. His contributions in the training of men like Keppler needed to result in more that a free drink now and then. He must be decorated. He would know what to do with the distinction of an award, how to use it to further his political and social standing. Not like poor Keppler who had consistently turned down promotions and transfers to better assignments. The boy was a good soldier, but he was obviously a poor judge of opportunity. Keppler could have been a Colonel by now, possibly serving in the Wolf's Lair itself! Instead, Manser had to call in some favors to ensure Keppler would accept a promotion to Sergeant, and be forced into a transfer under his command.

'If you don't know how to make use of your success my friend, then I do.' Manser fingered the edge of Keppler's file. It was filled with nominations for medals and reports of heroism beyond the regular duties of a soldier. His medical records were there, showing the locations of each battle wound. It even held a top-secret sub-file on his father who was thought to be a communist sympathizer.

Manser threw the jacket onto the desk in front of him, poured a glass of scotch, and raised it to the manila folder containing the military history of one Johann Keppler.

"Here is to our future partnership." He drained the contents of the glass and slammed it down onto the mirror shine of his desk. Winning the Knights Cross for the actions of his unit would be just as rewarding as winning one himself. The doors were about to open for him and Manser could hardly contain his elation.

Chapter 3

Sergeant Keppler looked at himself in the cabin mirror of the transport ship. It was their fourth day at sea and they were supposed to be landing in Kiel within a few hours. Russian submarines and aircraft had hunted them relentlessly since their departure from the bridgehead two days ago. The ten ships in the convoy had been reduced to seven. Keppler could still see men, now little black dots, bobbing in the fiery water screaming for help as the rest of the convoy made best speed out of the area.

They could not stop to help the others or they too would become victims of the submarines. This was a type of warfare unfamiliar to Keppler; however the results seemed the same. They had been on alert since their departure, but Keppler had been too tired to care.

He had slept in a bed with sheets. He could not believe it. As he stared at a reflection that was shaven, hair cut, and dressed in a freshly pressed uniform, Keppler wondered at the stranger in the mirror. It had been several months since he had seen his own reflection. The faint recognition he felt for the ghostly image in front of him was haunting.

One of the crewmen had thrown his old uniform overboard after they departed the bridgehead. He had made a joke about getting rid of it before the lice thawed out. Keppler was happy to be able to take a bath and clean himself up. Keppler looked like he was ready to return to the human race.

The Knight's Cross hung just inside his collar with oak leaves, swords, and diamonds around its ribbon. Keppler looked at it with disdain. He felt no pride in it, even when The Fuhrer himself had pinned it on him.

'Humph,' he thought 'why do they put so much weight on such a small piece of tin?' The first time he was nominated for this award, Keppler had shrugged it off. He had seen most of his friends killed in a battle that was more like bitter street fighting. All he had done was survive the event. In the end, he had been credited with holding his position and saving lives in the

Kompanie. 'What lives?' Keppler thought irritated. The only other survivor of the battle had been Georg.

'Georg,' Keppler had tried not to think about his friend, but the weight of the name came crashing down into his consciousness, 'how could I just leave him there?' He could feel Georg's eyes staring at him. He realized that he was gripping the edge of the sink and staring into his own eyes. 'Is he dead?'

Keppler tried to push away the guilty feeling of being here in this moment: standing in a warm cabin, sleeping on a bed with sheets, wearing a new uniform free of lice and rips, having his haircut and his face shaven. Squeezing his eyes shut, Keppler tried to find something else to think about, but nothing offered to take the place of his friend's face.

The ship's claxon sounded and Keppler was ripped from his guilt-ridden meditation. Opening his eyes, he listened to the running feet out in the hallway beyond his door. The sailors rushed to their stations at the sound of the alarm.

Keppler's heart did not beat any harder at the sound of the alarm and the fear outside his door could not touch him. He was numb to it all. He turned back to the bunk and crawled into the sheets without taking his uniform off. 'If I die today, I'll die in bed,' as he rolled over and went back to sleep.

Chapter 4

06th December 1944, Nuremberg Germany

Corporal Hearn gathered up his gear and slung it over his shoulder. He turned to face his tearful mother as she stood in the entryway.

"Be careful my boy." She choked.

"Don't worry, Mom. They won't get me the way they got Father." Hearn regretted the words before they were out of his mouth. His mother's tears began to flow again. He crossed over to her and put his free arm around her shoulder. "Mom, please, I have to go. Don't be like this. I'm with all the other guys and they won't let anything happen to me."

"But you are all just boys Adler." She shook under his arm.

"No Mother, the enemy has made us into men by removing our fathers." He felt her stiffen under his arm as she resolved to stop crying.

"Come back to me Adler. I couldn't bear it if I knew you were never coming back." She leaned over and kissed him on the cheek.

"I'll be back Mom, and when I do come back the enemy will have been driven from our boarders and the Reich will have been saved." Hearn felt pride in his words. They were the same words he had heard from Captain Manser the night before at their Kompanie meeting.

Manser had given a brilliant speech to his new "men" and rightly so after he explained why.

"The heads of your homes have been removed by the plague of Capitalists and Bolsheviks that have come to ravage your homeland and your families. Germany now looks to you to deliver them from the murderers who stalk our boarders." Just thinking about the speech made the hair on the back of Adler's neck stand up on end. He was filled with pride to be wearing his new Wafen-SS uniform. He was ready to go and deliver Germany.

Adler knew his mother's views towards the war and the Third Reich, and hoped with all his heart that she would not voice them at this time. As a soldier, he could not ignore his responsibility to arrest those who were not fully supportive of the movement. He had heard his mother speak in the past, but if she were to speak those same words right now, he could no longer turn a blind eye. Hearn noted, thankfully, that she held her tongue and kissed him again, this time on the forehead.

"I love you son. Come back to me." She backed away from him, looking him up and down as if it was the last time she would see him.

"I love you too, Mom," he clicked his heels together and raised his right hand, "Heil Hitler!" Adler turned and left their house. It was really his aunt's house, but he had learned to call it his own after they moved here. Their home in Hannover had been bombed and destroyed in an air raid on the city. Having nowhere else to go, he and his mother took up residence with his aunt.

Hearn had been honored to stay in his cousin's room, who unfortunately had been killed at Stalingrad in 1942. His uncle had also met the same fate, both of them serving with the sixth army in Russia. Hearn had also felt a closer loss with the death of his father at the hands of American paratroopers during the invasion of Normandy. Now, Adler Hearn was determined to do his part and add his name to the honor roll of his family.

Adler Hearn walked to the sidewalk where Dieter waited for him. Dieter Bergin had become his best friend since moving there. He was one of the first ones to welcome Adler to the Hitler Youth when he transferred to the new city. Captain Manser was impressed with Adler's skills and abilities that he had honed in his previous Hitler Youth Kompanie. Manser had promoted him to the rank of Corporal within the first week after helping Bergin locate some runaway Jews. They had found them in the basement of a sympathizer's home. The arrests made the front of the paper, along with Bergin and Hearn's smiling faces.

Finally, he was going to help lead his truppen into combat- something he had been training for since the age of ten. Now at the age of fourteen, he was a man, and ready to serve his country. Captain Manser had given him a command and he intended to do his duty.

Dieter saluted Hearn as he approached, and Hearn returned his salute.

"Are the men ready?" he asked.

"Yes Corporal." Dieter answered.

Adler looked beyond Dieter Bergin to the truppen formed up on the street. They were all wearing their new pea style camouflage uniforms with the Wafen-SS insignia sewn proudly on each one of their collar boards.

"Form up Bergin," Hearn said lightly to his friend who ran over and came to attention beside the others. "We are marching over to the barracks where we are going to be outfitted with equipment from the storage lockers. Then we will be transferred by truck to Frankfurt." Adler looked at his men with pride. After four years of drilling and endless marching, Adler was determined to make a new name for this truppen. They would no longer be called 'asphalt soldiers', the name given to them because of their marching drills. Now they would have duties beyond marching, more akin to tracking down rogue Jews and sympathizers. They were going to become true German soldiers.

"Truppen, right face." In complete solidarity, Adler's truppen turned on their heels and faced right. "Truppen by the left, march." Their new hob-nailed boots tapped out in unison on the pavement as they marched towards the barracks to be outfitted with the rest of their equipment. Adler Hearn permitted himself a smile as he marched beside his men. Their day had finally come.

Chapter 5

Keppler stood by the docks waiting for his ride, which was an hour overdue. The Captain of the cargo ship was about a stones throw away from him and was engaged in a heated argument with a Wehrmacht officer. It seemed the Captain and his men were going to be drafted into the infantry, as there were not enough supplies to be transported to justify the current assignment of his crew. As a result, he was to turn command of his ship over to the port authorities and report with his men for infantry training and equipping later that day at Kiel's base. Keppler had a hard time keeping the smile off his face.

'What is it coming too when we have to draft our navy into the army? Things are indeed becoming desperate.' He noticed a man walking across the large concrete dock towards him. 'Could this be my ride?' The cold air coming off of the ocean was piercing, and the man walking towards him was hunkered down in a great coat.

"Are you Sergeant Keppler?" the man asked as he drew close enough for Keppler to hear him.

"Yes." Keppler reached inside his tunic, the warm air surrounding his hand for a brief moment as he pulled out his order of transfer from Captain Albrecht. The driver looked at it casually and gave it back to Keppler. Keppler once again invaded the warmth under his coat as he put it back.

"Sorry I'm late Sergeant, but the British and Canadians have been pushing hard into Amsterdam and General Blaskowitz has been gathering up men and equipment from all over the place to supply Army Group H," he stopped speaking and Keppler noticed the driver was staring at the Knight's Cross around his neck.

"Where have you parked?" Keppler snapped, pulling the driver from his trance.

"Well, that's the problem Sergeant. Some SS captain took my Kubelwagen and until I can get something else, we're both on foot."

"That's just great," Keppler said. "Well, you lead the way."

"Yes Sergeant!" The driver wheeled on his heel and headed off in the direction he had come. Keppler glanced over towards the ship's Captain as he followed the driver. The Captain was standing there alone now, watching the back of the Wehrmacht officer as he walked away. The fear on the Captain's face could not be hidden as he realized he had no choice but to report for infantry duty with his men. Keppler could not bring himself to feel sorry for the Captain. He could not bring himself to feel anything at all.

It took some time but the driver finally secured some transportation. They were now traveling down a snow-covered road towards Hamburg where Keppler could catch a train to his new assignment in Frankfurt. The ride was anything but warm, as the only transportation the driver could secure for them was a BMW R-75 motorcycle with a sidecar. Transportation was scarce, but they were able to acquire the motorcycle because no one wanted to drive it in this weather.

"I'm sorry about the sidecar Sergeant," the driver yelled through his frost-covered scarf, trying to compete with the wind and the thumping of the 746cc engine.

"It's quite alright," Keppler replied. Ice worked to keep his eyes shut as balls of frozen breath struggled to fuse his eyelashes together. The harsh wind in his scarf-covered face reminded him of the weather on the Russian front. They came up fast on a convoy of trucks headed for the docks and the driver almost put them in the ditch trying to maneuver around them. They slowed to a crawl through the snow trying to get past the trucks.

'This is going to be a long ride.' Keppler thought to himself watching the truck tires sliding around on the road. Suddenly without warning, bullets were raking into the trucks and Keppler's driver gunned the throttle on the motorbike causing the back end to slide side to side as he attempted to gain some speed. The back tire spun in the snow despite the chain wrapped around it and the back end began to creep over to the ditch, turning the bike sideways as it continued to crawl painfully up the road.

Keppler looked up into the frozen sky to see a British Spitfire coming out of its dive from which it had strafed the column.

"He'll be coming around for another pass!" The driver yelled, trying to regain control of the bike. It gained speed down the line of trucks towards the open road ahead and it looked like they were going to make it.

Without warning a driver from one of the trucks jumped out of his cab in front of them and the motorbike ran the panicked truck driver down, shooting the front tire into the air and spilling Keppler from his perch in the side car. When the back tire collided with the truck driver, it slammed the front of the motorbike into the frozen earth and sent the motorbike over onto its back. Keppler's driver was trapped under the bike, unconscious from the spill. The driver of the truck was back up and running with a pronounced limp away from the scene, panic painted across his face.

Keppler stood up and realizing that he was unharmed from the throw, ran over to the driver pinned under the motorbike. The convoy had stopped and the occupants of the trucks were now in a mass exodus and running towards the tree line, trying to get as far away as possible from the stalled column. The zipping sound of 20mm bullets came streaming into the trucks a second time as Keppler labored to move the bike off of the unconscious driver. The mob of drivers and supply men were almost all out of sight now, hunkering down in the tree line twenty meters away. One of the Spitfire's 20mm auto cannon rounds hit the mirror of the truck nearest Keppler, disintegrating it and sending a shard of metal into his cheek.

Keppler ignored the pain and the zipping sound of bullets whipping by him as he shoved with all his might against the 670kg bike. He moved it enough that the bike, carried by its own weight, slid further down the icy slope of the ditch. The clapping sound of the plane's auto cannon reached Keppler's ears, which caused him to relax a little. Hearing the sound meant that the Spitfire was now moving past him and was strafing further up the column. He pulled the driver up as the man began to come around. Keppler half dragged, half carried him into the tree line on the side of the road.

One of the men from the convoy reached down into the ditch to help Keppler get his half-conscious driver into the cover of the trees before the Spitfire came around for its third pass. On the third pass one of the trucks exploded as 20mm rounds punctured its gas tank. The heat from the explosion waved over Keppler as he finally found some cover behind one of the trees.

"That was the bravest thing I've ever seen," it was the driver who had helped Keppler pull the wounded man to safety.

"Well if that's the bravest thing you've ever seen, then you haven't kept the same company as I have." Keppler could not keep the bite out of his voice. He could not understand these men who scampered into the trees at the first sign of trouble, thinking of no one but themselves.

The convoy driver recognized the scorn in Keppler's voice and quickly retreated further into the woods. Keppler tended to his driver who had clearly shattered his leg. He was almost fully conscious now and was moaning in pain. Looking around, Keppler decided that it would be best if his driver stayed unconscious. When no one was watching, he balled up his fist and punched the driver in the side of the head, sending him back into the dark abyss he had been trying to crawl out of.

"Trust me, the head ache you'll have later on will be much better than coming too with your leg like this." He whispered into the driver's ear.

The Spitfire seemed satisfied with the pillar of smoke it had created in the column of trucks and did not come around for a fourth pass. A Captain quickly appeared out of the trees and began barking orders to the transport crews. They moved supplies from the damaged trucks to the undamaged trucks as fast as they could, and pushed the disabled vehicles into the ditch.

As they were moving goods, Keppler noticed a doctor shuffling out of the trees with some other stragglers. He called the doctor over to where he sat holding his injured driver. The doctor turned out to be General Blaskowitz's personal surgeon returning from leave in Berlin. He immobilized the driver's leg and helped Keppler carry him to one of the trucks that was ready to move out.

After loading the driver into the truck, the surgeon grabbed Keppler by the arm and pulled him in close.

"Let me have a look at that cheek of yours." He pulled out a clamp from his jacket and gripped the piece of metal fragment that had imbedded itself in Keppler's cheek. Keppler stood silent as the surgeon removed the object. The pain was not much, at least in comparison to what he had endured in the past. "Hmm, you're obviously used to pain. I hope you can stand getting a few stitches without anaesthetic as I have none to give you." Keppler simply nodded an affirmative to the doctor who then pulled a few stitches into the wound. Keppler winced a couple of times, but for the most part the cold air had numbed his cheek and he barely felt the needle. "There, that should do. You won't be entering any beauty competitions, but I'm sure where you're going there won't be any chances for such things," the doctor smiled at Keppler, patting him on the shoulder. At the sound of the Captain screaming for the doctor to hurry, he turned away and moved on down the line of trucks.

"Thanks Doc," Keppler said. The doctor raised his hand in a partial wave without turning to look back. Keppler moved over to the motorcycle, on its side immobilized like a turtle on its back. He got it upright, but could not start it. 'Great, I'm going to have to find another ride to Frankfurt.' The newly loaded trucks were already pulling out of the area heading back the way Keppler had come. They left the immobilized vehicles in the ditches for the falling snow to bury. Keppler started to walk towards Frankfurt, the falling snow already covering the tire tracks made by the convoy on the road.

An hour later Keppler was sitting in the passenger side of a supply truck headed for Frankfurt. The driver, a newly drafted Hitler Youth, had picked him up just past the site of the Spitfire attack. The carnage of the exploded truck's burnt-out shell and other disabled vehicles had spooked the boy. As a result, the driver was anything but cautious.

"Do you drive this way because you would be more comfortable dying in an accident on the road than being shot?" Keppler asked as he leaned back and pulled his cap down over his eyes. The driver shifted gears with a grind to slow down a little for a corner.

"No, I drive like this because I want to put as much distance between us and the attack site as possible. The Spitfire might come back you know." The driver's voice was shaking as he skidded into the turn and then straightened the truck out punching down hard on the accelerator.

"Well you can't outrun a Spitfire boy, and you sure as hell can't outrun death. When it's your time to go there won't be any speed or skills that will keep it from happening, so my advice to you is to relax. Besides, how the hell am I going to get any sleep with you skidding all over the road and grinding gears?"

Keppler heard the boy grunt at his words, but he also noticed that the youth slowed down and took the rest of the road with a little more caution. Keppler closed his eyes and fell asleep.

Chapter 6

10th December 1944, Frankfurt train yards

"Sergeant, wake up." Keppler woke up to the youth shaking him. He jumped up in the seat and reached for his Mauser 98k rifle. He stopped short of chambering a round and looking for a target when he remembered he was in the cab of the truck. "We've reached Frankfurt Sergeant, this is as far as I go." Keppler looked over at the Hitler Youth who rubbed his eyes and then opened his door.

"I see you got us here in one piece," Keppler said to the youth that was climbing down to the cobblestone courtyard where he parked the truck.

"I always deliver," the youth said sharply and slammed the door shut.

'Hmm, I guess they don't train them to have a sense of humor,' Keppler thought. It finally hit him; he was in Frankfurt. The knot in his stomach he had managed to ignore since his departure from the bridgehead returned. He relaxed the grip on his rifle and opened the truck door. Dropping to the ground and closing the door behind him, he began to take stock of his surroundings.

Men and equipment were being loaded onto train cars one hundred meters from where Keppler's ride had parked the truck. There were supply trucks all over the place and Hitler Youth were moving equipment and supplies to the train cars as fast as they could.

Keppler set out, surprised at how quiet Frankfurt had become. There were no lights. The blackout was in full effect, to give allied bombers as little to sight in on as possible. He needed no lights. He knew the way by heart and walked along well-known roads. Bombs had damaged some of the houses, but for the most part it looked hauntingly familiar.

Keppler reached the house he was looking for, but could see no signs of life inside. He checked his watch and realized it was late, almost one in the morning. Walking up to the wooden door, he held his breath and knocked.

Gabi had looked magnificent the last time he had seen her. She wore a red ribbon in her hair and a blue dress. He had been on medical leave after being

29

shot in the leg back in 1943. He spent a week with her before being shipped back. Gabi had given him an embroidered hanky that he had worn around his neck ever since. On the ship he tried to get it as clean as possible, but it only washed out to a dark gray rather than its original white.

She looked so elegant the day he left. He remembered the moment clearly, having played it over and over in his mind. A few of her blond hairs escaped from her bun at the back of her perfect head. The golden threads waved up and down across her cheek in a gentle breeze. Her deep blue eyes had filled with tears as she kissed him goodbye.

He knocked again on the door and waited, fearing for a moment that they might have moved. The door to the house opened a crack and a familiar voice asked who was calling. Gabi's mother was peering out into the darkness at the black form on her step.

"Mrs. Felis, it's me, Johann Keppler." The door opened a little wider as she looked him up and down.

"Johann, is it really you?" her voice, barely audible, trembled as she reached out to touch him.

"Yes, it's me." She ran her fingers over his face, and then grabbed his collar pulling him closer to see his face in the darkness. Her eyes grew big as she released his collar.

"It is you!" she blurted out. Just then, a familiar figure came into the doorway behind the older lady. Keppler looked up and saw Gabi.

"Johann?" Her soft voice pierced Keppler to the very center.

"Gabi." He held his breath.

"We were told you had been killed." Gabi pushed out of the door past her mother and embraced Keppler. He was stunned.

'Dead?' He thought. 'How could the army report me dead, especially after I just received a transfer?' The smooth, soft body of Gabi pressing against him caused his mind to whirl. He embraced her, smelling a familiar odor of perfume faintly on her neck that awoke his senses.

"I'm certainly not dead."

"Oh Johann, I thought I would never see you again." She kissed him on the mouth and he could taste the salty tears running down her cheeks. He kissed her back and felt a hunger for her rising up from his stomach.

"Well," he said breaking away for a moment, "there has obviously been some mistake." He kissed her again and Mrs. Felis, now recovered from her initial shock, herded the two of them inside.

Mrs. Felis got the door closed and lit a candle. In the dim light both Mrs.

Felis and Gabi stood back to get a good look at Keppler.

"Johann Keppler, don't they feed you in the army? You're as skinny as a rail!" Gabi's mother complained.

Mrs. Felis moved over to the cupboard and opened it. Keppler noticed it was empty except for a block of cheese covered in cheesecloth. She pulled it down and took a knife out of the drawer to cut off a piece.

"Oh no, Mrs. Felis, I don't need any cheese," Keppler lied. It looked great and he did want some, but he knew it was harder for civilians to get food than soldiers. He pulled a sack out of his pack and gave it to Mrs. Felis. "I brought this from the mess hall in Kiel. I thought you might be able to use it." She pulled the cloth back to reveal a smoked ham.

"Oh Johann, what a treasure!" Gabi clapped her hands and kissed him again, just happy to have him in the house with her- back from the dead. "What happened to your cheek?" Gabi asked, pointing to his fresh stitches.

"Oh, it was just a small accident I had on the way here, nothing much," he said drawing his lips back into a smile.

Mrs. Felis took the knife and cut a slice of the meat for each of them and then a slice of cheese. As Keppler held up his hand in protest, Mrs. Felis crammed the slice of cheese and meat into it, "Don't try to argue with me my boy, just hush and eat."

The trio stayed up most of the night after Keppler informed them he would have to leave in the morning.

"Tell us the truth Johann, how are things going, really? The war, I mean." Mrs. Felis asked Keppler. He paused for a moment and then asked,

"What have you heard?"

"They tell us that our boys are holding the Russians and in some places they are actually pushing them back. What wonderful news!" Mrs. Felis exclaimed. Gabi held Keppler's hand and looked back at him, waiting for him to support the reports they received.

"They lie," Keppler shook his head with disgust. Gabi jerked slightly as his body tensed. "We are losing ground almost every day. In some places the lines are so thin that the only reason the Russians haven't pushed through is because they have currently outrun their supply lines." Mrs. Felis went pale. He did not need to look at Gabi to know her reaction. He could feel her grip tighten around his hand.

"You mean we're losing the war?" Gabi asked.

"Yes." Keppler could not break it to them any easier. It was the simple truth. "I think we will be forced to surrender within the next six months."

"But the Fuhrer will never surrender," Mrs. Felis' eyes stared blankly at the wall behind him.

"He is a fool." Keppler could not believe he said it out loud, but had no desire to take it back.

"Johann, you must not say such things!" Gabi said, looking around the room as if someone might hear their conversation.

"I am only telling the truth. Of course the truth will get you killed if you say it in the wrong company," he looked at Gabi, who also sported a pale face.

"I never imagined I would hear you say anything like that. You used to be such an ardent supporter of the Party and their cause."

"I was a fool as well. I believed all they told me, but I have seen things you two would not believe." He looked down at his boots, willing himself to be quiet as he had already upset them and said too much.

"What have you seen?" Mrs. Felis leaned in close when she asked the question.

Keppler looked up from his boots and met her eye before he answered.

"Horror," he paused there hoping the word would be enough, but she did not back down. Mrs. Felis pressed to know more. She was like a priest who got paid a commission for confession. Keppler did not know why but he finally broke and started to tell her, "I've butchered innocent people." Keppler almost choked on his words he could not believe he was telling the truth. "We made war on innocent civilians as much as we did against soldiers." Shame waved over him. He felt as if he were at the judgement bar of God having to confess his crimes against humanity.

"I see," Mrs. Felis said, pulling back a little from Keppler.

"We don't deserve to win the war," Keppler said, echoing the same phrase Georg had said many times.

"Johann Keppler!" Gabi said, gripping his hand harder, "you must not say these things!"

"We're going to lose the war." Mrs. Felis turned to face Gabi.

"Mother, don't say that!" Tears sprang from Gabi's eyes.

"Gabi is right, Mrs. Felis. Don't be caught saying that no matter how true it might be. The truth will get you killed." Keppler had regained control of himself and his tongue. He waited for Gabi to regain some composure before he continued, "The Russians are coming and we will not be able to stop them. You both need to be prepared for that. With a little luck, you will be overrun by the Americans or the British before the Russians get here." Keppler took a small silk black pouch out of his tunic and passed it to Gabi. "I want you and your mother to keep this."

Gabi opened the sack and held it upside down above her open palm. Keppler's original Knight's Cross with Oak Leaves, Swords, and Diamonds fell onto her hand.

"But this is your medal Johann, you earned it! The Fuhrer himself pinned this on you! I can't accept this." Gabi tried to give it back.

"No Gabi!" Keppler pushed her hand back towards her and folded her fingers over the medal. "I want you to keep it. Those are real diamonds in the pin, 2.7 carats worth. You and your mother will need all the bartering tools you can find. I'm sure that thing can fetch something of value for you. When things get worse, and believe me they will, you will need it." Keppler was staring hard into Gabi's eyes trying to make her understand. "The copy they make us wear in combat is good enough for me." He motioned to the medal hanging around his neck. Gabi folded the precious medal back into the silk sack and tucked it away in her dress. They all sat in silence for a long time.

Keppler noticed that the room was getting lighter as the sun was coming up outside and sprinkling light through the tattered blinds that covered the windows.

Mrs. Felis glanced at Keppler and Gabi holding hands and faked a yawn, "Well, sorry to retire on the two of you, but an old lady has to get her sleep." She rose up and kissed Keppler on the forehead, "Come back soon to us Johann, my Gabi needs you." Without another word she walked up the stairs to her room and the kitchen fell silent.

Gabi reached across the short distance between them and grabbed his other hand, holding them both in hers. He looked up into her deep blue eyes and he could see a pain that he had long become numb to. Her touch and her smile were perfect and her voice was just as he remembered it, but he had left a part of himself behind in Russia, a casualty of war. He did not know what it was that he had lost there, but he could feel it missing regardless.

Gabi stood up and pulled Keppler to his feet. She kissed him gently on his lips and turned to walk to the back of the house where Keppler knew her room was. He followed along behind as she pulled on his arm. He was sexually excited, knowing what was to come, but also troubled. He loved her so dearly, but he was not the man she had fallen in love with. He was a shell of what he use to be, unable to feel anything for the human condition.

Once in the back Gabi dropped her housedress. He gazed at her as if she were a foreign land. The smooth white beauty of her skin was still molded in the perfect way, just as he remembered in his dreams. Her eyes beckoned him forward to hold her in this last hour together. Keppler felt himself pulled forward and they pressed together. For a brief moment, the pain of the Russian front was lifted from his soul and Johann Keppler felt alive once more.

*****

Keppler finished dressing by pulling on his boots and watched Gabi as she lay face down on the bed. She was asleep, tired out from the excitement of the long night. He leaned over and kissed her lightly on the cheek. He thought of waking her to say goodbye but he wanted to stay a little while longer in her dreams, and live there vicariously. He let his hand run lightly down her back and grabbed the covers pulling them up around her so she would stay warm in the chilly house.

"I love you Gabi," he whispered it softly into her ear, and he knew he meant it. Keppler had worried about this moment, unsure if he was still capable of loving anything or anyone. Gabi had helped him remember how. Unwillingly, Keppler walked quietly out of the room and closed the door.

Once he was outside the house and walking to the train station, the feelings resurrected by Gabi slowly fell away like the last few leaves of a tree in an autumn breeze. Leaving Gabi and coming back into the reality of war was allowing the numbness to return. He was losing the capacity for love and tenderness once again, as they crawled back into their hiding place- only a memory. Those feelings had no place where he was headed.

Keppler stopped by the cemetery where his parents had been buried. He brushed the snow off of the top of their headstone and stared at the engraved names in silence. Death was familiar to him; it was living he had a hard time dealing with. Glancing over to his brother's grave, next to his parents, Keppler tried to remember what his brother looked like. It had been a long time since he had seen him, and the memory would not come. Keppler turned away and exited the cemetery. He was only a few blocks away from the train station. He listened to his hob-nailed boots tapping on the frozen asphalt and realized how solitary a single pair of boots sounded on the street.

Chapter 7

10th December 1944, Frankfurt train yards

The station was packed with soldiers. Most of them were in complete Kompanie formations, all in new uniforms with new equipment. Keppler looked at their patches and saw that they were part of the 62nd Volksgrenadier Division.

'Hmm, I've never heard of that division before.' Keppler noticed, as he got closer to them that the majority of them were speaking Polish. 'Pollacks in German uniforms? Having to draft the naval personnel into the army is bad enough, but recruiting Pollacks to fight for us? Desperation is all running rampant.'

Keppler felt a loss for his German heritage. His hand reached down to the Hitler Youth knife he had strapped to his belt and started to hum one of the old songs. He sang quietly as he walked to the boarding platform, but the song faded before he got there. He hated the words. He hated the music. He hated the lies.

'What have we become?' Keppler had no time to think any more on the matter as the train was being loaded and he had to push forward to get into the car. 'Like cattle,' he thought. Suddenly the memory hit him like a concussion grenade. It always came without warning, but usually he could push it away. Today he was not so lucky. Keppler dropped into the seat of the passenger car trying to clear his mind, but this time the harder he resisted, the faster it flooded into his consciousness. The interior of the car melted away and he found himself standing at a train station far away on the Russian steep.

It was always the same image, as he watched the scene unfold while helplessly standing still. One cannot change the past. Children and women were crowded together, pushing up against him. He fought with the other SS soldiers to contain the crowd. They held their rifles out in front of them like a makeshift fence. Their battalion commander had gathered the civilians at the station by forced march to send them back to Germany. Keppler's eyes fixed on a young boy of about seven who stood in the midst of the screaming and crying women and children. Unlike the others the boy did not cry or resist, he stood completely still. The boy's eyes were already locked on Keppler when he noticed him. They seemed to burn into his soul. Keppler tried to look away, but the memory would not allow him to. He was paralyzed, just as he had been at that moment. He had to watch. His eyes remained fixed with the boy's.

One of the officers in charge waded into the crowd and hollered for order and discipline. The women did not stop their attempts for freedom. He pulled the small boy off of his tiny feet and drew a lugar from his leather holster. A scream caught in Keppler's throat. His fingers ached for his weapon to shoot the officer before he could finish the act. Of course he could not. This is the way it had to play out, consistent with the true events. The boy continued to stare at Keppler despite the cold barrel of the lugar being pressed to his temple.

There was no sound in Keppler's memories as the pistol discharged its bullet. Silence reined all over the platform as the tiny form hung limp in the officer's arm. The boy slowly dropped to the platform below. The sound of the child's body hitting the wooden slats of the platform, however, was thunderous.

"Can I sit here?" Keppler jolted in his seat, pulled mercifully from the memory, and looked up at the Pollack standing above him.

"What?" Keppler asked, feeling the sweat running down the side of his face.

"May I have this seat beside you, Sergeant?" The man's German was very broken, but Keppler understood.

"Sit where ever you like." Keppler, annoyed, waved beside him and the Pollack dropped down into the seat. He had no real hatred for the Polish people, at least not that he knew of. The invasion of their country was quick and decisive, and as Keppler remembered it, he did not loose any of his friends to the Polish. Why did he feel such anger at this Pollack's presence beside him?

Keppler leaned against the window and hoped that the exhaustion from the night's activities would cause him to fall asleep. Unfortunately, sleep did not come. He watched out the window as the 62nd Volksgrenadier soldiers loaded their supplies into the baggage car linked in front of them.

'What right do they have to wear that uniform?' Suddenly it dawned on him. 'I don't want to share the field of battle with these men. Who are they compared to Georg and the others? What do they care about the Fatherland?' He thought of Gabi and her mother entrusting Germany to these men, these foreigners and it made him furious. He turned from the window with a jerk, and stared at the Pollack beside him. Georg was lying in a frozen hole wearing Russian rags and this man, not even a German, sits here in a warm train car wearing a new uniform! The man turned to see what the commotion was and froze. Keppler glared at him, wishing he had met him on the battlefield as an enemy rather than on the train as a comrade in arms. His muscles were tingling and his hair stood up on the back of his neck with the effort to remain motionless. He played his desire out in his mind, grabbing the Pollack by the hair, exposing his throat, and stabbing him in the jugular with his knife.

The Pollack saw a struggle in Keppler's eyes and the smile on his face faded to fear. He felt danger emanating from Keppler and chose, with sound judgement, to leave immediately. He gathered up his gear in one fluid movement and stood up as if shot to his feet. He joined the slowly shuffling crowd moving down the aisle of the train towards the other end of the car where some of the seats were still empty.

Keppler lowered his eyes to look at the new boots he had received on the ship. Shame consumed him as he imagined Georg shuffling along in appropriated enemy boots too small for his feet.

'Why is there so much equipment available for these men, and for me, but Georg and the others must rob the dead for clothes and boots just to stay alive?' His anger slowly melted. It was not the Polish that blistered this hostility. It was the situation the leaders of this land had created. That was the tragedy of it all. Soldiers on the front, like George, had been abandoned and Germany now looked to its former enemies for deliverance. The Reich could no longer do it alone, and they had turned their backs on their own people to win the war. Keppler cursed the name of Hitler under his breath and wondered what he would do if he ever met the man again. He had turned the country over to those who could not hope to defend it.

Despite the crowded train, the seat beside Keppler remained empty. It seemed that word had spread to the others riding in the car the empty space carried too high a price. Keppler stared out the window at the snow-covered countryside for the rest of the trip to Frankfurt.

Chapter 8

10th December 1944, Frankfurt staging area for the 12th SS Panzer Division

Hearn walked down the length of his troops, looking each one over. He wanted to make sure the truppen was in top form before being inspected by their new truppen leader. Their new sergeant was rumored to be a veteran from the Russian front. More than this though, was the rumor that he had won the Knight's Cross with Oak Leaves, Crossed Swords, and Diamonds. Hitler himself is the only one that can make the presentation of such an award. To these boys, this incoming Sergeant was a god to them.

Hearn collected all postcards made by the German postal service to commemorate the few recipients of this award. He was sure he would recognize his face if the man were one of the recipients. Hearn had only dreamed of having such a leader and was thrilled over receiving such an experienced superior. His men would benefit greatly from this man. They would triumph in battle.

"Bergin, tighten up that strap on your webbing! It looks sloppy." Dieter Bergin did as Hearn commanded, tightening the strap on his leather webbing a notch. "That's much better." He moved on down the line, as he had been doing for the last twenty minutes, pacing back and forth to make sure that everyone was ready for the reception of the Sergeant.

A sergeant appeared briefly in the doorway and Hearn thought for a moment that it may be the man they were waiting for. The face even looked familiar, perhaps from one of his collected postcards. He called his truppen to attention and awaited inspection. However, after a quick glance into the room, the sergeant left the doorway and continued down the hallway of the barracks.

Disappointed, Hearn waited a moment and was about to tell his truppen to relax when the sergeant returned and entered the room.

"Truppen attention!" Hearn barked out and the truppen, already at attention, tried to straighten even more. Hearn felt his heart in his throat. 'It's him!'

Hearn thought, recognizing the face from one of his postcards.

"Do you know where I can find the third truppen?" The sergeant was looking at Hearn, waiting for an answer.

"Third truppen reporting for duty Sergeant!" Hearn clicked his heels together and stiffened himself to the point that he thought he might actually snap in half.

The sergeant looked puzzled as he came further into the room, looking intently at Hearn's men.

"You are the third truppen of the 18th motorized Kompanie, 6th battalion, 12th Panzer Division?" The sergeant looked like a horse had kicked him in the stomach when he asked the question. He walked up to Hearn's formation of immaculately dressed men and looked at the shoulder patch on Dieter's arm.

Adler Hearn had a moment of panic. Maybe Dieter had a thread loose or something was wrong with the patch. The sergeant seemed unimpressed. He walked around the stiff group, looking them up and down as they stood at attention. 'What more could I have done?' Hearn despaired. There before Hearn stood a true hero of the Reich. He ached to think that he had made a bad first impression.

Chapter 9

Keppler stepped off the train and found a driver waiting for him at the station office.

"I've been waiting for you Sergeant. All of the other non-commissioned officers have arrived and are already training their men.

"I had a long way to come, and the transportation around here is unreliable to say the least." Keppler was annoyed at the driver and the war.

"Is it true Sergeant that you won the Knights Cross with Oak Leaves, Swords, and Diamonds?" The man asked looking at the award hanging inside the neckline of his tunic. Keppler ignored the man's question, tired of his company already.

"Where did you park?" Keppler did not try to hide the disdain from his voice.

"Over here, Sergeant." The driver led Keppler over to a Kubelwagen and jumped into the driver's seat. "I have orders to take you straight to your truppen when you arrive."

"Fine," Keppler said as he dropped into the seat. The driver gunned the engine and they shot off into the crowded streets of Frankfurt.

It did not take them very long to get to the barracks. The streets were full of armored vehicles from the 12th Panzer division. Keppler marveled at seeing so many Tiger and Tiger II tanks, intact and operable, in one place. He even saw a couple of Panther G's, which were a rare sight, as were all non-Russian tanks on the Eastern Front.

"Where did all of this equipment come from?" he asked the driver as they pulled up to the front of a long barracks building marked "F". Keppler felt anger looking at all the equipment wondering why none of it made its way to the East.

"We're preparing for an attack. The Fuhrer is going to push the Capitalists back into the sea." Keppler quickly tuned the driver out; realizing all he would hear from him was official Nazi party propaganda. He grabbed his gear out of the back seat and got out of the Kubelwagen as the driver droned on and on about the glory of the Reich and the power about to be unleashed on the American and British armies that were fragmented and divided.

Ignoring the driver, Keppler entered the barracks alone. Inside, he walked down a hallway and paused to look into one of the rooms. He found a group of Hitler Youth in the room but dismissed them, assuming they were some of the bases' auxiliary staff used for cooking, driving, and guard duties. He moved on down the hall but became confused when he found no one else in the building.

'Where could the damn truppen be?' He thought as he walked back down the hall to the youth he had seen. 'Maybe they can tell me where my men are.'

Keppler entered the room and the oldest one, who wore the rank of corporal, called them to attention.

"Do you know where I can find the third truppen?" he asked the corporal.

"Third truppen reporting for duty Sergeant!" The boy clicked his heels together smartly and came to attention. Keppler could not believe his eyes.

'This must be some kind of joke.' He walked closer to the group. Then he noticed they were not wearing the uniforms of Hitler Youth but the combat fatigues of the 12th Panzer Division. "You're the third truppen of the 18th motorized Kompanie, 6th battalion, 12th Panzer Division?" His question was more a thought out loud than anything requiring an answer. He walked over to the first boy in line and looked at the patches on his arm. The patch was indeed the 12th Panzer Division.

'What kind of truppen is this?' Keppler was starting to get the picture now. He could see the need for experienced leadership and the haste with which he was shipped here to take command of a truppen. 'I expected a truppen of naval men, not children.' He was speechless as he walked down the length of boys standing at attention. What could he say to them? Go home to your mothers? The oldest of them could not be more than fourteen years of age!

He came to a halt in front of one of the younger ones. "What is your name?"

"Mapes, Sergeant."

"How old are you?" The boy looked offended at the question, but snapped out a response with perfect discipline.

"Twelve years old, Sergeant."

"What is your name?" Keppler asked, side-stepping to the next youth in line.

"Lubbert, Sergeant."

"Your age?"

"Ten, Sergeant."

Keppler felt sick to his stomach.

'The High Command could not be serious about this. Could they?'

"Ah Sergeant, I see you have found your men. What do you think? They do the Reich proud, don't you agree?" Keppler recognized the voice immediately. His stomach twisted into tighter knots.

He turned to see a ghost from his past. Captain Manser stood in the doorway, looking slightly more worn than the last day Keppler had seen him five years ago. Keppler had been taken under his wing at the tender age of ten and raised for six years under his tutelage to the heights of Hitler Youth leadership. Now five years later they were together again, Keppler a highly decorated sergeant, and Manser, a newly appointed Captain to the 12th division.

"Come Sergeant, I have some things to show you before you begin the training of these soldiers for combat duties." Manser wheeled on his right heel and strode out of sight towards the front of the barracks. Keppler walked towards the open door to follow the Captain. Keppler's legs felt like rubber.

'They're just kids,' he thought. "At ease Corporal, as you were," he managed before he left the room.

Outside Keppler took a deep breath and tried to clear his head. There was a time Keppler had thought Manser was a great man, but the Eastern Front had changed all that. Keppler had found out for himself that the German people were not invincible and certainly not supermen. He had seen Manser's teachings put into practice on the Eastern Front and become witness to atrocities he could have never imagined.

Manser had talked Keppler's entire group into joining up together for service. Because he had believed Manser, Keppler found himself at the advanced school for combat leadership wearing an SS uniform on his seventeenth birthday. It had been five years since that time and Keppler now found himself a non-believer in the Nazi ideology. It had taken a lot of innocent blood to wash the ideas from his head, and the price had cost him his soul.

"Well Keppler, you've certainly become a great soldier," Manser turned to look at Keppler, "I'd like to think I had something to do with that." Manser turned back before Keppler could respond and continued across the compound to a smaller building marked "G".

Keppler could not think of anything to say to his childhood mentor.

'Do I still fear him?' Keppler followed Manser to the barracks. As a youth, Keppler fought hard to keep from being a disappointment to Manser. Keppler had excelled in all his studies under Manser and later went on to graduate top of his class from battle school.

Manser pushed the door to the barracks inward and stepped aside so Keppler could enter first. Keppler allowed himself to be herded into the room and listened to the door as it shut behind them.

"You have risen to the top again, Keppler. No one could ever keep you down." Manser's praise in the past would have caused Keppler to puff out his chest with pride, but three years of Eastern front experiences had washed away any concern for Manser's opinion.

"I see you still carry your Hitler Youth knife, the one I gave you." Manser had crossed over to a small map on the wall. "And the Knight's Cross looks good on you, especially with the Oak Leaves, Swords, and Diamonds on it. Naturally I was impressed when I saw a picture of my greatest protégé on the front page of the paper with the Fuhrer pinning the cross on you. I even bought one of the post cards featuring your face."

Glancing at Keppler, Manser waited for his former pupil to attribute some of the award to him, but Keppler's face remained stone. "You and me Keppler, just like old days." Manser smiled, ignorant of the sergeant's coolness, and shoved his finger into the map on the wall. "Take your men on a hike to this location and begin their training. You will only have one week to make them ready for combat duties. They are good men, as you will see. I have trained them myself. All they need is a little guidance from you and they will be ready for anything." Manser crowed.

Keppler felt rage boil up inside him, but he knew he had to keep it in check. Any outburst towards Manser would be fatal.

"Yes Sir!" He even managed to click his heels together, as in the old days. Manser looked like he was going to burst with pride.

"Good Keppler, I knew I could count on you! Who do you think got you transferred here in the first place?" Manser was very pleased with himself and his attempt to bring Keppler further under his thumb with gratitude. Manser was a master manipulator, and now Keppler could see him for what he was.

"I won't keep you any longer. You can get to know your men without my interference." With that, Manser exited the room and Keppler was left staring at the map.

He felt dizzy. Keppler was not used to so many emotions. On the Eastern Front emotions were predictable: fear, anger, and anguish. Of course all of these emotions became blended over time and created a familiar, constant numbness. However, at present there were so many things to deal with. Here, his enemies did not come after him with guns, but instead with smiles and handshakes. This was a war Keppler did not know how to fight.

He left "G" building and crossed back over to "F" barracks. Inside, the Hitler Youth came to attention as he entered the room, stiff as boards and waiting for their orders.

"Corporal, get your truppen geared up and ready to hike in ten minutes. Meet me back here, and bring your map and compass." The young corporal looked disappointed at the order, but was quick in hiding it. He turned on his heel and barked out orders to the others to get their gear and meet back in full attire. The group of boys ran out the door and down the hallway to carry out their orders. For the moment, Keppler was alone and wished it could stay that way.

The truppen was back and fully geared faster than Keppler had hoped they would be. He tried to focus on the task at hand. He could not afford to let emotion carry him away.

"Corporal, move them out. We're to hike up to the top of hill 454. I want to examine you with the…" Keppler caught himself and bit off the word 'boys' before he said, "men." He hated himself for saying it.

Corporal Hearn moved the truppen out of the building and across the asphalt parade square that had been carefully cleared of snow to the side gate of the compound. Soon they were moving up a gentle snow covered slope. Keppler was glad he had told the Corporal to move the truppen out. He was not sure he would have remembered all of the drill commands, as he had not been on parade for a very long time. In contrast, the youth marched impeccably. They were model marching soldiers.

Hearn broke out into song "Let the flags fly in the glorious sunrise that guides us to new victories or into flaming death…" Keppler cut him off before the rest of the truppen could fully join in with him.

"Corporal," he snapped, "You will maintain silence as we march!" Keppler could not believe how harsh he had been and called the truppen to a halt. He tried to soften his tone to make up for his outburst. "This is not a parade we are training for. This is not a game. This is not going to make you famous and immortal." The youth were listening to him, intent on gaining some deep insight from this war hero as they saw him. "This is…" Keppler paused to find the right word, "real."

The truppen looked confused.

"I want you to break formation and spread out. Space out, four meters between each of you. You will maintain absolute silence." The truppen moved and spread out. "You, what's your name?" Keppler pointed to one of the boys.

He snapped to attention and clicked his heels together as he answered, "Wagner, Hyronimus Wagner, Sergeant!" Keppler bowed his head trying to keep his composure.

"How old are you?" Keppler could not help but ask.

"I just turned thirteen Sergeant," the boy thrust out his small chest.

"Private Wagner, this is the field. Don't any of you ever snap to attention when out here. You'll get your officers killed doing that. There are no parade squares where you are going." Keppler could see that the comment crushed the boy, but he did not care. If they wanted to live through the coming weeks, they would have to learn. "Wagner, take point. You will walk up front of the truppen and maintain a distance of at least ten meters." Wagner visibly resisted the urge to snap too and nodded his affirmative running off to take the point of the truppen.

As they moved through the snow, Keppler sidled up to one of the boys in the troop and pulled him aside. "Mapes," Keppler remembered his name from the barracks, "when you step in the snow, do it with your toe pointed down so it breaks as little of the surface as possible." He showed the youth what he meant by performing the maneuver for him first. "See how little noise it makes when you walk this way?" Mapes nodded his head and tried it for himself with success. Keppler moved on and took the time to show each truppen member how to walk in snow without making it crunch underfoot. The boys were learning a skill that had cost many lives to develop on the Russian front.

After they walked through the snow for about an hour, Keppler stopped the truppen and called them over. Examining their faces he could see the determination they had to do their duty. These boys exhibited the same ideological propaganda that he believed when he first entered the SS. He could see it oozing out of their eyes and if given the chance it would spew out of their mouths. These kids were fed bowls full of lies and they ate it up in their innocence.

"Are you all prepared to die?" Keppler asked, knowing the answer before it came.

"Yes Sergeant!" they all bellowed at once. In their youthful chorus, Keppler could hear the faint echo of his friends answering Manser who had asked that very same question of them over and over many years ago.

"You," Keppler pointed to the smallest boy "what's your name again?"

"Lubbert, Sergeant," he had to push his helmet up on his head higher so he could look at Keppler fully from under the massive brim around him eyes.

"Lubbert," Keppler paused to add emphasis to his question, "what is death?"

"It is the highest honor I can give the Fuhrer and the Third Reich!" The answer was a carbon copy of the words Keppler also had memorized long ago.

"And if you die who does your death benefit?" Lubbert paused at Keppler's question trying to think of a correct answer, for it was a question he had never considered before.

"My country?"

"Who thinks Lubbert's death would benefit Germany?" A few of the truppen raised their hands, but none of them said anything unsure of the exact answer. "If Lubbert's death would benefit Germany then why don't we just kill him right here and now?" Keppler chambered a round in his Mauser 98k with amazing speed and brought the barrel up and level with Lubbert's face. There were gasps from some of the youth and Lubbert's eyes grew wide, but his ingrained discipline would not let him move away from the end of the barrel. Silence gripped them all as Keppler stayed poised to shoot Lubbert, waiting for an answer.

"It would be a waste."

Keppler turned to see who had made the statement. It was Wagner. Keppler smiled and dropped the barrel of his rifle down towards the ground.

'Maybe' Keppler thought, 'there is some flicker of humanity Manser did not manage to root out of these boys.'

"That's right Wagner. It would be a waste." He looked around at the truppen to make sure he had their complete attention. "If any of you die, it is a waste, not an honor." He could see some of them physically pull back and then look around to see if anyone else heard the sacrilegious words. He spoke the unspeakable but no one dared to challenge his authority. After all this was Johann Keppler, a household name throughout Germany, known for his bravery and service to the Reich. "No one secures a victory by getting killed." Keppler lowered his rifle.

"If victory can't be secured then death is the only honor left." Keppler looked over to Hearn who had made the statement. Again, it was an echo from so many years ago.

"Soldiers who believe that don't live very long, and when soldiers don't live long, they can't win battles, and if battles aren't won then the war is lost." Keppler could see that this was a new way of thinking for these boys who had been indoctrinated by Manser. "I want to teach you how to stay alive so you can fight longer for the Reich. It benefits no one if you die on the first day of the battle." Truthfully, Keppler did not care about the Reich, but he knew no other way of getting these boys to accept a desire for life. "From now on you are all under direct orders from me to stay alive and not get killed until I tell you differently. No one is allowed to die unless you get permission." Keppler looked around to see if his words were sinking in, and to his satisfaction, many of the boys were nodding in approval. "Good. Let's get moving. You have a lot to learn."

The youth amazed Keppler. They listened to his instructions throughout the day and needed very few reminders. By the end of the first day they were moving and acting like a combat truppen. Unlike some of the other groups they had encountered on hill 454 where the youth marched and sang songs about "victory or flaming death," Keppler's group had sound discipline, keeping silence and proper spacing.

Keppler set the boys up in feigned ambushes on the other groups that were parading around the hilltop; he set his truppen up to watch in silence as the other groups marched by oblivious that they were being watched down the barrels of rifles. After one of the groups passed by one of their mock ambush sites, Keppler came out of his hiding spot and stood out into the open where the other truppen had just passed unawares.

"That is what will get them killed out in the field and there will be no glory in it."

The lesson was learned and the boys under his command adapted to the new idea that staying alive was more beneficial to the welfare of Germany than dying an early death. Keppler spent the entire day instructing them on ways to move and seek cover without being detected. As night fell he showed them how to keep watch and stay warm in the bitter cold that came with the setting of the sun. After setting them up in their positions, he moved over to a tree to lie down. He was emotionally drained from his efforts to teach the boys about the value of their lives. He had seen the results of Manser's teachings on his friends and he vowed to curb that belief in these children before they went to war.

Keppler tried to get some sleep, but it did not come easy. He dreamt briefly and then woke with a jolt, expecting to hear gunfire or artillery, but all was silent. He glanced around for the familiar form of Georg, but suddenly remembered where he was. Keppler closed his eyes again willing himself to fall asleep. He soon fell into another dream.

He was at the movies with all of his friends. The film on the screen was familiar. It was a propaganda film put out by the Nazi party depicting the patriotic nature of the Hitler Youth. They had all gone to see it many times. Keppler's friends were all young, just as he liked to remember them.

On the screen before them, they watched the film's hero Heini. It was near the end of the movie and Heini lay bleeding on the street. The communist brutes had chased Heini down and done their work with a knife. Heini's friends, arriving late, drove off the communist beasts and gathered around their dying friend. "Our flag," Heini said raising his hand and pointing upwards in delirium "flutters before us, it leads." And with that the hero of the film, Heini, died.

As the film ended, Keppler looked at his friends in the movie house. The pleasant dream had turned into a nightmare. His friends still sat in their seats, but each one sported the fatal wound that had claimed his life on the Russian front. His friends still appeared as their youthful selves, but with horrific wounds of war. Alarmed at the sudden change of events, Keppler looked back up to the front of the movie house. He watched Heini rise up from the dead. His blood stained Hitler Youth uniform was transfigured into a flag for the other boys to follow and all of his friends rose up, despite their deadly wounds, and marched through the front of the movie theatre. They were ghosts following the flag. Keppler was left alone in the dark theatre.

Keppler's heart jumped a little as Heini looked directly into his eyes and walked off the screen to confront him. The theatre melted away and it was just the two of them standing face to face with blackness surrounding them. Heini opened up the flag that now draped him, revealing the deep wounds inflicted on him with the knife,

"See what they did Keppler?" Blood frothed out of the side of his mouth and Keppler awoke with a start again.

The night was quiet. He listened hopeful for familiar sounds of gunfire but again there was nothing, 'Too quiet…there is too much time to think.' Keppler stayed awake in a leaning position against the tree, resolved that sleep was going to give him anything but rest. 'I haven't though about Heini for a long time. That was eleven years ago.'

When the 1933 Socialist party film was debuted, Heini became a role model for all boys to follow. Heini became the inspiration for boys all over Germany to join the Hitler Youth. Keppler himself had seen the film so many times in the theatre that he could still recall the entire motion picture line by line as if it were yesterday. The young boy Heini, uncertain of which youth group to join, chooses to join the Hitler Youth against his parent's wishes. Risking his life for the cause, Heini delivers flyers to the communist community. Later chased through the streets by the communist party boys, he is caught and stabbed repeatedly. In the climactic end of the film, Heini uses his last breath to advocate the cause.

Keppler remembered the feeling of pride that swelled up inside him every time he went with his friends to see the film. He felt pride to be German. He felt transformed. He was not a boy, but a man in charge of his life and the destiny of a nation. Heini instilled in him a desire to serve the Fatherland. Keppler did not feel that pride or desire now, but he could still remember the intensity he had felt for it back then.

His father forbade him to join the Hitler Youth, but Keppler had learned from Heini that he did not need or want his father's guidance. Heini had shown him that all parents were weak and unable to lead. The film had taught him that the weakness of parents was to be overcome with the strength of his fellow companions.

With some regret, Keppler reflected on his last interaction with his father before he was killed in an explosion at the ammunition factory where he worked. His father was enraged when Keppler came home in his new SS uniform and informed his parents he was going to battle school to become a soldier and serve the Party. Keppler warned his father about his unpatriotic attitude and threatened to turn him into the authorities if he persisted in his resistance. His father looked like he had been shot at his son's rebuke. It was the only time Keppler had seen his father slump his shoulders in defeat. They never had the chance to speak again.

'Enough memories!' Keppler pushed away from his leaning position and walked around the truppen's positions. The youth were well disciplined, that much was certain. They were all in the exact positions he had told them to assume. Half of them were awake and the other half sleeping just as he instructed. The ones that were awake maintained silence as he walked around their positions; they looked at him as if he was a ghost gliding among them.

Keppler thought about his resolve to teach these boys to survive and kill. It was a hard apprenticeship to accept. It was almost more than his conscience could bear, but duty demanded he do it. He felt a deep obligation to the boys' survival. Germany's future depended on these boys living until Germany lost the war. While his duty demanded that he make these children into soldiers, his conscience begged him to get the boys away from here and away from the coming battle that would try to devour them. Unfortunately there was no way out for him or the boys. All Keppler could do was instruct them like they were new combat replacements on the Russian front. He would have to force himself to ignore the fact that none of them needed a shave at the end of the day, nor would they need one in the morning.

Chapter 10

Hilltop 454, Frankfurt Staging Area, 12ᵗʰ SS Panzer Division

Corporal Hearn watched the Sergeant as he walked by. Despite his desire to tell the Sergeant how much he admired him, Hearn did not say a word. He had been told to be silent, and so he remained mute. There was no opportunity to speak to Dieter yet, but he knew that Dieter and the others respected their Sergeant, this hero of the Fatherland. He closed his eyes and pictured the post card he had tucked away safely at home with Keppler's face on it. He tried to imagine the heroic deeds the Sergeant must have done to be awarded the Knight's Cross with Oak Leaves, Swords, and Diamonds by the Fuhrer himself!

Hearn reflected on Keppler's words that he spoke earlier in the day. Even though it sounded like treason to say that death was not a proper substitute for victory, Keppler proved his point. This man was clever, that much was clear. If he followed in his footsteps, Hearn was sure Keppler would make him a hero. He tried to imagine his own face on a postcard and broke into a wide grin.

When he was looking down the barrel of his Mauser 98k earlier he had allowed himself to lightly caress the trigger as the oblivious singing group of Hitler Youth moved past them. He had imagined that they were a platoon of American infantry or British paratroopers. It would have been so easy. Hearn could hardly contain his excitement over the days to come when he would prove himself in battle.

Hearn knew his father would have been proud of him. If his father had been given the same kind of teacher as Sergeant Keppler, perhaps he could have lived to be a great hero too. It was as if Manser had taken the truppen as far as he could and now Keppler was going to finish the job. He would make them into household names that Germany would celebrate. Hearn sat quietly in the snow playing out the heroic deeds that would be done in his mind. The excitement was enough to keep him awake all night.

*****

In the morning Keppler started drilling them again on the methods they would use when advancing into combat and how to move with tanks. He showed them how to seek shelter in an artillery barrage and how to cover each other when on the attack. The training continued like that for the rest of the week. The training engrained a new method of movement and protocol in the boys. Keppler took them to new heights of awareness that Hearn had not dreamed possible. Unlike the other truppens they ate in the field, they slept in the field; they did everything in the field. Even when the weather got worse and worse with heavy snow falling and wind whipping through the trees they stayed out in the field while the other leaders took their truppens back down the hill to the compound. Keppler kept them out and taught them the skills of survival they would need in the days to come.

It was not until they were to depart that Keppler finally brought them down and allowed them to rejoin the regiment. They had one final hot meal at the kitchen that night and Keppler allowed them to sleep one last time in their beds. In the morning, they were to be sent out to their new positions and prepare to attack the enemy.

On that last night Hearn lay in his bunk awake, unable to contain the excitement he felt over their coming victory. The long awaited day would come with the dawn. He managed to fall asleep, but woke with a jolt. He looked over to the foot of his bed and saw Sergeant Keppler sitting on a footlocker staring at him. Hearn leaned up on one arm to address the Sergeant, but Keppler quickly stood up and walked away without saying a word. Hearn shrugged off the incident and managed to fall into a shallow sleep before the entire unit was called to gather their gear up and board their transportation.

Hearn led his truppen out at Keppler's request to the idling half-tracks that were to speed them to their jump-off point. The other divisions had left yesterday, and were now moving up behind the 12th Volksgrenadier Division to await the breakthrough. The day of Germany's deliverance was at hand.

Chapter 11

"Sir, I would like permission to take my truppen up to the front and let them observe the attack on Losheimergraben." Manser turned from his staff to look at Keppler, and then he broke out into a smile.

"What an excellent idea Sergeant. You have done a superb job with the men, but letting them wet their appetites for victory by watching the Volksgrenadier attack will be the crowning event on their training." Manser turned back to his staff, "Everyone, I would like you to meet my former pupil, Johann Keppler, winner of the Knight's Cross with Oak Leaves, Swords, and Diamonds." The other officers in the circle needed no introduction to Keppler whose arrival to the division had sparked a wave of encouragement throughout the ranks. They all nodded at him, admiration evident in their eyes.

"With your permission then, I will attend to my men." Keppler begged his leave. Manser nodded and Keppler left the circle of officers. He hated officers. He had been given the opportunity many times to become one, but always managed to evade promotion. The last place he wanted to end up was in the uniform of an officer. Returning to the boys, Keppler informed them that they were going to be moving up with the 12th Volksgrenadiers to observe the attack. The boys were beaming with excitement at the news. Keppler led them down the road with the last reserve Kompanies of the Volksgrenadiers.

The trip to the jump-off point was a quiet one as Keppler insisted the truppen maintain sound discipline. They stood out as they walked by Volksgrenadiers who were busy laughing and joking with each other. Keppler took his boys to the tree line and set them up personally so they could have the best view of the events and maximum coverage. It was a risk to bring them to the front, but they would be here soon enough and he needed them to observe a lesson that words could never teach them. They were about to learn the true definition of horror.

The 12th Volksgrenadier Division was starting its attack along a three-kilometer front. Keppler had chosen to observe the attack against the train yards at Losheimergraben because his boys would have the best coverage from enemy shelling and return fire.

Keppler could see after their arrival that victory here would be a miracle. The officers of the Volksgrenadier Division seemed as inexperienced at combat as the men under their command. He watched in dismay as a captain formed his Kompanie up on either side of the railroad track leading to the rail yards and began to march them off towards Losheimergraben in a column of twos.

He wanted to scream at them and tell them marching into battle was going to get them all killed, but he knew better than to say anything. Instead he crawled around to his boys and told them they were about to see a tragedy. He wanted them to learn from the mistakes they were about to witness.

The Americans waited a painfully long time before they reacted to the marching Kompanie of German infantry. Eventually they began to fire into the gray-green ranks of the Volksgrenadier. The Kompanie's formation broke and the soldiers sought cover in the ditches and depressions around the tracks. They then began to fire back and the battle for Losheimergraben began in earnest.

The poorly led German infantry had little hope for success. Keppler watched as the Americans moved up a mobile artillery piece and began to fire it into the pockets of attackers. They then fired their 60mm mortars at maximum elevation, bringing the deadly rounds down right outside the perimeter of the town. Any of the infantry lucky enough to get past the small arms fire and the mobile howitzer had to then negotiate with a hailstorm of 60mm shrapnel.

After about a half-hour of fighting, the shattered remains of the German Kompanie began to find their way back to the tree line. Some of the Volksgrenadiers broke with panic and did not stop running once they hit the trees. Some of them ran by Keppler's boys, their eyes wide with panic leaving their equipment and wounded behind, fleeing for their lives. Keppler surveyed the faces of his truppen and to his satisfaction he only saw fear.

Behind the boys more Volksgrenadiers formed up in the woods, preparing a second attack. Keppler went back and found out they were going to try to synchronize their attack with the 990th regiment from the 277th Volksgrenadier Division, who would hit the rail yards from the north. He decided to keep his boys on a little longer to let the lessons they were learning penetrate deep.

The second attack was doomed from the start. Keppler watched through binoculars as the 990th regiment tried to make its way through barbwire, a minefield, and artillery shelling that was brought down on their position. As a result, the attack was anything but coordinated.

The grenadiers from the newly arrived Kompanies of the 12th Volksgrenadier Division moved out into the same open ground where over eighty bodies from the previous attacking Kompanie lay. Keppler watched the boys cringe at the sounds of the heavy guns and small arms fire. The attack began to peter out half way to the rail yards and the grenadier regiment went to ground just like the first one did, firing back at the Americans who were dug in deep.

A couple of tanks from the 12th SS Division came up to give support to the failing momentum of the attacking grenadiers, but American artillery drove the tanks back into the cover of the woods. Then, after about another hour of fighting the second attacking regiment began to pull back having sustained heavy losses.

Keppler watched the boys more than the fighting in front of him. They were all pale and open mouthed at the spectacle before them. 'Good,' he thought, 'better to give the honor-in-death routine Manser indoctrinated them with the glamour it deserves.'

He noticed a transfer in the enemy's salvos and looked back to see the Americans shifting the bulk of their fire to the north. The 990th regiment had finally made it through the minefield and barbwire. They were starting their attack an hour late.

'If it had been better organized' Keppler thought, 'it might have worked.' He pulled his truppen back out of the tree line. They had seen enough.

He marched them back the half kilometer to their own Kompanie staging area with the 12th SS Panzer Division as it waited for the infantry to break through to the Malmedy road. The truppen was eerily quiet as they marched back to their Division. Keppler had made his point.

Once back with the Kompanie, Keppler gathered his boys around him.

"Learn from what you saw today. German soldiers are not invincible and there is nothing glorious about getting slaughtered. Keep your heads and move the way I taught you and you will have a chance to stay alive. If you buy into the superman idea and try to march through enemy bullets you will die needlessly." He could see the boys were taking in everything he had to say. Keppler knew he was again directly attacking some of the things Manser taught, but he did it purposefully, having seen many casualties among his own friends attributed to Captain Manser. He refused to let the same thing continue to happen.

"Get ready to move out!" it was Lieutenant Lehrer, their Kompanie commanding officer. Keppler and the boys looked up to see the Lieutenant, hovering over them. He reached down and patted Hearn on the shoulder. "I always said they should have sent us into the train yards first. We would have saved the grenadiers a lot of unnecessary casualties," Lehrer said. Hearn looked down at his boots, choosing not to answer.

They loaded into a half-track and waited for the news that the grenadiers had broken through the American lines, but the word never came. The waiting became torturous, even for Keppler as they listened to the sounds of battle. The daylight began to fade and the grenadiers had not yet broken through. The division was scheduled to be speeding up the road by now on their way to Malmedy. Instead they were sitting in a half-track trying to keep warm.

Night finally fell amid the rise and fall of small arms and artillery. They finally received their orders to stand down. The Volksgrenadiers had failed to break through the American positions. Keppler breathed a sigh of relief as he realized that the boys would have one more night to remain boys.

*****

Wagner lay on the cold ground and tried to get some sleep. The excitement of last night and the terrors he had seen today made him restless and ill. He was sure he would never be able to sleep again.

"Wagner, is that you?" He sat up at the whispered voice. He knew the voice well; it was little Lubbert.

"I'm here Lubbert." He watched in the darkness as Lubbert came the last few feet through the snow the way Keppler had taught them. Lubbert was so light thought that he hardly broke through the snow at all. He flopped down beside Wagner and looked around to make sure there was no one else in earshot of them.

"I'm scared Wagner. I don't want to be a soldier any more."

"I'm scared too, but we have to fight. You can't just choose to stop being a soldier because you are worried."

"Okay," Lubbert whimpered after he said it, trying to muffle a cry.

"Don't worry," Wagner pulled Lubbert in close putting his arm around Lubbert's tiny shoulders, "I'll keep you safe." Wagner was not sure now if he could deliver on such a promise.

"You saw those men today Wagner. No one can be safe!" Lubbert had quit crying, as if he accepted the fate Wagner had now come to fear.

"Well, those men didn't have Sergeant Keppler leading them into the fight, now did they?"

"No."

"Don't worry Lubbert, you'll see, everything will be just fine." Wagner doubted his own words after what he saw today, but he had to say something to ease Lubbert's fear. Saying he did not want to be a soldier anymore could prove disastrous if Manser were to hear about it.

"Can I stay here with you?"

"Sure, no problem," Lubbert wiggled down into the snow and stared off into the darkness beside Wagner. Being three years older than Lubbert, Wagner was like a protective big brother to him. He had always assumed that he would be able to protect Lubbert when they went to war. He had also thought that he would become a great hero. He had imagined flags fluttering, and drums beating out their marching songs as they drove the enemy before them. Everything he had imagined in his daydreams did not come close to what he had witnessed only a few hours ago. He still shook slightly thinking about it. His biggest fear had been that he would not get a medal during his first few days of fighting. Now his fear had changed to a more realistic concern that he might run away in a fight or possibly get killed. Even death had changed faces from the flag-flying honor Manser made it out to be, to the shredding of flesh from bones like he had witnessed. The world was changing before him and Wagner was becoming a reluctant eyewitness.

Chapter 12

17 December 1944 day two of Autumn Mist

The fighting started early in the morning before the sun came up. The Volksgrenadiers from the 12th Division attacked just before dawn trying to make up for the already painful delay in the timetable. Lieutenant Lehrer approached Keppler's truppen as they were finishing their breakfast. The boys tried to chew while pensively listening to the distant sounds of combat.

"Keppler, get your men ready to move out." He walked by the group and patted Hearn on the helmet. "We'll show them what we're made of, eh Hearn?"

Keppler watched Hearn out of the corner of his eye as Hearn turned pale and looked back down at his boots, not wanting to betray his fear, especially to the Lieutenant.

"Keppler, Captain Manser wants you to lead the assault. You will have your truppen, Horst's truppen, and Klaus' truppen to support a few tanks we are loaning to the attacking regiment of Volksgrenadiers. The Volksgrenadiers are not experienced at moving with armor, so you have the privilege of being the first ones from the Kompanie to engage the enemy. Congratulations! After you achieve a breakthrough, the Captain will bring the rest of the Kompanie up to exploit it. You will be supported in the attack by three Panthers from Captain Breuer's Kompanie." The Lieutenant moved off to inform the rest of the men about their movement forward.

"Okay, you boys remember what I said about moving with tanks?" The boys nodded at Keppler. He had spent half of their training period on hill 454 teaching them how to move with tanks. Keppler hoped with all his might that his training of the boys would keep them alive. "Okay, breathe deeply and make sure your rifles are ready for action. Don't go to ground unless I tell you too. The best way to stay alive is to keep moving." With that, he stood up and moved out down the same road they had walked the day before as spectators. Klaus and Horst's truppens joined them on the road and they all moved towards their jump-off point.

On their way, the boys passed several of the surviving attackers from the 12th Volksgrenadier Division huddled behind trees in small groups. Some tended to their injuries, while many others had already succumbed to their wounds and lay dead by their comrades.

'This is not a good start,' Keppler thought.

The Panthers had already been moved up and were waiting with their engines idling at the tree line. He positioned the three truppens around the tanks and readied for the attack. He realized that he had been so nervous for the welfare of his boys that he had not had time to be afraid. Slowly the numbness he knew so well came over him like a warm blanket. Keppler was ready to go into combat.

Keppler watched as the first of the tanks lurched forward towards the American positions. He felt tremendous responsibility towards the boys. He had wanted to keep them out of this war, but knew no way of doing that. He had settled for teaching them how to stay alive as long as possible and now he was about to see if the training would accomplish that goal.

The roaring of the Panther's engine was deafening, its black diesel smoke pouring out into the crisp snow filled air. The ground shook under his feet as he moved his truppen out from the tree line behind the iron monster, its treads churning up the frozen earth making a white and black mishmash of the snow and dirt ripped from its peaceful blanket.

He glanced back and noticed the boys were moving just as he had taught them. They were hard even for Keppler to see in their white camouflage pullovers. He took some heart that the American infantrymen would have a hard time targeting them.

The American positions opened up first. Tracer rounds ripped through the falling snow and the sounds of machinegun fire began to tear through the growling of the Panther's engine. An anti-tank round clanged off the side of a Panther and ricocheted into one of the Hitler Youth from Horst's truppen. The boy was ripped in half and the snow was showered with red mist behind him in a wide fan shape.

The Panther rocked to a skidding halt and its turret slowly turned to fire back. Keppler motioned for his truppen to get down just as another anti-tank round pinged off the thick armor of the tank's turret. The Panther tank lurched on its treads slightly from the recoil as its 75mm gun boomed in response.

An explosion erupted in one of the buildings by the rail yards and a pillar of smoke poured out of the shattered house, rewarding the Panther's shot. They had scored a direct hit on the gun. The Panther wasted no time throttling its engine full out and continued on its course as the turret straightened out to face its main gun forward again.

Small arms fire from Losheimergraben intensified as they came into range of the American smaller arms. Carbine rounds raced all around Keppler with a familiar zipping sound. He felt anxious for the welfare of his truppen and wanted to keep his boys in cover, but he knew their survival depended on them pressing on.

Keppler could see the Americans now, some of them draped in white camouflage, and others standing out in their green fatigues. He drew a bead on one of them as he ran ammunition forward for one of the machineguns. Keppler breathed out and pulled the trigger as he ran. The green form crumpled to the ground behind one of the rail tracks and was still.

Behind him he could hear the cracking of rifles from his boys. They were shooting back at the American defenders. Their days of innocence had come to an end. The Panther tank in front of him lurched hard to the left as its tread spun off, an American 37mm round hitting the Panther in the track.

The shot had come from an American light tank, an M4A1 Stuart. Keppler could see the wisp of smoke rising from its barrel that had branches and netting draped over it for camouflage. The small tank remained almost out of sight behind a rail car.

"Get down!" His truppen flopped down into the snow in unison as he motioned them down with his hand. He brought his rifle up and sighted on another green clad figure near the Stuart tank. The American was firing his carbine from inside a rail car. Keppler squeezed the trigger and the enemy soldier's form flew backwards out of sight into the wooden boxcar. Another 37mm shell hit the Panther tank. The round, unable to penetrate the Panther's thick armor, went zinging by Keppler and impacted into the ground behind, blowing up dirt and snow into a geyser.

The Panther had sighted in on the American light tank and fired. Its 75mm round had no trouble breaking through the thin armor and the American tank exploded as its magazine went up. The M4A1 Stuart's turret blew off the hull and flew fifty meters into the air. The airborne turret came crashing down between its shattered remains in the rail yard and the immobilized Panther.

Keppler motioned his truppen forward into the American positions and he ran full out through the snow towards the rail yards, firing as he went. He felt the heat from the destroyed Stuart's burning turret as he passed it. The remaining Volksgrenadiers who took heart from the direct hit of the Panther, followed him in his charge. The entire regiment was up and attacking in force.

The American 60mm mortars had resumed their firing, but the Germans had closed with the Americans to the point that the mortars dare not bring their rounds in any closer.

Everything seemed to slow down for Keppler as he ran. Another American went down clutching his side where Keppler had shot him. Rounds whizzed by him, but Keppler did not care. He kept on plodding on through the snow. Aim, fire, eject casing, slam a new one home, aim fire, eject casing…. Keppler worked his rifle as if he was a machine. He rarely missed.

The American lines were breaking in the rail yards and the enemy soldiers were running through the boxcars and buildings, away from the attacking Volksgrenadiers and SS. Keppler dropped down into a shallow foxhole in the American lines. He sighted in on another form as it fled for the rear. He fired and it went down skidding into a crumpled heap.

Keppler took another clip of rounds and shoved them into his rifle as he looked around for more targets. The attack had petered out to sporadic shots. There were erratic loud claps as some of the rounds from the destroyed American anti-tank gun burning in the house cooked off, but the shooting, for the most part, was in a lull.

'The boys!' It was the first time Keppler had thought about them since he had charged the American lines. He turned around and saw that they had followed him and were taking up positions in the deserted foxholes and firing pits of the Americans in the rail yard. He did a quick mental count of the truppen and felt they were all accounted for. Relief swept over him.

"Kompanie forward!" It was Manser. He charged across the open field in the lead of their Kompanie waving his lugar like it was a sword. Keppler almost burst out laughing at the ridiculous sight of him. He looked back at his truppen and motioned them forward, moving up and taking the point himself. There were fresh tracks through the snow-covered ground from the retreating Americans and some blood trails.

Keppler was cautious, not wanting to fall victim to a rear guard ambush. He stopped and waved his truppen into cover again at the sight of an American lying prone on the ground. He watched the man for a moment and realized that he was dead. He waved his truppen forward again and stepped through the snow with wariness.

He had never fought the Americans before, but he had heard about them from some of the replacements on the Russian front. They reportedly broke easy in battle, but supposedly rallied just as fast and would take up the fight again before the smoke from the first round cleared.

As if on cue a Thompson sub-machinegun opened up and sprayed into Horst's truppen. They had been walking close together, taking no care to maintain spacing. They all fell to the ground dead or wounded before the machinegun's magazine was empty. Keppler saw some movement to his front as another American moved to sight in on the downed truppen. He was close to Keppler, only about twenty meters away behind some rail ties stacked on the ground. The enemy soldier obviously did not see Keppler coming or he would have shot him.

Keppler brought his rifle up and sighted in on the man's forehead just below his helmet line and pulled the trigger. The enemy soldier's head snapped back with the impact of the bullet and sent him sprawling to the snow covered ground. A second American appeared and drew a bead on Keppler as he chambered another round into this rifle. Keppler knew he would never get his weapon up in time but instead of getting shot, Keppler watched as the American was hit in the upper chest and crumpled to the ground. Keppler glanced back to see Wagner, his face as white as a sheet still in the firing position from which he had just shot the enemy soldier.

Three more forms to Keppler's left darted back through the boxcars and stacks of rail ties, one of them holding a Thompson machinegun. Keppler brought his rifle on line and fired at the one with the machinegun, but he missed. The American rear guard was running back through the yards, and Keppler was not about to go running after them. He looked behind him again and noticed that Wagner had now gotten to his feet, but he was still staring at the dead soldier he had shot.

"Thanks Wagner," Keppler said in a low voice. The youth looked at him, and then back to the dead American. Keppler remembered the first man he ever killed. There were countless others in between but it was the first one he would always remember. He walked back to Wagner and put his hand on the boy's shoulder. "It was either him or us." He wanted to tell the boy he would get used to it, but he did not want Wagner to get used to it. He did not want any of these boys to get used to killing. Hearn moved up behind Wagner and patted him on the back without saying a word.

Keppler turned and took up point again. He heard nothing from his truppen as they advanced cautiously from boxcar to boxcar, but some of the other truppens in the Kompanie made up for the lack of noise, yelling and stomping through the snow covered rail yard in search of the Americans. 'So much inexperience.' Keppler mourned. The 12th SS Panzer Division had started its attack.

Chapter 13

Rail Yards, Losheimergraben, Belgium

Wagner looked at the dead American. He had anticipated this moment for a long time, and had looked forward to it. He had imagined the entire event from start to finish. However, something was missing here. Wagner thought he would feel pride at the killing of his first enemy soldier, especially after his own father had been so badly wounded by Americans. He had killed one, but no pride would come, no matter how much he willed it. He felt something else instead. He actually felt guilt. He had killed a human being. Sergeant Keppler had told him not to worry, that the American would have killed them both if he had not shot first. That seemed like it would have felt better than having taken a life.

'Maybe the American got the better end of the deal.' Wagner thought and he wished he could crawl into a hole to hide. He was the first one in the truppen other than Keppler to shoot anyone and the others looked at him with envy, perhaps even some trepidation. He was the first of the boys to cross that unseen line from childhood fantasies into naked reality.

Wagner tore his eyes away from the dead American and tried to regain his focus on the duty at hand. Wagner looked on as Keppler moved cautiously down the line. He followed his lead, knowing that mimicking Keppler would be his best chance of staying alive. Several shots rang out and Wagner hit the ground, his heart thumping loudly in his chest. His helmet had slipped down over his eyes when he hit the dirt and he had to shove it back up onto his head before he could see anything. Someone was screaming, and he could not tell where the rifle shots were coming from. He stared down the length of his rifle barrel looking for a target but nothing appeared. As the shots intensified, he shifted his aim to the left. Wagner saw him. It was an American with a cigar jutting out of his mouth, firing from the top of one of the train cars.

The American did not notice Wagner aiming at him, as he was busy shooting at someone else to Wagner's rear. Wagner tried to pull the trigger, but froze up. He watched the American shooting and then refilling the magazine in his carbine and then shooting again. No matter how much Wagner tried to pull the trigger it did not happen.

Suddenly, the rifle bucked in his hand. It was so unexpected that it caused Wagner to jump and his helmet flopped down over his eyes again. As he shoved the helmet up, he could not see anyone on top of the boxcar anymore and the shooting had stopped. The American was gone. Wagner hoped that the man had simply run away, but he knew better. He had sighted in on the man's face and somehow his finger had finally squeezed the trigger of his weapon. Wagner was a good shot and there was no doubt, he had killed again.

The firing intensified further down the line where some of the other truppens had formed up on their left, but to the front all was quiet. Hearn flopped down beside Wagner and scared him half to death.

"Wow, Wagner, that's two you've nailed so far." Hearn spoke reverently, in awe of his friend. "Sergeant asked me to come and get you. He needs you to go with him and flank the Americans. He said he wants you because you don't seem to have any trouble hitting what you're shooting at."

Wagner felt his stomach do a flip-flop and settle like lead. He did not want to go anywhere, especially if it involved shooting more people. He opened his mouth to scream at Hearn and tell him to go to hell, but all that came out was:

"Where is he?"

Hearn gestured to Wagner's front, "He's up there about twenty meters in amongst some rail ties. You'd better get going. We have to stay back here and guard the flank."

"Take care of Lubbert for me."

"We're all watching him." Hearn gave Wagner a thumb up.

Wagner's legs felt wobbly as he ran in a crouch towards the area Hearn had pointed out. Out of the corner of his eye he saw the man he had killed sprawled out behind a boxcar. The sight spurred Wagner into a careless run. His mad dash was brought to a sudden halt. A hand grabbed his tunic and pulled him to the ground.

"Easy boy," Keppler said, looking around them, "calm down a little and try to keep from making so much noise. Don't shoot unless I shoot first. If I run, stay right behind me. Clear?" He looked Wagner in the eye and saw Wagner bob his head in affirmative.

Instantly, Keppler was up and moving through the rail yard, headed to the rear of the shooting behind the American ambush. Wagner shook and felt tears welling up again. He was a killer.

He had heard about the atrocities that prisoners endured under the American's capture. Manser had gone into great detail how they used ancient American Indian torture tactics to break a man down. Manser had shown them pictures of the Indians holding knives and wearing war paint. The savages appeared in Wagner's nightmares for a long time after those lessons. Wagner realized, with some alarm, he would not have anything to tell them if they did catch him because he did not know anything of value. In that case, they would probably torture him to death.

Keppler waved Wagner to the ground and he thought his heart was going to jump out of his chest. He was shaking so badly now he was not sure if he could hit anything further than a few meters away from him. Keppler was aiming at something and he followed Keppler's rifle to a spot where some Americans were holed up. They were spaced out underneath a burning boxcar and had pinned down a large group of grenadier and SS truppens advancing on the area. There were six of them firing into the buildings to their front; firing at German troops; firing at his countrymen. It was at that moment Wagner felt a wave of calmness flow over him. The Americans were killers too. He brought his rifle up and sighted it in on one of the enemy soldiers.

Instead of jumping when Keppler's rifle cracked, Wagner too pulled his trigger. The impact of his 7.92mm round sent a puff of snow and material up into the air when it hit one of the Americans. The 12.8g bullet slammed into the man at 755 meters per second and smashed him into the raised tracks he was using for cover. The man's right leg grounded into the gravel and the body slid down the raised embankment before he became still.

Wagner ejected the spent round from the chamber in his rifle and slammed in a new one. Keppler had shot another one of the Americans before Wagner had even reloaded. All three of the remaining Americans jumped up and turned just as Wagner pulled the trigger again, hitting a fourth one in the throat. The impact of the round bounced the man off of the side of the flaming boxcar and deposited him face down onto the ground. It was only then Wagner realized the man had dropped his weapon and had had his arms in the air. The two remaining Americans continued standing with their hands in the air surrendering to them. Wagner felt the guilt all over again. He had killed four men within five minutes and one of them had been trying to surrender!

Keppler told Wagner to cover him and stood up. The Sergeant walked over to the surrendering American soldiers and prodded them away from their cover with his rifle. Wagner remembered that he had not reloaded after his last shot so he chambered a fresh round, and cursed himself for forgetting. He was shaking again.

A gurgling sound came to Wagner's ears. He walked over to his last victim who had received the bullet in the throat. The American soldier churned his legs back and forth and lay face down in a growing pool of blood. With the toe of his boot, Wagner flipped the man over. The American had both hands clutched around his throat, trying to stem the flow of blood, which oozed out between his fingers. The American's eyes were wide with horror, realizing that death was in attendance. He tried to speak, but only a low gurgle was released. Wagner felt nauseous at the sight.

Some of the older men from Klaus' truppen came rushing forward to the captured position. A group of them gathered around the downed American beside Wagner and watched the man writhe in the crimson snow.

"Did you see that?" one of the men asked, "This little guy nailed him from twenty meters!" Wagner grimaced as a renewed flood of shame wave over him.

Wagner's mind flashed back to a time when he was in the Black Forest with his cousin and a group of other boys. They had captured a squirrel in a tall metal bucket. His cousin had said it would be a good idea to kill the squirrel and Wagner volunteered to do the deed. He grabbed a large branch off the ground and raised it up bringing the end of the branch down onto the squirrel. Wagner had been aiming for its head but because the squirrel was running around he missed. Instead of a quick blow to the head Wagner hit the squirrel in the hip. The blow from the branch crushed its hind end into the bottom of the rusty pail. Wagner did not know that squirrels could scream until that moment. It screamed with a piercing howl of pain and he saw the color drain from the faces of the other boys. Wagner raised the branch again, his arms shaking, and brought it down finishing the job. He swore he would never kill anything again after that. The squirrel's screams still haunted him sometimes at night. He supposed that nightmare would now be replaced.

Feeling out of control of his body, Wagner brought his rifle up into the air and brought the butt of his weapon down into the American's face again and again until the gurgling stopped and the man was still. He was horrified at himself, but he had to end the noise of the American. He had to bring the man's suffering to an end the same way he wanted to end the screaming of the squirrel. Wagner looked up and realized that the group of men had grown completely silent. They looked at Wagner with unease. Wagner watched their pale faces, similar to his cousin and the other boys in the Black Forest.

He turned and the group parted to make way for him to leave the grizzly circle. Wagner walked out of the throng of soldiers and straight to Keppler, who was standing beside Captain Manser. Keppler was turning over their prisoners.

Manser was looking at the two Americans who had been knocked to their knees. Wagner could tell by the look on Manser's face that the fate of the Americans was already decided. He wanted to turn and run, but he had nowhere to go. He walked right over and stood beside Keppler. Keppler was arguing that the two soldiers might be able to offer some information and should not be killed. Manser, tired of the argument, drew his lugar and shot both of the men in the forehead.

"We are here to conquer these Capitalists, not hold them by the hand after they lose the stomach for battle." Manser turned and ordered the Kompanie to continue forward. Keppler looked at Wagner and jerked his head for the boy to follow him. They walked back over to the truppen members who waited in a defensive position where they had left them.

"Did you get any more, Wagner?" It was Mapes who asked the question, his voice full of admiration for the newly born soldier he saw walking beside Keppler. Wagner tried to smile at his friend, but he could not manage anything more than a stare.

"Let's go!" Keppler snapped, "And don't forget your spacing!" The truppen got to its feet and moved out through the rail yards. Wagner fell back behind them as far as he dared and then knelt down to throw up. He did not have much in his stomach but that did not seem to matter. He continued to wretch after the small contents of his stomach had been emptied. He felt dizzy and wanted to pass out. He noticed that he had blood on his hands and he was trying to wipe them off on his trousers when he felt a hand on his shoulder. He looked over to see Keppler kneeling beside him.

"It's okay boy, you had no choice." Wagner looked at Keppler as he spoke the words and could not hold back. He dove into Keppler's chest and clung to the man. He yearned to fight back the tears, but they came anyway. Keppler, unsure of what to do hugged the boy back. Wagner got control of himself faster than he thought possible and wiped his eyes with the back of his sleeve.

"I'll be okay Sergeant. Please don't tell the others!" Keppler nodded an affirmative at Wagner's request.

Wagner thought he saw sorrow in Keppler's eyes as he picked up his Mauser rifle, but the Sergeant quickly averted his gaze so Wagner was not sure. Wagner followed Keppler's lead and picked up his own rifle and trailed his truppen leader back to where the others waited. They advanced through to Losheimergraben without any more incidents. It seemed that the Americans had withdrawn for now, but Wagner feared it would not last for long.

Chapter 14

Losheimergraben Rail Yards, Belgium

After they had taken the rail yards and Losheimergraben, the Kompanie paused for some rations of sausage and cheese. The 12th Volksgrenadier division was moving through the town to continue the advance and Keppler was glad they had a moment to rest. The boys gathered around Wagner, wondering what it felt like to shoot someone, but Wagner did not answer their queries. He just ate in silence.

A runner from Captain Manser came up to Keppler and briefly spoke to him while the boys hungrily devoured their rations. Keppler dismissed the runner and waved the truppen over to him.

"Division is going to swing our Kompanie around to the left to take some higher ground. The enemy decided to make another stand between Murringen and the forest edge on the southeast side of the town. They've been trying to take the ridge all morning and they need a fresh unit to make a run at it." Keppler hid his worry as he gave the news to the boys.

"Let's go." Keppler stood and led the boys to the left flank as the 18th motorized Kompanie shifted position. The Kompanie moved through the 12th division's positions towards the ridge.

It took about an hour to move through the lines of German infantry and tanks. Around noon they could hear the small arms fire from the hill, and could see smoke drifting down through the trees, sliding like fog. The sounds of battle included the divisional artillery pounding the unseen ridge.

Keppler brought his truppen to a halt. Before them the ground began to rise slightly and the truppen realized they had reached the base of the ridge. The shooting was louder now that they had reached the base. The loud clap of the division's 21cm heavy artillery rounds crashing through the trees at the top and exploding with ground shaking thunder occasionally drowned out the smaller arms.

"Keppler, I want your truppen to lead the way up." Manser had arrived in the truppen's position without warning, as always, clutching his lugar like a sword. "We need this ground! It's a hill that marks the end of the ridge. If we can take it, we'll be able to turn the American flank!"

Keppler was annoyed with Manser. He knew that Manser was a disaster with tactical planning. He refrained from showing his exasperation with the Captain as he answered him,

"Yes Sir." Keppler motioned his truppen forward and they adopted the proper spacing before moving up the hill behind their sergeant. A few meters into their climb, they began to encounter the dead. German and American uniforms blended together in a pile of bodies. The boys tried to maneuver around the corpses while the bitter cold turned their faces numb and burned in their throats and lungs with every breath.

Lubbert and Wagner were on the far right side of the advancing truppen as they moved up the hill. Early into their trek Lubbert came upon a dead German officer, his lugar still clutched in his lifeless hand. Lubbert bent down and picked the pistol up, tucking it in his belt. The pistol was huge compared to his ten-year-old frame. Lubbert looked at Wagner and shrugged his shoulders. Wagner tried to smile at him, but could not get the corners of his mouth to turn up.

The truppen had moved half way up the hill when Keppler dropped to his knee, waved the others down, and brought up his rifle; someone was coming towards them. The sound of someone crashing through the brush became louder and louder. An unarmed soldier finally appeared, clumsily fighting through the trees and knee-deep snow.

Keppler let his rifle drop from the target as soon as he realized the lone attacker was a German soldier in full retreat. The man looked frantic and was running full steam down the hill. He was missing his helmet and his weapon, and did not say anything to the others as he ran by. Keppler waited a few moments to make sure enemy soldiers were not following the man, and then resumed his climb. The sound of gunfire intensified as they moved up, and they knew they were close to the American skirmish lines. The other Kompanie attacking the hill was splintered and fought from different positions around the top without any real effectiveness.

The smoke was thick. Some of it came from burning trees that had caught on fire in the bombardment, and some of it from the smoke canisters thrown to cover attacks on the machine-gun emplacements the Americans had around the top of the hill. Keppler could tell by the sound of them they were .30 caliber guns, and there were at least two of them. He looked anxiously back at his truppen. They awaited his order. The snowfall became heavier and added to the limited visibility on the hill.

Keppler dropped onto his belly and started to crawl the rest of the way up the slope, through the deepening snow. The cold was familiar to him as he moved. A brief flash of George came to his mind, but he forced it out. There was no time to wonder about his friend now. He stopped crawling when through the thickening smoke, he could see flames spitting out of the front of one of the machineguns as it sprayed bullets down the opposite slope. Pulling out one of his stick grenades, Keppler motioned for the rest of the truppen to stay put. He then crawled ten more meters to get into range of the pit. He unscrewed the cap at the end of the stick, and pulled the string to activate the fuse on the grenade. He waited patiently, and then threw the stick in an arc towards the machinegun pit.

There was a flat thump and the pit fell silent. Keppler was about to congratulate himself when all hell broke loose. Two other machineguns that had been sitting silent on the hill suddenly opened fire. Bullets whipped around him. He wanted to burrow into the ground and get below the level of the dirt to find cover, but there was nowhere to go, and he did not dare move. The zipping sound of bullets buzzing by his head became a constant hum and he could not believe he had not yet been hit.

*****

Bergin saw the two other machineguns open up on the Sergeant's position and realized that Sergeant Keppler needed help. He had felt useless in the train yards and envied Wagner for his courage to fight. Bergin did not know what came over him, but seeing the Sergeant pinned down was more than he could bear. He pulled out one of his own stick grenades and decided to charge the pit closest to him. Clutching the grenade in his right hand and holding his rifle in his left, he yelled for the others to cover him. The rest of the truppen started to fire blindly into the smoke towards the spurting flames of the machinegun fire, unsure of what else to do.

The spotter in the machinegun pit started slapping the gunner on the helmet and the machinegun turned to face Dieter's charge. Dieter Bergin's right hand went numb as a round from the machinegun hit him in the wrist. Then he felt the heat from a second round as it punched through his left shoulder and spun him around. As he hit the ground, the wind knocked out of him and everything hazed into a gray blur for a moment.

The loud clattering of the American .30 caliber machinegun seemed to fade out to a thumping no louder than a heartbeat in Bergin's ears. He had blood in his eyes and he went to wipe it away with his right hand but something scratched his cheek instead. He looked at his right hand puzzled, only to realize that it was missing and a piece of broken white bone stuck out from the cuff in his wrist's place.

Bergin knew he should be horrified at the scene, but he felt nothing. He dizzily tried to steady himself as he got up. He found his shorn right hand lying on the ground close by, still clutching the grenade. Somehow he had lost his rifle. Despite his confusion, Bergin knew what he had to do.

His left shoulder joint had been shattered from the .30 caliber round. With some effort, he used his left hand to open the fingers of his severed hand and retrieve the grenade. He gripped it, bent over in agonizing pain, and pulled on the exposed fuse with his teeth. The grenade began to smoke as the fuse burned towards its head. Clutching the grenade in his left hand he stood up and ran towards the machinegun emplacement. There was no way he could throw the grenade with any accuracy. His dizziness was worsening, but somehow his feet continued on. He could hear someone screaming, and realized that it was his own voice making the sound as he charged.

The spotter in the pit with the gunner slapped frantically on the gunner's helmet to get him to turn the gun back and finish the job, but Bergin had gained too much ground. Bergin tumbled into the hole with the Americans mechanically, almost as if in slow motion. The grenade in his hand exploded.

*****

Hearn had seen Dieter go down. Hearn felt ill as he sighted in on the American position and fired his weapon. He chambered a second round and then a third. Out of the corner of his eye he saw movement. It was Dieter! He was up and charging the machinegun nest with a live grenade! Hearn became frantic. He jumped up and started to charge forward as well, determined to give Dieter the cover he needed to finish his run and throw the grenade.

"Throw it Dieter!" he screamed, "you're close enough now, throw it!" Dieter continued on with his charge, himself screaming at the top of his lungs. It was then that Hearn noticed Dieter was missing his right hand, and his left arm was hanging useless by his side. Dieter could barely hold onto the grenade, much less throw it.

Hearn hit the dirt just ten meters from the pit as Dieter fell into the hole. The heat from the grenade's explosion chased off the intense cold for a brief second and brushed over his body. Hearn jumped up, eyes searching for his friend. In front of him sat a smoking hole full of arms and legs. Hearn fell to his knees. It felt like someone had kicked him in the stomach. 'Not Dieter! Not here! It wasn't supposed to be this way.' He threw up in the snow.

The last enemy machinegun began to strafe the hill, and some of the rounds buzzed by Hearn's head. Hearn felt rage bubble up inside him. He wanted to kill all of the Americans. He could not rest until he had done just that. It was like someone had flipped a switch inside of him. He slammed a fresh clip of rounds into his rifle, stood up, and walked towards the last machinegun pit. He chambered and fired his weapon as he walked, taking no noticed of the rounds zipping by him.

Suddenly, Hearn was slammed to the ground, the air forced from his lungs as a stray artillery round smashed into the hill and showered him with frozen dirt lumps and snow. There was more firing as Hearn tried to get up. He could tell by the intensity of the shooting that the truppen was rushing the machinegun nest and he wanted to attack with them. Spots swam before his eyes and he could not focus. The swarming spots forced him to lie back down and be still.

*****

Keppler watched in horror at Bergin's sacrifice. His attack on the machinegun pit allowed Keppler to crawl back to the rest of the truppen, and he gathered them up for a rush on the last emplacement. It was then he realized that Hearn was missing from the group. Keppler feared the worst, but knew they had to get the last machinegun emplacement before it sighted in on them and killed all of his boys.

There was a small rush from the other side of the hill. One of the other truppens from the previous Kompanie was making an attack in an attempt to take out the last gun emplacement. The American gun shifted its fire to meet the threat. Keppler saw an opportunity. He jumped up and rushed forward, the rest of the truppen charging with him. He raised his rifle and shot the spotter in the head, sending him overtop the gunner. An artillery round hit the hill and Keppler felt a wave of heat wash over him as the concussion from the explosion hit him in the chest and sent him careening backwards.

*****

The explosion knocked down Wagner as well, but the boy was quick to renew his attack, jumping back up and running the last few meters to the pit. The machine-gunner was the only American left alive in the hole and he struggled with the belt of ammo feeding into the chamber of the weapon. Wagner arrived at the rim of the firing pit, aimed, and fired, but his rifle clicked with a miss-fire. The round did not go off.

The enemy soldier turned at the sound of the miss-fire and started to frantically pull on the flap covering his .45 pistol. Wagner jumped into the sandbagged pit, swinging his rifle like a baseball bat into the head of the machine-gunner. The solid walnut stock of his weapon knocked the man over and Wagner raised his rifle again to bring it down into the soldier as he still struggled to get the pistol free. Wagner froze. The man's image had turned into the squirrel in the bottom of a bucket. It then morphed into the gurgling American from the train yards. He watched helpless, his arms frozen above him holding the rifle up to hit the man, but nothing happened. It all seemed to be happening in slow motion as the American got the pistol free and started to bring it up. Then a single shot cracked out in the cold air and the enemy soldier's chest blew apart before Wagner's eyes. Wagner came out of his trance and regained control of his limbs, lowering the rifle. He looked up to the edge of the pit. Little Lubbert was struggling to his feet, one hand still clutching the liberated lugar. The recoil from the pistol had hit Lubbert in his helmeted head and knocked him to the ground. Lubbert stared into the pit at the dead soldier, the barrel of his pistol still smoking.

"Lubbert, thank you." Wagner felt his senses coming back to him. "I don't know what happened." Lubbert did not say anything. He stared pale-faced at the American he had gunned down. Wagner grimaced, knowing exactly what Lubbert was going through.

Wagner crossed over the dead bodies in the bottom of the pit and took the .45 from the dead American hand. He thought a pistol might come in handy like it had for Lubbert. Wagner then rifled through the man's equipment belt and took all of the extra magazines he could find for the pistol. When he was done, Wagner noticed the corner of a chocolate bar sticking out of the man's left breast pocket. There was some blood on the wrapper sprayed there by Lubbert's shot, but Wagner could care a less. It had been a long time since he had had any chocolate. He drew the bar out and presented half to Lubbert who crouched at the edge of the pit.

"Let's share this."

Lubbert took his half of the bar and devoured it greedily. "See if they have any more," Lubbert said with some chocolate smudged on his bottom lip.

Wagner searched the dead, but found nothing. It was then that they noticed the silence. The machinegun emplacements had been taken. Wagner and Lubbert left the firing pit to join the others in their search for Hearn. They found him collapsed in a heap near a tree. He was alive, but a gash in his left cheek went so deep it laid the cheek open and exposed some of his teeth. Keppler called for the Kompanie doctor, but they sent a litter instead to take Hearn down off the hill.

Manser showed up just as they were taking Hearn down off the hill.

"Well, Sergeant! Looks like you didn't bother to wait for the rest of us!" He was smiling from ear to ear with pride. "Did you loose very many men? They look pretty good to me." He said surveying the truppen loosely gathered around Keppler. "You did a fine job here." He then raised his voice so the rest of the truppen could hear him. "All you men did a fine job!"

For the first time, Wagner saw Manser in a new light. He realized what a hateful man this leader was. There was no compassion, no humanity. All he displayed was greed and ego.

Keppler bit his lip, willing himself not to say anything that would get him or the truppen in trouble.

"You can take a rest here Keppler. I'm going to send Sergeant Klaus' truppen the rest of the way up the hill. Some of the scouts say there is an enemy bunker up there. We'll let someone else do the fighting for the next little while, what do you say?" Manser waved Klaus over. "Klaus, do you think you can do as well as Keppler's men?" Manser prided himself on promoting competition within the Kompanie, but Klaus was a veteran just like Keppler, and could not be bothered with Manser's manipulation.

"We will do as you order us too," Klaus said, exchanging a glance with Keppler.

"Good! Then I order you to take the top of this hill!" Manser yelled, unhappy with Klaus' lack of enthusiasm. Klaus turned and walked back to his truppen where they waited near the edge of the clearing. "Get some rest Keppler." Manser continued. "I'm sure I'll need your truppen soon." The arrogant

Captain turned and strode back down the hill. Keppler congratulated himself on not plugging him in the back as he walked away.

Keppler's truppen sat down to rest. They watched as Klaus' truppen moved through their positions towards the top of the hill for a final push on the hill. Klaus' truppen was made up of older men who most likely were drafted from home guard units, maybe even some navy men. Keppler noticed they all looked at Wagner with some alarm as they passed the youth. Word about Wagner's exploits at the train yard had been going around the Kompanie all day. They hardly noticed the bodies they stepped over, being solely focused on his boys. Amazingly to the older men, these Hitler Youth appeared to be hardcore killers.

Already the boys in Keppler's truppen were beginning to look like veterans, especially compared to the truppen now going past them to experience their first solo fight.

"Wagner." Keppler called out. Wagner got up and ran over to Keppler.

"Yes Sergeant?" Wagner crouched down by the truppen leader.

"You're promoted to corporal." Keppler could see the fear in Wagner's eyes at the idea.

"Yes Sergeant." Wagner replied shakily. Wagner returned to his captured hole. Lubbert and Wagner had managed to push and pull the dead Americans out and they had the hole all to themselves.

"Congratulations, Wagner," Lubbert said with a shiver. He was pale from the last hour's activities, or maybe it was the intense cold.

"I don't think I like it very much," Wagner said. He normally would have been happy at a promotion, but after the events of the day he could care less. 'After all' he thought, 'it's Hearn's position, not mine.' Hearn was a natural leader and the truppen liked him. Wagner was unsure he would be able to fill his boots now that he was not here.

Lubbert looked at his friend and nodded in sympathy. "Hey, Wagner…"

"Yes?" Wagner looked over at his friend.

"Do you think I'll die as bravely as Bergin did?" Lubbert was sincere in his question.

"What makes you think you're going to die?" Wagner asked.

"I haven't seen anything that's made me think I'm going to live." Lubbert said matter of factly. As if to emphasize his point, shooting started up the hill as Klaus' truppen made a rush on the bunker.

Wagner did not know what to say. He stood there in the hole, quiet with his friend. He could not argue, because he felt the same way. He just hoped

Klaus's truppen took the position at the top of the hill because he did not want to go up there.

Chapter 15

South East Side, Murringen, Belgium

Night fell on the Ardennes. The snow had been coming down lightly all day, and with nightfall came more snow. Word came down from the top of the hill that Klaus' truppen had taken the bunker, but with heavy casualties. Keppler's truppen was ordered to hold their positions and Manser transferred his command to the captured bunker at the top of the hill.

After dark Keppler went to Wagner and asked him to take charge of the truppen as he had been called to a meeting in the command post. Keppler walked up the hill to the bunker. Outside the bunker were dead Americans, stacked like cordwood. Inside the bunker, warmth emitted from an oil heater Manser had liberated along with the bunker.

"Ah Keppler, come, sit." Manser waved to a small wooden stump near the heater. The Division Commander was there sitting beside the heater as well, Keppler remembered his name was Colonel Fagan. The crowded bunker was full of the Captains and Lieutenants of the Kompanie. Keppler wondered why he had been summoned here, as he was not an officer.

"Keppler," the Colonel began, "Lieutenant Lehrer was killed in action today. You will be his replacement." The Colonel flipped Keppler his new rank insignia for his shoulder boards. Keppler wanted to throw them on the ground. He wanted to argue that he was not officer material. Of course he did not, knowing that arguing with Fagan would be foolish and out of line. This time he would not be able to dodge the promotion.

"Our advance is moving according to schedule. Our American prisoners have all expressed great surprise at our attack." The Colonel paused and Keppler took the moment to look at Manser. He had killed all the prisoners their Kompanie captured and Keppler waited for Manser to react at the reference to prisoners, but Manser was busy brushing lint from his tunic. The Colonel continued, "The entire Corps is going to push onto Bullingen and Malmedy tomorrow in a three pronged attack. We need to free up the roads into these areas for our panzers in the rear. To the south we will be supported by the 3rd Parachute Division and to the north the 12th Volksgrenadier Division. We can't get more than two or three tanks down the roads at a time, so the infantry is going to have to do most of the pushing until we can get to the main roads." The Colonel pulled out a map and spread it on the ground indicating the current positions of the three German Divisions involved in the attack and small black arrows showing their proposed routes of advance.

Keppler took a deep breath. This whole plan seemed weak to him. 'As soon as this weather breaks, allied planes will be all over us.' He kept his thoughts to himself, but he knew as he looked around that he was not the only one who realized the precarious situation they were about to enter.

"Captain Manser, your Kompanie will head down this road and make sure it is secure for our tanks to follow. The 277th Volksgrenadier infantry regiment will add strength to your own infantry and help support the division. We have a lot of armor to move and a short time to do it in, so I expect large amounts of ground to be covered tomorrow." The Colonel's brow furrowed as he examined the map. It was clear to Keppler that even the Colonel did not like this plan, but like everyone else, he followed orders from someone.

"Captain Breuer, you will follow closely with your Panthers and give support to the 18th mechanized Kompanie's advance." The Captain nodded and leaned in closer to look at the map. It looked like he was trying to wish the lines of advance into a different direction. "Time is precious gentlemen. Let's not waste it." With that, the Colonel folded up his map and readied to dismiss them. He paused, "General Model has repeated the Fuhrer's words: 'Forward to and over the Meuse!'" The Colonel then raised his right hand, "Heil Hitler!" The rest of the men in the bunker raised their hands, including Keppler and all responded,

"Heil Hitler!" Keppler's declaration resembled more of a mumble, along with over half of the other officers. Only a few of them, like Manser, said it with enthusiasm. With that they were dismissed.

Keppler felt some relief as he stepped out into the cold air. It was not as hard to breathe out here as it had been in the crowded bunker. He had to stand still for a moment in the darkness and let his eyes adjust to the night. He noticed that Manser had moved up beside him.

"I recommended you for promotion myself Keppler. You will make a fine officer." Manser could not help but take the credit for Keppler's promotion. "I had expected you to make officer long before now, especially after you received your medal from the Fuhrer, but I guess we all have to wait until our time. Getting a field promotion is not something to be taken lightly. There are not many who get that privilege." Manser took a deep breath and rose up onto the balls of his feet with his hands behind his back. He settled his feet back down before he continued. "I expect the resistance to be even lighter tomorrow than it was today, and as long as this weather holds we don't have to worry about the American P-38's and British Mustangs taking a toll on the tanks." Manser acted like he had planned the entire attack himself, and Keppler was tired of his company.

"No disrespect Sir, but I need to see to the platoon and promote someone in the truppen into my former position." Keppler tried to keep the sting out of his voice but was not sure he had been able to hide it.

"Of course you do Lieutenant." Manser did not seem to notice Keppler's disdain and moved on down the hill ahead of Keppler as if he had somewhere else he needed to be in a hurry. Keppler breathed a sigh of relief and moved off down the hill to the truppen's position.

He went straight to Wagner's hole and told him he was promoted to Sergeant and was to take command of the truppen. Even in the dark Keppler could see the color drain from Wagner's face.

"Sir, I think someone else in the truppen is better suited for the job." Wagner argued.

"And I think someone else in the platoon is better suited to be the Lieutenant, but I still have to do the job because I was told too." Keppler made the promotion final by throwing his old shoulder boards to Wagner. "Promote whomever you want to as corporal. We move out tomorrow, down the road ahead of our armor. Get some rest. You're going to need it." Keppler left the truppen to check on the others of the platoon that were settled into the hill. He dreaded this promotion, but he could do nothing about it.

*****

Wagner watched Keppler leave and felt sick to his stomach again. Lubbert stood silently in the hole with him and watched Keppler go.

"I can't be the Sergeant." Wagner argued to himself out loud.

"Well don't make me Corporal, Wagner. I don't want it." Lubbert looked worried to the point that Wagner thought he might run out of the hole and never return.

"Don't worry Lubbert. Ten years old is a little young for a corporal. I think I'll make Mapes a corporal." Little Lubbert slouched in relief. Wagner could not understand it. A week ago, all he wanted in the world was to receive a promotion and become a hero. Now he did not want the responsibility of command. He did not want to be a hero either. He just wanted to live through all of this and go home.

"What are we going to do?" Lubbert asked as he sat down in the bottom of the frozen foxhole.

"Get some sleep, just like the Lieutenant said." Wagner slid his new shoulder boards on. "I'll be right back." Wagner crawled out of the hole and over to the other positions to make sure the truppen was situated the way Keppler had taught them. When he came to Mapes' hole he threw in the corporal shoulder boards and told him of his promotion. Mapes did not say anything. He just put them on and stared at Wagner in disbelief. Wagner informed the truppen of tomorrow's coming push and urged them to get some rest. He took the first watch and did not wake anyone to relieve him, as he could not sleep. Before first light Keppler was among them and told Wagner it was time to move out. They were heading to their jump off point.

Wagner sent Mapes ahead with the truppen and took a moment to throw up in the bottom of one of the captured American foxholes. He joined the truppen before they hit the bottom of the hill, sliding his bolt in his rifle the way he had seen Keppler do so many times to make sure it was not frozen shut.

Chapter 16

18 December 1944 day three of "Autumn Mist"

The heavy snow during the night made the road ahead of them look like a white river stretching out through the trees. Keppler had been briefed by Manser and knew that he would not have enough command of the situation to keep Manser's incompetence from becoming a liability to the men in the Kompanie.

It was becoming clear to Keppler the reason for the promotion. Manser knew Keppler had far greater battle experience and as long as he could keep Keppler close to him, it would be hard to tell who was making the decisions. Keppler's promotion had been a career move by Manser. Manser wanted to win the Iron Cross vicariously and he was willing to pay for it with the blood of others.

Manser made Keppler sick. He was ambitious and stupid, a combination he had seen in many on the Eastern Front. The problem was that they hardly ever ended up dead themselves. They had others killed in their place. There was a small hope, deep down inside Keppler that he might be able to counteract some of the poor decisions Manser seemed determined to make, but so far his advice had been ignored.

Keppler waved his arm forward, signaling to the truppen leaders that it was time to go. They had been waiting for his signal and moved out as soon as he gave the order. He watched as Wagner's truppen moved on the left side of the road cautiously, the way they had been taught. Keppler was responsible for the whole Kompanie, but he felt the most responsibility towards his old truppen. Manser had come up with the bright idea of blazing a hole in the enemy lines with infantry first and then letting the tanks exploit the breakthrough. Keppler thought it was a foolish move. It would slow them down and take away two of their best weapons, speed and surprise.

The other platoons that Manser had insisted act as flanking units had a harder time keeping up in the deep snow and dense brush. The platoons had been ordered to flank the road through the forest. Several times Keppler had to stop his truppens on the road and wait for the flanking units to catch up. It was not going fast enough for Manser's liking.

"Keppler, we have a timetable to keep too. Why are we stopping again?" Manser had his hands on his hips.

"Sir, if you want to lead the attack with infantry then we have to keep our flanks covered or we could walk into an ambush. If you would just let the armor lead then we would be able to move much faster and with less risk." Keppler did not care that Manser was mad. Let Manser demote him for all he cared.

"I want you to get these men up the road Lieutenant. If we run into an ambush then we'll bring up some Panthers and deal with it." Manser was angry, but he did not raise his voice.

"Sir, if you bring Panthers up into an ambush sight you'll get them knocked out, plain and simple. We need to use their speed to shoot up the road ahead of us. Speed is the key to victory here." Keppler tried not to smile at the angry red glow Manser's face adopted. Here was Keppler telling Manser that his current strategy was poor and ineffective and he was doing it in front of other officers.

"I am giving you a direct order to get these men moving up that road. Now move them out! We are not using the tanks until we encounter resistance." Manser had to clench his teeth to keep from yelling. His words come out in a hiss.

"Yes Sir. Just remember that I'm doing this under protest." Keppler moved away from Manser before he could respond. He motioned the truppens forward and the Kompanie continued down the road. They had scarcely moved fifty meters when a .30 caliber machinegun opened up and three of Horst's truppen went down on the right side of the road. Small arms fire pounded into the truppen a moment later as they tried to find cover and they were almost completely wiped out in the second salvo. Two survivors tried to make a run for the other side of the road, but were gunned down completing the annihilation of Horst's truppen.

The ambush seemed to be contained to one side of the road so Wagner's truppen was able to clear out of the ditch on the left side and into the trees without being fired upon. Keppler dove into the ditch with the support truppens when the firing broke out. He could hear Manser yelling for the Panthers to be brought up the road and he cringed. Keppler grabbed a sergeant next to him by the front of his coat and pulled him in close so he could be heard above the gunfire "Get across the road and try to flank their position before those Panthers arrive!" The man stared a Keppler for a moment, frozen to his place by the chugging sound of the American .30 caliber as it chewed into the road above them. The sergeant finally moved and called his truppen to action. They were up and running across the road to the other side as Keppler and the other truppens moved up to the top of the road and opened fire to give them some cover.

Two of the truppen went down while they crossed the road to the trees. One of the men was dead and the other had his stomach shot out. The wounded man began to scream and writhe on the frozen road, turning the snow crimson red around him.

The rest of the truppen made it into the trees and disappeared from sight as they moved deeper into the woods. The men with Keppler slunk down below the road as more rounds poured into their position from the American machinegun. The screaming of the wounded soldier on the road was having its effect on the men. One of them started to cry.

Without warning one of the young privates, a Hitler youth from Manser's command staff, sprang from the ditch and ran for the wounded man. He grabbed the writhing man and tried to move him back to cover. Keppler rushed to the top of the road and began to fire, trying to cover the boy.

The wounded man screamed in piercing agony as the boy tried to move him. The .30 caliber waited a moment before it ripped into the youth as he attempted to pull the man to safety, tearing his tunic open and throwing him dead onto the road behind the screaming wounded soldier. Keppler ducked back down just as the machinegun turned on his position and grinded up snow and asphalt.

The wounded man continued to cry out and scream in agony amid the chugging of the machinegun. The ground started to shake and the squeaking of tank treads could be heard. Manser's call for the Panthers had been answered. Keppler prayed that the truppen he sent across the road would be able to take out the ambush before the tanks arrived.

On the road, the wounded man pleaded for someone to help him. "The tank is going to run me over! Please God help me!" Keppler knew the tank would never see the wounded man on the road in its buttoned up state. The fate of the wounded man on the road was sealed. There was nothing to do for him and if anyone attempted, they would meet the same fate as the boy who so foolishly tried to pull him to safety.

As the tank got closer and the noise increased, the cries of the man on the road were drowned out, heard only faintly above the treads and the roaring engine of the first Panther.

A shot rang out from the American side of the road and a distinctive clang told of an anti tank round hitting the Panther's armor. The turret of the tank was turning. Keppler could hear the whine of the electric motor as it tried to bring its gun on line before the anti-tank gun fired again.

A second shot from the anti tank gun hit the Panther and a muffled explosion above Keppler's position verified that the tank had been taken out. Black smoke started to boil up into the crisp air on the road above them. There was no return fire by the Panther and the anti tank gun fell silent. There was no longer screaming from the wounded soldier on the road and Keppler knew that he had fallen victim to his own prophecy. The tank had run him over.

He chanced a glance at Manser who was staring at him. Manser looked at Keppler with venom, as if he had planned the ambush in conjunction with the Americans just to prove himself right. Manser was in a rage, but knew better than to say anything. Keppler looked away and tried to figure out their next move.

Just then firing broke out among the trees on the other side of the road and Keppler took the moment to bring the others into action. The truppen he sent across the road must have made contact with the Americans. He waved the rest of the Kompanie forward and sprung to his feet. He raced up the bank of the road and past the burning wreck of the Panther. The pungent smell of burnt hair and skin rolling out with the smoke from the smashed Panther caused his breath to catch in his throat.

He made it to the tree line safely. The shooting in the American position was growing in intensity and Keppler moved the remaining truppens in quickly to relieve the others.

He almost ran straight into the anti tank gun because it was so carefully concealed. Its crew had taken up their rifles and were firing behind them in the direction of their attackers so they did not see Keppler and the others come upon them. Keppler and the men with him opened fire and the anti-tank crew was instantly wiped out. They moved on, but by the time they got to the machinegun nest all they found were dead American bodies, and Wagner's truppen waiting for them.

Wagner had crossed the road further up and circled around behind the American defenders. They had taken out the machinegun without any casualties of their own. It was Keppler's old truppen that had attacked, not the one sent across the road. Keppler felt elated and proud of Wagner. He had shown more sense than the others in reacting to the ambush. Keppler could not keep from grinning.

"We flanked them Sir," Wagner stated proudly.

"You sure did." Keppler replied.

After some searching, they found the truppen Keppler had sent across the road in a flanking maneuver. The other sergeant had sent his truppen further into the woods on the American side for cover. The weak-willed sergeant had told his truppen to hold up and they had remained there even when the assault on the American position had begun. The sergeant was shaking and said his men had come under heavy fire and were pinned down. Keppler examined the area and found no trace of enemy activity. Keppler almost shot the man for cowardice. He could not stand cowards, but instead he demoted the man and moved him to another truppen.

Back on the road Manser was trying to get Captain Breuer to send up another Panther to clear the burning hull of the destroyed tank, but Breuer wanted to wait and make sure the area was secure. He did not want to loose any more tanks.

Keppler emerged from the trees with the Kompanie, just as their flanking truppens showed up at a dead run. The men in the Kompanie were tired, and the day had just begun. He looked down into the ditch where Horst's truppen had been hit. The ten gray-green forms with their snow capes splattered in blood lay twisted in various positions of death. On the road, two more of the truppen lay still. Manser had killed them just as much as the Americans had. 'If they had waited for the flanking truppens to move into the trees, or if Manser had agreed to let the armor lead…' Keppler stopped thinking about it. He could not afford to get angry with Manser right now.

"Okay, let's get back into our positions. Klaus you'll take Horst's position." Keppler had been holding Klaus' truppen in reserve since they had taken such heavy losses yesterday while attacking the bunker at the top of the hill. He now had an almost entirely new truppen from the battalion reserves.

They took up their positions and moved out. Keppler did not bother to look back at Manser, even though he could feel the Captain's eyes boring holes into the back of his head. The mistake in tactics could not be passed to Keppler as he had protested the move officially and Manser knew it. Everyone in the vicinity had heard Keppler make the protest, so there was no one to take the blame except for Manser.

The Kompanie moved further up the road, careful to remove the bodies off to the side so the Panthers following them would not further desecrate their fallen companions. The only body they could not move was the one flattened under the disabled tank. Manser did not argue about their progress anymore. Keppler would halt the advance on the road and wait for the truppens in the trees to move up, and switch the units around to keep the men in the trees from becoming exhausted. The process was painful to Keppler, but if Manser insisted on advancing with his infantry instead of tanks it had to be this way. On this narrow road they could not afford to encounter any more ambushes.

Around mid-day, Manser was informed by Battalion Headquarters that he needed to stop and wait for the support companies on his flanks to gain some ground. It seemed disheartening to Keppler that out of the entire Division Manser's Kompanie had been moving the fastest. The others were encountering little resistance, but they were having a hard time getting through the deep snow in the woods and needed about an hour to catch up. Manser looked up into the gray sky full of falling snow and cursed.

"Keppler, lead a patrol up the road and see if there is any sign of the enemy." Manser was hungry for battle. He wanted his Kompanie engaged and nothing else would satisfy him.

"Yes Sir." Keppler felt some relief actually to be getting away from Manser for a little while. He rounded up Wagner's truppen and Klaus' truppen for the patrol and moved them out down the road. He made sure they spaced themselves accordingly and had two point men, one from each truppen ahead of the troop on each side of the road.

They had moved up the road about half a kilometer when Keppler suddenly had a feeling that they should leave the road and move into the trees. He conferred with Klaus who agreed. He did not want to be on the open road much longer. They took both truppens into the trees and continued moving forward on the right side, keeping just in sight of the road through the trees and brush. It was harder to move in the deep snow, but Keppler felt better about their position.

Ten minutes later Keppler brought the patrol to a halt and had them take up firing positions inside the tree line. He heard armor coming down the road and could hear someone yelling in English. Keppler positioned the men into an ambush and they waited. Soon a small platoon of American soldiers came into view. They were moving down the road followed by a Bradley tank destroyer.

Keppler watched as the youth sighted in on the unsuspecting Americans, who obviously had no idea they were so close to the German advance. Keppler gave the signal and his patrol opened fire at virtually point blank range. The results were deadly. The American soldiers on the road writhed under the hailstorm of lead, all of them hitting the pavement without firing a shot. The Bradley gunned its engine and spun off the road into the far ditch trying to turn around. Keppler shot the man in the turret as the driver tried to get away, but the Bradley bogged down in the ditch on the other side of the road. It still moved, but they were in a bad position.

Keppler ran from the tree line and up onto the road with a grenade. He threw it at the open hatch where the man he had shot lay across the top of the turret. His grenade missed the opening as the Bradley lurched forward trying to retrace its path back up onto the road and escape.

Keppler's grenade exploded with a flat bang and seemed to egg the driver of the Bradley on to safety. The rest of the patrol arrived and they all threw grenades towards the opening on top. They were forced to flop down on the road before the grenades went off and did not get to see the results until they stood back up. The track was blown off the Bradley, its engine stalled, and its barrel was shoved into the tree-side bank of the ditch. A small white piece of torn bed sheet was improvised into a flag and was waving out of the top of the driver's hatch.

"Does anyone here speak English?" Keppler asked.

"I do." It was young Lubbert who had moved up to join them on the road. "My family used to live in London because that's where my dad worked before he brought us back to Germany. We came back to answer the call of the Fatherland." Keppler stared at the small boy. He had no idea Lubbert's family had come from England.

"Tell them to come out with their hands up," Keppler said.

Lubbert gave the instructions in English and a single pair of hands came up out of the driver's hatch, followed by a wide eyed, shaking American soldier.

"Tell him to come up here and to keep his hands raised in the air." Keppler was beginning to hate the fact that they were still standing out in the open on the road. "Wagner, take the patrol back into the tree line set up a defensive position." Wagner moved off and did as he was told.

The American arrived at the top of the road, his arms held high.

"Ask him if there are any more Americans in the tank destroyer." Keppler waited while his question was translated into English, and a response was given. Lubbert turned to Keppler and shook his head in the negative.

"He says they're all dead."

"Ask him if there are any more coming down the road."

Lubbert asked the prisoner and the prisoner gave his answer shaking his head no while he spoke.

"He says that they were separated from their company early yesterday and that they were on their way to reinforce Murringen. He says he hasn't seen any other American units all morning." Keppler eyed the man cautiously trying to see if he was lying.

Lubbert spoke to the man briefly again and then turned to Keppler. "He says he did not know Murringen had been captured by us." Keppler looked down the road in the direction the Americans had come from. He felt exposed on the road.

"Let's take him with us. Tell the men we're heading back." Keppler threw a grenade into the open hatch of the Bradley and the explosion was a muffled thump inside the armor. Keppler then took the prisoner himself and marched back down the road from where they had come, leaving the carnage of their ambush behind them. When they rejoined the Kompanie, Keppler turned the prisoner over to the military police before Manser could execute him. Then he reported their findings to Manser.

"If the Americans don't know we broke through then the roads should be clear!" Manser looked like a small child on Christmas morning.

"But Sir, we can't take the word of a single American soldier that the road ahead of us is clear." Keppler argued. Manser looked at him with the same glare he had given him earlier that day before the first ambush. Keppler fell silent.

"Load your men up into the half tracks. We're going to advance down the road and secure it at the cross roads before the enemy realizes what's happening here." Manser ordered.

Keppler felt his stomach sink. They were going to go charging into the crossroads without any regard for security, not to mention the direct orders from division to await their support companies' advancement. Instead of spearheading an attack with armor, Manser wanted to lead it with half-tracks.

Keppler reluctantly ordered the Kompanie into the half-tracks and soon after they were speeding down the road towards the important intersection that headed for Malmedy.

Keppler opted to ride with Wagner's truppen, still feeling a deep commitment to keeping his boys alive. He told them what to do if they were ambushed and they all sat ready for the shot to come at any moment.

They were several kilometers from the crossroads when the first anti-tank round hit the lead half-track. The American gunners had jumped the mark and fired too soon. They could have cut off the whole column. Their driver brought their half-track around the burning shell of the forward vehicle and Keppler readied himself to jump out over the side.

Another round from the anti tank gun hit the fourth vehicle. It was one of the only Panthers Manser had agreed to mix in with the half-tracks. The Panther tank was hit in the side and blew the tread off of it, turning it into a roadblock. The half-track they were in came to a skidding halt in the ditch and Keppler leapt over the side. The others followed him as he scrambled up into the tree line.

Keppler expected the trees to be full of American soldiers, but there was no one there. He positioned the truppen in the trees just as small arms fire broke out on the other side of the road, raking into the other truppens. They jumped from the trapped half-tracks on the road between the immobilized Panther and the burning hull in front of them.

The drivers of the trapped vehicles were halted on the road; perfect targets for the anti-tank gun, and the infantry were cut down by machinegun fire as they leapt for the ditches. Once again the brilliant strategic mind of Manser had led the Kompanie into a bloody trap.

The immobilized Panther fired into the tree line and the small arms fire withered somewhat from the American position. The anti-tank gun fired and hit the Panther again, disabling the main gun. The tank crew jumped out and ran for the ditch. All but one made it to safety.

German bodies lay all over the road between the immobilized Panther and the destroyed half-track. The rest of the column behind the ambush site had unloaded its infantry and they were already into the trees on the other side advancing on the American positions. A group of Americans tried to cross the road. Six of them ran straight for Keppler's position and were gunned down by Wagner's truppen. Machinegun fire was sporadic now and it sounded like the Americans were retreating through the trees.

Keppler cursed under his breath. These hit and run tactics would hurt them more than the stand up fights. He gathered the truppen up and searched their side of the woods for any signs of enemy soldiers, but it was clean. Up on the road, Captain Breuer was raging at the loss of a second tank and Manser was calling for something to come and clear the road to allow them to continue their advance on the crossroads.

Just then Colonel Fagan drove up in a kubelwagen and called Manser over to him. He spoke quietly for a few minutes and then got back into his command vehicle and left the scene. Manser, looking flushed, called Keppler over to where he was standing.

"I have decided that we will hold here until the rest of the Division gets into position." He huffed off, leaving Keppler open mouthed. Manser was losing control. Keppler spent his time directing the set-up of defensive positions while they waited for the support companies to arrive on their flanks.

They took the time to clear the wreckage and bodies off the road. After two hours of waiting they were cleared to advance again. The 277th Volksgrenadiers arrived by truck and took the lead. Keppler was more than happy to give the lead role to the grenadiers and wait behind in the half-tracks for a break through at the crossroads. The Kompanie had advanced six kilometers in five hours at a cost of 45 dead and 12 wounded, not to mention the loss of two Panther D's and three half-tracks.

While they waited, Breuer ordered the gas tanks emptied on the disabled vehicles, as there was such a shortage of fuel. Normally the vehicles of the 12th Division would have been left running in the cold to ensure they would be able to operate at a moments notice, but right now everything was shut off to conserve the precious fuel supplies they had left.

The sounds of fighting up ahead rose and fell in waves. The 277th had stepped into a fight and had been trying to break through for over an hour and they were still struggling to get into the American held position. After several failed attempts, they started to call for tanks to help support their attack.

"Keppler, I want you to take one of the assault platoons up and support the Panthers. We can't afford to lose any more." Manser almost huffed his command to Keppler as if to say 'don't you dare say anything to me about the losses we sustained today.' Of course, Keppler kept his mouth shut. He knew he did not need to state the obvious. There was already talk in the Kompanie that Manser was going to get everyone killed and that he should hand over his command to Keppler. Such talk was very dangerous for Keppler, and he knew it.

Keppler wanted to leave Wagner's truppen behind, but they belonged to the only intact platoon after the day's events. He took the four truppens from the platoon, including Wagner's, and moved out in support of the tanks. They went up the road as far as possible and then Keppler stopped the tanks.

"Wait here until we determine a safe rout for you to come in on." Keppler had to yell to be heard over the idling diesel engine. The tank commander nodded his head, obviously relieved that Keppler knew how to work with tanks.

"Okay, let's find out who's in charge here." He led the platoon into the trees and made contact with a group of grenadiers who were stocking up on ammo in the rear.

"Where's your commanding officer?" Keppler asked a corporal among them who was filling his webbing with fresh rounds for his rifle.

"Dead Sir, killed an hour ago right over there." He pointed off into the trees towards the sound of the heaviest fighting.

"Who's in charge of the attack?" Keppler asked.

"That would be Captain Dippel. He's right over there." The corporal pointed to a group of trees further into the forest where a truppen of Volksgrenadiers had dug in.

"Thanks," Keppler said as the corporal nodded and smiled, running back through the trees with his arms full of ammo for the others in the line.

Keppler walked over to the makeshift command post and asked for Captain Dippel. The Captain came over and started to make excuses right away as to why they had not yet made a breakthrough of the enemy positions.

"Captain, I'm not here to grill you, I'm here to lend a hand. I have three Panthers on the road back there waiting to be deployed, but first I need to know what the situation is. What are the enemy positions?" The Captain looked stunned.

"I'm not sure of the enemy positions right now." He stared blankly at Keppler.

"You mean to tell me you don't know what the defenders have set up around here?" Keppler was feeling incensed at the Captain. "Haven't you been up to the line to figure it out for yourself?" The Captain retreated back into his command post shaking his head and saying that he was needed to direct the battle from back here.

Keppler huffed and walked away from him. He could tell he was not going to get anything done by working with this guy. "Klaus I want you to take some of your truppen up to the line and find out what's going on up there. Find a place for us to deploy these Panthers so we can make a hole in these defenses." Klaus nodded and ran off towards the fighting.

"Wagner, you go back with the tanks and wait for my orders to move out. When you find out where I need them, move with the tanks the way I taught you, got it?" Keppler asked.

"Yes Sir," Wagner said and led the truppen back through the trees to the idling steel monsters on the road.

Klaus came back soon after to report,

"There is at least one American company in the trees up ahead and they're dug in pretty deep. Looks like they mean to hold onto the crossroads if they can. They even have a couple of tank-destroyers up there waiting for our armor to show up."

"Where are the tank destroyers holding up?" Keppler looked back towards the tanks, trying not to worry about the boys.

"Right near the crossroads." Klaus replied.

"Okay, ready the men to move on the position. First take out the tank destroyers, then we'll bring in the Panthers." Klaus moved off to prepare the men for their attack. Keppler walked back over to the useless Captain and asked to speak with him again. The man presented himself carefully, eyeing Keppler's SS insignia.

"I need you to give me a platoon. Do you have one in reserve?" Keppler asked.

"I have one in reserve. I was just about to commit it to the center for a charge on the American positions." He replied trying to prove that he was doing something proactive.

"Well, give them to me instead." Keppler insisted and the Captain relayed the orders. Soon Keppler was standing in front of his platoon, minus Wagner's truppen, and a platoon of Volksgrenadiers.

"I want you to split up into teams by mixing the truppens. I want panzerfausts with all of the groups. We're going to take out their tank destroyers so the Panthers can come up." The men did as Keppler commanded and mixed together without any need for guidance from Keppler. They looked like a good group.

The groups were ready and Keppler moved them out through the trees. As soon as they got near the crossroads they came under heavy fire from machineguns and small arms. The Americans were dug in deep and did not want to lose their positions. They knew the importance of the crossroads.

Two Volksgrenadiers went down and Klaus picked up their panzerfaust. He moved into position while under heavy fire and used the panzerfaust on the nearest enemy machinegun emplacement. After the frozen lumps of earth and snow settled, there was a smoking hole left where the gun had been.

The rest of the attackers seemed to take heart in Klaus' attack and opened up on the Americans. The firefight was fierce and Keppler noticed that in some places his men were only ten meters away from the defenders. The weight of the two platoons hitting the crossroads was more than the defenders could contain and soon the German infantry were overrunning the foxholes and firing pits. Then the American tank destroyers started to fire at Keppler's men. Keppler grabbed one of the Volksgrenadiers and told him to go and get the tanks. The man ran off towards the road.

One of the holes liberated by a small group of Volksgrenadiers and SS took a direct hit and everyone in the hole was killed. The tank destroyer was bringing its main gun back around to target the road when it exploded into a ball of flame and smoke. The Panthers had arrived.

Keppler yelled out and raised his rifle in the air. The timing had been perfect. He watched as the American gunners frantically tried to bring their last tank destroyer back around to target the lead Panther, but they were too late. It took two direct hits from the Panthers that had moved up into the crossroads.

A bazooka round clanged off the lead Panther's hull, but Wagner and the others were there and overran the American position before the lone American could reload. The Panthers broke the back of the defense and soon the defenders were running through the trees. A few of them raised their hands in surrender and were prodded at gunpoint towards the rear. With their flank turned, the American company panicked and abandoned their position.

Keppler's platoon had little time to rest from their attack on the crossroads. The Volksgrenadiers had set up defensive positions and gathered up the American wounded for evacuation to the rear with their own wounded. Manser was already screaming for Keppler to load up and move out as the 12th Division was now being fully committed to the attack. Manser believed the Americans had fled but the enemy had simply withdrawn about 900 meters to more prepared positions to their rear. Manser was furious and was demanding a full break out.

Keppler told Wagner to keep his truppen in reserve and the platoon moved out on the left flank of the Kompanie that was now advancing with tank support to the new American lines. As they moved through the trees, Keppler could see countless dead enemy soldiers. The Americans were holding at all costs, and they were ruining the German timetable of attack with their stubbornness.

It did not take long to find the grizzly green defenders. Machinegun and rifle fire poured into their advancing ranks and Keppler watched several of the lead elements of the platoon go down. The fire from the American lines was so intense that he sensed the Kompanie was about to break, but Captain Breuer managed to bring up six of his Panthers and a couple of Mark IV's just in time. The tanks brought direct machinegun fire into the defender's positions.

Keppler hit the ground and motioned for Wagner to stay back in reserve; he wanted to keep them out of the fight if he could. Keppler then crawled up to the lead truppen and found Klaus nursing a wounded leg.

"You okay?" he asked. Klaus looked at him and smiled. Klaus was a veteran and knew the value of a leg wound. "Good for you." Keppler smiled back and patted him on the shoulder. He grabbed Klaus by his webbing and drug him back towards the Kompanie aid station and over the heavy din of shooting Keppler was sure he could hear Klaus humming.

*****

Wagner watched as the Kompanie moved out to take the American positions. The noise of combat was so loud that Wagner could not have been heard by the truppen, so he used hand signals to communicate orders to them. He told them to stay in place until called as Keppler had ordered, and they all seemed relieved at the command, not wanting to go into the thicker tree line where the Americans had decided to make another fierce stand. The trees they found themselves in were thinner and gave the tanks room to maneuver, but offered less cover from the thousands of rounds lacing around them. To the right was a small ravine-like road and to the left, more trees.

Before them, the Kompanie was exchanging fire with the Americans. Some of the men were no more than ten meters away from the foxholes of the enemy. Grenades arced through the air from both sides and small arms fire raged together into one harmonious roar.

Wagner and the others watched as one of the men in Klaus' truppen went down, clutching his side. Then another went down, and again another. Wagner examined the American positions and watched as an American rifleman shot two more of the attackers before the bolt in his rifle locked open. His carbine was empty and he ejected his magazine. The man was reloading when three SS arrived at the brim of his foxhole and all discharged into him like a firing squad.

Further down the line through the trees, Wagner saw another American, blood running down the side of his face, throwing frozen dirt lumps and snowballs at a truppen from the platoon. Some of the SS wrestled him to the ground and hit him in the head to gain cooperation as he was taken prisoner.

Wagner noticed that the Capitalists were not as weak as Manser had said they were. Some of them were beginning to withdraw, not because they did not have the stomach for battle, but because they were out of ammunition. Some of the fighting was turning into hand-to-hand combat as the Kompanie pushed right into the foxholes of the defenders.

"Take your truppen over to the road Wagner! The tanks are going to make a push up that way!" It was Manser. He had to lean in close and yell in order for Wagner to hear what he was saying. "Don't just stand there, get into the fight!" Wagner wanted to explain to Manser that Keppler was holding him in reserve, but he knew it would be pointless. Instead, Wagner nodded his understanding and felt his stomach turn over. He was going into combat again. He brought the truppen to their feet and they set out for the ravine road on their right. Wagner looked around hoping to see Keppler but he was nowhere in sight. He was going to be on his own for a while- that much was clear.

Three Panthers were moving up the narrow road, managing to keep two of them side by side for the push on the narrow fork ahead of them. It looked like a simple assignment. They were half way to the fork when all hell broke loose.

Shooting from the fork tore into their position and Wagner saw Mapes go down, doubled over and holding his stomach. Wagner hit the dirt and started to return fire into the trees The Americans were like ghosts. He only got quick glimpses of them as they twisted around the trees to fire and then whipped back into cover. Manser had sent them directly into a kill zone. The Panthers gunned their engines trying to move in to give cover to the exposed truppen and soon the majority of the small arms fire was pinging off their armor.

Wagner was about to crawl over to a screaming Mapes when a loud clang caused him to hug the snow-covered earth under him. A 35mm round passed so close overhead that Wagner was sure he felt the wind of it as it hit a tree to the truppen's rear and sheared the trunk in half. He thought they had all escaped unharmed from the shell until he heard someone else crying out in pain. It was Saxony. He was competing with Mapes' shriek for help over the din of shooting. Saxony was a big burly boy and at age thirteen had been mistaken for a much older soldier from time to time. Seeing someone as brawny as Saxony go down was disheartening. One of the toughest soldiers of the truppen was now cradling a shattered leg, riddled with tree bark and 35mm shell.

The Panthers reacted swiftly to the enemy tank shell that hit the tree. Two brought guns about to target the Sherman tank that had recently fired.

The lead Panther rushed his shot and missed the Sherman completely. The second Panther also rushed and the 75mm round ricocheted off the Sherman's front, carving a large gapping scar that ran lengthwise across its armor. Another incoming 35mm round hit the lead Panther. This one was a direct hit, but did not penetrate the thick front armor of the tank. The Sherman's second round sent shards of zimmerit coating flying from the armor through the air, some of which pelted Wagner's helmet. This coating was designed to keep anti-tank mines from sticking to the Panther's hull.

Almost in succession, another 35mm round was fired from an additional Sherman further up the road, but it too failed to penetrate the Panther's thicker armor. The American tanks had been waiting in silence for the Panthers to come up the road so they could spring their trap, and now Wagner's truppen was caught in the middle of it. The lead Panther ignored the second Sherman and its main gun fired again, scoring a direct hit on the first Sherman. It exploded, rocking the massive chassis on its treads.

During the clash of the steel beasts, Wagner finally found the opportunity to crawl over to Mapes who was screaming in agony so loud that he could be heard every once in a while over the thundering battle. Wagner tried to pull Mapes' hands away from his wound to see how bad it was, but Mapes was clutching it too tight and Wagner gave up trying. He looked around for help, but everyone was concentrating on staying as low to the ground as possible.

"I need some help here!" Wagner screamed, but the noise of battle drowned out his plea. About a hundred yards further back, Oney had crawled over to Saxony and was trying to pull a large piece of tree trunk out of Saxony's leg as the wounded youth squirmed on the ground. The truppen was slammed hard with American small arms fire and Wagner knew they would all be hit soon if they did not get more support.

The lead Panther was blocking the path of the two tanks behind him so he gunned his engine and moved about ten meters further up the road before losing a tread to another 35mm round from the remaining Sherman. The movement left enough room for the other two Panthers behind him to come up. They both moved around and took out the last Sherman tank at near point blank range.

Wagner gripped Mapes' shoulder and yelled in his ear for him to hold on. He waved the truppen forward. The Panthers were now spraying the American positions with machinegun fire and it gave the truppen the respite they needed. Wagner was up and running, trying to get the truppen to fire into the trees, when a bazooka round hit the third Panther in the side and broke through the armor. The tank lurched once after the explosion and was still. Wagner continued to urge the rest of the truppen to shoot their rifles and soon the truppen's rifle fire joined the remaining two Panthers. It seemed like the tide had finally turned in the firefight. The outgoing rounds slashed into the trees and the incoming fire tapered off until there was no more return fire. It was at that moment everything seemed to stop. The sound of shooting dropped off to a few random shots and Wagner's ears rang in the silence. The hatch of the immobilized tank, its tread laid sprawled on the ground, flew open and a tank commander appeared.

"See if there are any more left in there," he barked at Wagner, pointing to the tree line on the other side of the ravine road. Wagner nodded and waved his truppen forward. As they entered the tree line, it became obvious there were no defenders left. Arms and legs were strewn around red painted shards of bark and shattered equipment. He came out of the shredded trees, willing himself not to get sick again and waved an all clear to the tank commander who then jumped out of his Panther too assess the damage done to his track.

Wagner brought the truppen back across the road to where Mapes had been shot. It had grown strangely quiet over there and Wagner feared the worst. He ran up the bank and over to Mapes who now lay still. Wagner pulled Mapes' hands away and saw that he had been holding his intestines in. Some of them spilled out like freshly wrapped sausage onto the ground. Mapes' eyes stared blankly in death at Wagner.

He quickly put Mapes' hands back over the wound before the rest of the truppen arrived so they would not have to see it. They were all quiet and pale. In the background, stretcher-bearers had come to collect Saxony whose leg was riddled with shrapnel. The wound was bad. Saxony would live, but he was out of the war. His screaming had stopped when he finally passed out from the pain. With medical attention attained for Saxony, the focus of the truppen was now on the crumpled form of Mapes.

"Is he dead?" Aiken asked, his voice quivering.

"Yes." Wagner replied, almost choking on the word. Aiken crossed over to Mapes and started to cry, holding his best friend's head in his lap.

It was at that moment Wagner realized little Lubbert was nowhere to be seen. He frantically searched for him and with relief finally found him on the other side of the ravine, sitting in the red stained snow, dead Americans all around him.

Wagner stood above him and watched as Lubbert anxiously rubbed snow on his boots.

"What are you doing?" Wagner asked.

"I can't get it off. It just won't come clean." Lubbert was shaking uncontrollably and rubbing his boots with snow in both hands, trying to get blood off of them.

"Come on Lubbert, we've got to go. We can't stay here." Wagner reached down and pulled Lubbert to his feet. Lubbert's blank face looked at Wagner.

"It just won't come off Wagner. Mom will never let me wear these boots in the house again." Lubbert was still shaking as he pulled his arm away from Wagner and crossed back over the road. Wagner reached down and picked up Lubbert's rifle. Wagner was worried about Lubbert. He had never seen anyone act that way before.

"Lubbert, here, you forgot your rifle." Lubbert turned and took the rifle from Wagner, then continued on his trek to the top of the embankment where the rest of the truppen had gathered around Mapes' body.

"Shouldn't we bury him?" Aiken asked tearfully. Wagner did not know what they should do and was about to tell them so when Manser showed up.

"What are you all standing around for?" He looked down at Mapes' body and then back to the truppen. "He's dead and he's not going to get up, so what are you waiting for? Let's get going!" Manser pointed his lugar into the trees where the Kompanie had advanced. "The fight is that way!"

Wagner waved the truppen forward and they followed Manser through the captured positions towards the sporadic small arms fire that seemed to permeate the entire forest around them. More tanks had come up the road and were moving past the immobilized Panthers. It seemed that the 12th Panzer Division had finally breached the lines of the 99th American Infantry Division and were beginning their lighting strike towards Malmedy, albeit 48 hours late.

*****

Darkness was approaching and the Americans had completely withdrawn from the trees across an open field where the Division artillery chased them until they were out of sight. The Kompanie received orders to dig in, occupy the captured positions of the enemy, and wait for morning.

Keppler sat back in a captured foxhole, looking at Wagner who had decided to share the hole with him. The boy had succumbed to exhaustion and was sleeping, unaware that Keppler was watching him. Keppler felt sick at the sight. 'A boy in charge of a truppen of other boys all forced to be men. Already, he was a veteran of combat.' He wondered what would become of Germany after they lost the war. Their future seemed to be dying with them and there was nothing he could do about it. News had reached them shortly after they bedded down for the night that Saxony would live, but the doctors had amputated his leg.

Everyone else seemed elated at the breakthrough and declared that the great offensive was on, but Keppler did not buy into the illusion. Once the weather cleared, the Americans would bring their air power into play and it would all be over. Some of the soldiers thought this attack was going to be a repeat of the invasion of France in 1940, but this was a different army than the one that had originally invaded France. This one was made up of boys and tanks with limited fuel supplies. 'Germany is in her death throws and no one sees it.' Keppler thought.

Lubbert worried him as well. He had seen the boy earlier sitting with his back against a tree, talking to himself and wringing his hands together. Keppler wondered how a ten-year-old boy could deal with being immersed into this level of death and destruction. War always got to you, one way or another. If you lived through the battle, it still found you, wanting to claim your soul. Keppler wished he could cry for him- for all the boys, but no tears came.

During the night, the hard-pressed 277th Volksgrenadier Division moved up into the line with the 12th SS Panzer. They stayed for some of the night, eating their chow and getting some much needed rest before moving out across the open field to renew attacks on the Americans at first light. The 277th was down to half their strength, having spearheaded the attacks on the American 99th division for the past three straight days.

Chapter 17

19ᵗʰ December 1944 day four of Autumn Mist

News was spreading through the lines first thing in the morning that the 1ˢᵗ Panzer Division had made a breakthrough at Lanzerath. Some said they would reach the Meuse by tomorrow. It was also rumored that Dietrich's lead elements had engaged American troops at Saint Vith, but Keppler knew better than to believe in rumors. Even if the advances were true, in the end Keppler knew they would amount to nothing.

Wagner came running up to Keppler as the Kompanie was preparing to move out.

"We can't find Lubbert," he gasped.

"What?" Keppler's mind started to reel as he thought of possibilities as to why Lubbert would be missing and where he could have gone.

"He didn't show up for breakfast and when I went to his hole Aiken said he hadn't seen him all night. Aiken thought he had found somewhere else to hole up." Wagner looked worried.

"Okay, when did you see him last?" The chances that Lubbert had been captured or killed during the night were remote as the 277ᵗʰ had been between them and the enemy lines, but there was always a chance that some American straggler had grabbed him.

"Last night, just after the 277ᵗʰ passed through. He was trying to clean his boots off and talking to himself."

"Get the truppen ready to pull out and I'll have a quick look for Lubbert." Keppler moved off through the trees to the rear of the Kompanie looking for Lubbert. The woods were full of frozen corpses and in the falling snow the dead looked like ice sculptures scattered among the shredded trees and churned up snow marking the path of the 12ᵗʰ Division's advance. He searched as long as he dared too but found no sign of him. He could not spare any more time.

Back at the Kompanie Command Post, Manser was raging on the radio at the forward elements of the 277th that had engaged the Americans earlier that morning, trying to take some high ground. The grenadiers were asking for tank support, but Manser told them they were not going to get it as the Division was going to skirt their position and break for open ground. He slammed the radio down in a huff and turned to Keppler.

"Load them up Lieutenant, we're moving out." Manser turned to leave after issuing the order.

"Sir, we're missing one of the men." Keppler stated.

"What do you mean we're missing one of the men?" Manser asked, turning back around to face Keppler.

"Lubbert disappeared and we can't seem to find him." Keppler reported.

"Did he get killed?" Manser asked sarcastically, raising his eyebrows to show his irritation with the matter. "You might not have noticed, but we've lost a few men in the Kompanie lately Keppler."

Keppler ignored the sarcasm and stood his ground. "No Sir, he wasn't killed yesterday. Both Wagner and I saw him just before dark and he was fine. Request permission to look for him." Keppler wanted to know what happened to the boy. He was the youngest one of the group.

"Request denied." Manser narrowed his eyes. "We can't spare the men to look for him. Load the Kompanie up. I want to be mobile in a few minutes." Manser turned and strode away, leaving Keppler to worry about Lubbert while he organized the Kompanie and got them loaded into the half-tracks.

Soon after, the Kompanie was headed at top speed up the narrow road towards the more open pavement of the Bullingen road. They could hear the fighting getting louder as they passed by the rear of the 277th and then fade as they skirted around the American position and headed for open country.

The snow made the travel on the roads more difficult and they had to watch to ensure that the column did not get too separated in the bad weather, but Keppler was glad for it. That meant that the allied planes would not be able to hit them today.

'Where could Lubbert have gone?' His mind would not let the thought alone. He feared the boy had run off. If he had, it would be a fate worse than death as his family would suffer along with him. Inwardly, Keppler hoped Lubbert had run away, far away, and with that hope he yearned to believe that Lubbert would not get caught and would escape the war. It was a hope that had little chance for success, but Keppler clung to it with all his might.

The Division made a sixteen-kilometer sprint, going farther in seven hours than they had in the last three days. As expected, however, the sprint did not last long. The half-tracks came to a skidding halt and the whistles started to blow as the infantry was dispersed. Keppler hit the ground, his Mauser rifle at the ready, as the boys scattered out of the back of the half-track. One of the companies from the 277th Volksgrenadier Division had come up with them and they were forming up in platoons and companies on either side of the road, preparing to move forward.

"Keppler!" It was Manser arriving on the run. "The Americans have blocked the road in force, we estimate Battalion strength. Ready your platoon to advance with the armor down the road. I want to punch a hole right through their lines before the sun sets!"

Manser was mad. Keppler could now see it in his eyes. Some men dealt with inevitable failure in different ways. Manser dealt with the impending failure of their offensive into Belgium by going mad. Manser rushed off to find the rest of the Kompanie leadership and get them to a ready position.

The truppen leaders from his platoon had found Keppler on the road where Manser had left him. They all waited for their orders. Keppler did not want the responsibility any more. He wanted to leave this place. He felt his emotions snap with the pressure of the last few days. Things were much simpler when he only had himself to worry about.

Two sig33 self-propelled artillery guns came up during the scramble of infantry and started to fire, their thunderous roar like the opening boom in an orchestra of chaos. The platoons in the woods began to move out in the growing darkness, trying to keep their textbook spacing and organization while they went through the trees, but the organization soon fell to confusion as units became mixed and soldiers became disoriented.

"Lieutenant Keppler? What are your orders, Sir?" Klaus had leaned in close to get Keppler's attention, favoring his bandaged leg, having refused at the last minute to be withdrawn with the wounded. Keppler pulled his gaze from the woods, stared at Klaus for a moment, and then answered.

"Lead the way, Klaus. We're going up the road, where else?" Klaus looked for a moment at Keppler, trying to find a connection, but there was nothing. It was like Keppler had turned himself off. "What other choice do we have?"

"4th Truppen, follow me!" Klaus yelled and his truppen moved out down the road behind him. Keppler turned to look at Wagner who was staring at him.

"What are you waiting for Wagner?" Keppler was feeling tired. He could not bear the responsibility any more. He had heard of Mapes' demise and the agonizing way he had died. At that moment he knew he could not protect the truppen any more. They were headed for the same fate as the rest of Germany no matter how hard he tried to keep them safe. It was too big for one man to control.

"Move out!" Keppler yelled, swinging his gaze to accuse all of the truppen leaders of inactivity. "What are you waiting for?" They all scrambled to organize their truppens, moving out down the road. The Kompanie stayed in their proper formation and spacing as they did not have to wade through trees to get to the battle. Keppler felt himself smile with regret. 'It'll cost us when we get to the American positions.' He looked at his platoon spread out over the open ground between the tree lines. 'What a waste.'

Keppler moved out at the head of the platoon, waving two runners over to him. "Make sure Klaus keeps behind the flanking platoons of the 277th. Let them hit the flanks before we bring up the tanks." The runner nodded and ran off for the lead elements of the platoon.

The choir of maschinepistoles (mp 40s), Karabiner Mauser 98k's, American carbines, and machineguns soon joined the bass thunder of the sig33's 15cm rounds. The trees flashed with the muzzle fire of weapons and were accentuated with the flat thumps of German stick grenades and the louder crack of American pineapple grenades. Keppler felt like raising his Mauser 98k and conducting, but instead he had to hit the dirt as their Kompanie came under direct fire from the American blocking force.

The runner beside Keppler had his head shorn off by an anti-tank round aimed at the Mark IV tank behind him. The blood that sprayed on Keppler's face felt warm in the cold air, and brought him out of his stupor. He rolled to his left and scrambled up the ditch back towards the rear truppen that was returning fire. A round hit Keppler in the helmet and spun it like a top on his head until it came to a rest backwards. He turned the helmet around the right way and kept going, unfazed by his close call with death.

Klaus' truppen had been the hardest hit. Hardly any of the men in the front were firing back. The ones that were not dead were trying to lie as flat on the ground as they could, attempting to get below the machinegun fire that battered into their position.

The reserve platoon came running up to lend weight to the attack and try to break the lead elements free. They came under intensive fire as well and had to go to ground, adding their weapons to the din. Three of the soldiers in the reserve platoon were carrying a Maschinenwehr 34 (MG.34) and set it up despite the heavy amount of incoming fire from the American positions. Soon the light machinegun was spewing rounds out and answering the

American .30cal fire incoming.

Keppler chambered a fresh round and waited for a clear shot. It took a little while, but he finally found a target in the trees. He centered his sights on an enemy soldier and fired. The man went down and struggled to get back up, leaning on his rifle. Someone else must have had the American sighted and hit him again and then again before he stayed down. Keppler ejected the used casing into the snow and looked into the open chamber that still smoked from the spent round. The numbness he usually felt like a warm blanket in combat became suffocating. He was struggling to feel, even enough to care about the fight he was in. Slamming another round into the chamber, he tried to find enough emotion to carry him through the battle.

His position was coming under heavier fire now so he slid back down the incline to the bottom of the ditch and crawled forward to try and get into a position to guide the forward truppens. As he crawled, he saw Wagner and what was left of his truppen, half of them firing, the other half-seeking cover under the intensive barrage of incoming rounds. He was almost to their position when Oney, one of Wagner's truppen, was hit in the face and his jaw blown off. He gripped at the wound with both hands trying to hold the shattered remains in place. His attempts to scream were lost and Aalders, on seeing Oney get hit, jumped up and started to run for the rear. It seemed that the sight was more than the youth could bear and he panicked.

Keppler dove for Aalders' feet, trying to get him out of the line of fire, but it was too late. Several rounds hit him at once and he writhed on his feet as the hot rounds pounded into his back and exited his front. He was dead before he hit the ground. Oney succumbed to shock and passed out in the bottom of the ditch.

Wagner held his ground though, and Keppler noticed tears running down the boy's cheeks as he continually reloaded and fired his weapon without shrinking back in the face of fire. Aiken lay beside Wagner, both of them holding their ground against the enemy. They were all that was left of the truppen. It was at that moment that Keppler's feelings returned from the dead. Seeing those tears on Wagner's face as he stood firm against the enemy caused a rebirth in Keppler. He felt immediately, and he felt deeply. Tears welled up in his own eyes for the first time in many years. Looking at the shattered body of Aalders just a meter away from him, his twelve-year-old features looking even younger in death, Keppler could not hold it back any longer. It was like a dam bursting inside him. He did not want to be here any more and the longer he stayed here the worse he felt. He wanted the madness to stop! Keppler jumped up and charged the American emplacements. He wanted to die, and he wanted to die now.

The rounds zipped by him, one of them even claimed his helmet for the second time, blowing it right off his head, but he remained unharmed. Keppler kept waiting for the magic bullet to strike practically praying for it. He held his Mauser rifle in his left hand and somehow had gotten a stick grenade in his right, the cap twisted off and the fuse activated.

He did not remember pulling out the grenade or even activating it. In fact later when he had time to reflect on the events he did not remember much about his charge into the American lines. There were just photographic-still memory images of the events: throwing the grenade; the explosion amongst the crowded defenders of the emplacement; soldiers going down on both sides; blood; the butt of his rifle shattering from an incoming round; the heel being shot off of his right boot.

During the whole event he knew he was screaming at the top of his lungs but the words were unknown to him. He jumped into the hole and raised his shattered weapon up, using it like a club. Soon there were German infantry all around him, charging the defenders and wrestling with them on the snow-covered ground. Keppler received a blow to the head and felt his face mash into the warm, moist, blood-covered chest of a dead enemy soldier at the bottom of the hole. The noise around him started to fade and he closed his eyes, surrendering to a darkness he hoped was death.

*****

Wagner watched horrified as Keppler got up and charged the enemy emplacement. The bullets raced all around Keppler, one of them taking his helmet off and another one shattering the walnut stock of his rifle, but he charged onwards holding a live grenade in his hand. Wagner flashed back to Bergin, flopping into the machinegun nest on the ridge. He tried to turn away so as not to watch but his eyes remained glued on the scene. Keppler's charge was a magnificent sight. The grenade was thrown and exploded among the Americans, and then Keppler was among them, fighting like a caged animal.

Wagner jumped up, almost out of control of his own actions. Aiken, the last of Wagner's truppen jumped up beside him and went down almost as fast as he had risen, shot in the head. Wagner charged without looking back at his dead companion. He felt spurred on by Keppler, who was risking his life for everyone else. He went to fire his rifle while on the run, but it jammed. Instead of trying to free the stuck round, Wagner dropped his rifle. As he charged across the road he pulled out the .45 pistol he had taken from the dead American.

As he ran, he noticed that the rest of the Kompanie was up and charging, following him and the crazed Lieutenant into the mouths of the enemy's weapons. Some of them were not as lucky as Wagner and Keppler, going down like Aiken before they could even build up momentum. Others made it part way before being riddled with bullets. The majority, however, reached the enemy lines and clashed with them at close quarters.

Wagner felt a moment of anxiety for the truppen, hoping they were following him, but then he remembered that there was no truppen any more. The last of them had fallen right beside him as he started his charge. They were all dead or wounded or missing. He ran across the open ground towards the enemy positions holding the pistol out in front of him like it was a shield. He fired the .45, the recoil more than he had expected, almost hitting himself in the nose with the kickback of the handgun. He had aimed at and hit an American infantryman as the enemy soldier clubbed a German soldier with an entrenching tool. Bringing the pistol back around to aim at another American, Wagner waded into the melee, but before he could fire, someone grabbed him by the arm.

Wagner was young, but big for his age, so when one of the American soldiers grabbed him by his pistol arm and threw him to the ground he was able to hold onto his attacker and pull him down with him.

Wagner lost his pistol in the scuffle and grabbed the American's wrist as he tried to bring a knife down into Wagner's chest. Despite the seriousness of the situation, Wagner felt surprisingly numb to the entire episode. Whether it was fatigue in the American, or his own adrenaline, he slowly overpowered the man, eventually breaking the man's grip on the knife.

As the knife fell to the bottom of the hole, the American ripped one of his hands free and took off his helmet, bringing it down into Wagner's face. The blow was hard but he barely felt it in the numbing cold. The American wrestled his other hand free from Wagner's grip and took the helmet in both hands, raising it up for another strike. Wagner ripped his Hitler Youth knife from its sheath and slammed it in between the man's ribs as Keppler had trained him to do.

The American did not scream, or make any noise at all for that matter. He looked down at the hilt of the knife sticking into him and then back at Wagner. The helmet in his hands fell to the frozen earth. He took the hilt of the knife in his now empty hands and pulled its seven-inch blade free from his chest. As if appraising the weapon at a pawnshop, the enemy soldier examined it, then fell over on top of Wagner and was still.

The pain in Wagner's face from the helmet blow began to surface but he did not react to it. He lay there under the dead American feeling the strange numbness exit his body through the tips of his fingers and toes until he was empty. Then, fear poured into him to take its place. Shaking, Wagner pushed the dead soldier off of him and crab walked to the wall of the emplacement, staring at the corpse before him. Steam spewed out from the chest wound and it looked like the cold was sucking the soul from the American's lifeless form. The eyes stared at him accusingly and Wagner looked away from the dead man briefly as if not looking at the body might make it go away.

When he did finally look back, he noticed something that made his heart jump. The dead soldier had an Indian head patch sewn onto his shoulder. It looked like some of the pictures Manser had shown them. It was a warning, just for him and he knew it. The Americans would hand him over to their Indian torturers for what he had done if they ever caught him. He looked at the other dead Americans in the pit with him and noticed they all wore the Indian head patch on their arms. Wagner knew it was a warning to all Germans. The American Indians would sooner or later exact revenge for this act.

The sound of fighting was not as severe and Wagner finally broke from his fearful trance to notice that a Kompanie of the 277th had come up from the rear to reinforce them. The Americans had broken and surrendered their positions, withdrawing through the trees.

Wagner looked down and realized he was sitting on a dead German soldier. He shot up as if he had sat on hot coals. Wagner did not know the man, but he felt like he had violated him somehow. He began looking for his liberated .45 handgun and found Keppler. The Lieutenant had a deep gash in the left side of his head from a rifle butt and he was just coming around mumbling names that Wagner was not familiar with.

"Are you okay, Sir?" Wagner looked into Keppler's right eye, as it was the only one open. His left eye was swollen shut and covered in blood from the head wound. There was a moment of confusion in Keppler's open eye but soon he shook his head and mumbled,

"Wagner? What are you doing here? Are you dead too?" Keppler reached out as he spoke and gripped Wagner's coat collar with his left hand to steady himself.

"You're not dead Sir. You were hit in the head. Are you okay?" Wagner could feel his own eyes swelling shut from the blow he received from the American helmet.

"Not dead?" Keppler said, slurring as if he were drunk. "Now that's a hell of a thing to say." With that he flopped back and was still. Wagner moved around to the side of Keppler and checked him. The Lieutenant was still breathing. Wagner realized he was having a hard time focusing on Keppler. He felt around in the bottom of the sticky, wet hole for the .45 pistol he had lost and finally found it, tucking it into his belt. By the time Wagner had fumbled his way back to Keppler's side the boy's eyes had completely swollen shut and Wagner found himself sliding in and out of consciousness.

During his delirium he became aware of someone shaking him. Wagner tried to focus and look into their face, but all he could see were dim outlines through his swollen eyes. He was attentive enough to know that he was being loaded onto a stretcher and slid into the back of a half-track, but he had no idea what was going on. All he knew was that the Indians would never take him alive; he would never allow that to happen.

The sounds of battle became less and less pronounced until they were gone all together. Wagner was not sure when they really stopped, as he continued to fade in and out of consciousness. All he knew is that suddenly the noises of battle had disappeared.

Chapter 18

Battalion Aid Station, Murringen, Belgium

The half-track took him to an aid station in the Division's rear. By the time they got there, Wagner's eyes were swollen so completely shut that he was blind to everything going on around him. He slid in and out of consciousness and was vaguely aware of being placed in a warm room. He did not know how long he had been there when he came fully around. He still could not see anything. He jerked slightly as someone placed an ice pack on his face and then the most amazing thing happened. He heard the voice of an angel.

"It looks like you took a bad blow," she said.

Wagner realized he had not heard a woman's voice, except for his mother's, in a long time and this voice was nothing like his mother's. He had been training for several months and there were not many women around the training grounds and Hitler Youth classrooms. Most women were busy in ammunition factories, or as firemen, and laborers.

"What's your name?" Wagner asked, almost embarrassed at the question, but needing to know what kind of name went with that voice.

"Jeannie," The voice said adjusting the ice pack on his face a little.

"Hello, Jeannie," Wagner said, wishing he could see her face.

"Hello," she replied, "hold this." She took his hand and placed it on the ice pack. Her hand was smooth and her fingers were small. "I have to help some of the others." He felt her weight leave the side of the cot where she had been sitting.

"You'll come back?" Wagner felt childish, but he really wanted to hear her speak again.

"Of course," and with that she was gone.

Somewhere in the room a man was screaming for God to help him, but all Wagner could think of was the soft voice of the woman who had been sitting beside him just a moment before. It was intoxicating. He lay back with the ice on his face and replayed her voice over and over in his head. He and the others had discussed the mystery of women, but none of them ever got very far. The truth was Wagner and his friends had never really been around women other than their own family members.

Several hours later a doctor came and examined Wagner. The doctor reported that his nose was crushed from the blow of the American's helmet. His cheekbones had also been fractured, but he would recover. It was painful getting his nose re-set and bandaged into place, but Wagner tried not to flinch and managed not to say a word. He normally would have screamed but he did not know if Jeannie was nearby and he felt the need to show how resilient he was.

He spent several days in darkness, his eyes swollen shut from the damage sustained by the helmet. During the days and nights, he faded in and out of sleep as the angel woman would come to him and talk in her heavenly voice. It was not until the fourth day in the hospital that Wagner opened his eyes and could actually see. He was lying in a cot inside a large mobile hospital.

He was happy to be able to see again, and the first thing he noticed was that his boots were off. He wiggled his toes under the blanket and reveled in the feeling for the moment. Then the pain in his face registered and broke his smile short. 'It's weird that I didn't notice my boots were off until now.' He thought. He spent his time looking at the shape of his toes underneath the blanket as they pointed heavenward.

"Are you feeling better this morning?" It was Jeannie, and finally, Wagner could see her. She was blond and short. Wagner had never seen an angel, but if he had, he knew it would have looked just like her. She was wearing a uniform for the League of German Girls, the female equivalent of the Hitler Youth. She had sounded like a woman, but now Wagner realized she was younger.

"No," he said matter of factly, "I feel like I was kicked in the face by a horse." Wagner was surprised at his response. He had not planned to say so much, but it all just came out.

"Well to tell you the truth, you look like you got kicked in the face by a horse," she said with a smile. Thrusting a tray forward towards him, she said, "I brought you something to eat, and don't worry, I cut it up into small pieces so it will be easier for you to chew."

Wagner felt a moment of panic hit him. He felt selfish and guilty all at once. He had not inquired about his friends in four days!

"Did they bring in a Lieutenant with me, a Lieutenant Keppler?" He shot upright in bed trying to look around as he asked the question, pain shooting from his face through every part of his body.

"I don't know," she looked worried at his sudden change.

"Could you please find out if he is here? Oh yeah, and also if they brought in a private named Kiefer Oney with a jaw wound or a private Erik Aiken with a head wound? I need to know if they're okay." Wagner felt like he had betrayed his fellow soldiers by not thinking about them earlier. Then he felt some shame at his outburst towards Jeannie, but she seemed used to it. Jeannie smiled again,

"I'll go and find out right now." Wagner felt some relief flood over him.

"Oh thank you. Thanks, Jeannie." He felt strange saying the name. He tried to smile, but the pain was too much. She bent down and left the tray in his lap before leaving to go inquire about his friends.

It felt like it took her forever to come back, but finally she did.

"There is a Lieutenant Keppler in one of the other wards. They're making a big fuss about him being a big hero who might be nominated for yet another Iron Cross for attacking a huge emplacement of enemy soldiers on his own a few nights ago." As she said the words Wagner felt his shoulders slump in relief.

"That's him," Wagner said, "is he going to be okay?"

"He took a pretty bad blow to the head, but the doctor says he will recover fully." Jeannie looked pleased that she could deliver good news. The truth of the matter was she did not get to give good news very often. So many of the soldiers wanted to know about their friends or the outcome of a battle and she just did not have the answers for them.

"What about Oney or Aiken?" he asked. The smile on her face faded

"They're not here that I could see."

"Do they have other hospitals? Somewhere else they could have been taken?" Wagner was beginning to fear the worst.

"Sure, they have medical units all over. You're friends may have been sent to one of them. Maybe they're in the same hospital together." Wagner could see the doubt in her face that the two missing privates would have been sent anywhere but here if they had survived their wounds.

"I didn't think you'd find Aiken here. He was shot in the head, but I thought there might be a chance." He let his sentence trail off at the end. "Thank you Jeannie." Wagner looked down at his tray of food still half full of food, his face too sore to finish it. She reached down and retrieved the tray, "Don't mention it." She winked at him and walked off down the ward. Wagner closed his eyes and tried to picture Oney as he wanted to remember him, hiking and singing songs together, but every picture ended with Oney getting his jaw blown off.

*****

Later that day Colonel Fagan arrived in the ward and Wagner heard his name mentioned by the Colonel. The doctor pointed to where Wagner was lying. Still trying not to feel anything above his neck, Wagner bemoaned the thought that the Colonel was coming over to see him. He did not feel like any visitors, especially an officer.

"Sergeant Wagner?" the Colonel asked standing at the foot of his bed.

"Yes Sir." Wagner answered. A week ago he would have tried to come to attention, but now he just looked up at his division commander.

"You are being awarded the Iron Cross second class for your assistance in leading the attack on the American defenses at the Bullingen crossroads." The Colonel clicked his heels together and raised his hand in the air. "Heil Hitler."

Wagner, too shocked for words, just stared open mouthed as the Iron Cross second class was pinned on his shirt by the Colonel. 'The Iron Cross? But I don't deserve a medal. I'm a killer, and I'm a coward.' Wagner thought.

"Don't you have anything to say Wagner?" the Colonel asked.

"Sir," he did not know another way to phrase it, "I don't deserve the Iron Cross. There are many others who were with me, and Lieutenant Keppler is the one who led the charge by himself." The Colonel stared down at him with a stern look for an uncomfortably long time before he bellowed out a deep laugh and slapped Wagner on the shoulder, causing profound pain in his face.

"Wagner! That's spoken like a true hero!" and with that, the Colonel turned to his staff and waved them out of the ward, following them down the row of beds. "A true hero!" He yelled again for everyone to hear just before he left the ward.

Wagner resisted the urge to throw the medal towards the Colonel's back as he walked away. Wagner looked on his medal with shame. 'Oney had his face shot off, but that wasn't good enough for a medal?' He felt a tear run down his swollen face and melt into some of the bandages. 'And what of Aalders who was gunned down, does he get nothing for his sacrifice. If Aiken had made it across the road with me wouldn't he be getting a medal too?' Another tear came and then another. He could not stop them as they fell silently, nor could he stop his hands from shaking uncontrollably.

Then someone was holding his hands and he looked up to see Jeannie. She was not smiling, but her face was warm. She just sat there and held his hands until they stopped shaking. When the moment passed and he regained control of himself she leaned in and kissed him on the forehead.

"I'll be back to see you in a while," she said softly and walked down the aisle.

Chapter 19

Battalion Aid Station, Murringen, Belgium

Keppler woke up in the hospital, unsure of his surroundings at first. He remembered seeing Wagner, his face smashed in. He remembered seeing blood all over the place and thinking he had finally been released from his slavery and given the gift of freedom; but now he realized he had survived his crazed charge on the American position. He tried to sit up but his head hurt too much. Keppler did not see what had hit him in the head. All he remembered was the slow fall to the bottom of the firing pit. He closed his eyes again trying to will his life away, but it just would not go from him.

"Keppler." He opened his eyes at the sound of his name and saw Heini standing at the foot of his bed. The fictional boy stood there with his blood soaked tunic draped open and his deep wounds from the communist knife stretched out across his torso like art. His ghostly form flickered a little the way it did when he was on the screen at the movie theatre.

"What do you want?" he asked, somewhat afraid of the boy.

"To be remembered..." Heini stated matter of factly. "I was created to be remembered."

"What do you want with me?" Keppler asked.

"Do you know what you have done?" The boy walked around the metal foot of the bed and placed a cold, dead hand on Keppler's foot. "You have brought me back, and made each of these children martyrs just as I was."

"Martyrs?" Keppler was confused. He had had visions of Heini before, but he had never talked to him so much before, and it was unsettling.

"A martyr, Keppler." Heini repeated. "Perhaps you would understand this appearance more." Before his eyes, Heini morphed into Dieter Bergin with his bone stub resting on Keppler's foot and a gapping wound in his shoulder. "Or perhaps this..." The form changed again to match Mapes, his bowels spilling out onto the white sheets of Keppler's bed. "Or this one..." Oney stood at the foot of the bed, his jaw missing.

"Enough!" Keppler screamed. He tried to get up and run. Heini resumed his own appearance and gripped Keppler by the shoulders, holding him down. Keppler could not push up against Heini's smothering pressure. His face was only inches away from Keppler.

"Protect them Keppler...you must protect them. That is your duty."

Heini was looking deep into Keppler's eyes. He changed shape one last time into the Russian boy from the train station. A trickle of dark blood ran down from the side of his head where the entry wound from the lugar appeared and dripped off his chin. "Do your duty Keppler. Protect them."

Keppler gasped. Heini was pushing him down hard into the bed, refusing to let him up. Slowly, Heini faded away and was replaced by two hospital attendants holding him onto the bed.

"Stay still Lieutenant!" One of them yelled trying to keep him from rising.

Keppler was so relieved at his new environment that he stopped struggling immediately. The attendants finally relaxed their hold on him and stood up.

"Just relax Lieutenant," one of the orderlies repeated, "The doctor will be by to see you shortly."

"Ah Lieutenant," it was the doctor arriving with a needle, "you have finally awakened." He came around the side of the bed and motioned one of the orderlies aside. Placing the needle down on the small table beside him, the doctor took out a light and flashed it in Keppler's eyes watching his dilation. Taking Keppler by the hand, he began to touch each finger and the palm, asking Keppler if he could feel the prodding. He moved to the other hand and both feet repeating the process. He asked Keppler to squeeze his hand and as Keppler did so the doctor smiled.

"You'll be fit in no time Lieutenant." He stood up and looked down at Keppler for a moment. "The Colonel was here and told me to give you this when you woke up." He held out an Iron Cross second-class for him. Keppler turned away from it like it was poison.

"Take it away. I don't want it." Keppler could not look at it.

"Oh, you might change your mind Lieutenant. I'll leave it here on the table beside you." He took up the needle and slid it in his pocket and left the medal on the small table. Then he shuffled off down the ward with the two orderlies in attendance and Keppler was left alone. He looked left and right to make sure Heini was not still there and when he was satisfied that Heini was gone, he allowed himself to relax. His head hurt deeply. Keppler fell into sleep without warning.

When he woke up, Keppler saw Wagner standing at the foot of his bed with his face covered in bandages. He gave out a small yelp at the site. He thought Heini was back to indict him again. He waited, but Wagner did not change form, he stayed the same.

"Are you feeling okay Sir?" Wagner said, his voice sounding a little funny from the bandages on his face and his half swollen cheeks.

"Fine Wagner." Keppler said realizing that his head still hurt and he was not hallucinating.

"What were you trying to do on the road?" The question accused him and Keppler knew he had already given his answer when he averted his eyes at Wagner's inquiry. Wagner paused reflecting on the expression on Keppler's face. "I see." Wagner replied. His was a mere comment without any accusation or judgment embedded into the remark.

There was a pause and Keppler continued to look away from Wagner's face, trying not to feel responsible for its puffed and bandaged black and blue appearance.

"Sir, are you responsible for this?" Keppler turned back expecting Wagner to be pointing to his face but instead he was holding out an Iron Cross in his hand. "If you are Sir, then I have to tell you, I don't want it." With that he placed it onto the blankets at the foot of Keppler's bed.

Keppler looked at the Iron Cross near his feet for a moment and then he started to laugh. He took his Iron Cross up off the table beside him holding it out towards Wagner. "And I don't want mine either Wagner, nor any of the other medals I've received."

At that moment Wagner understood more about Keppler than anyone else could have. He picked his Iron Cross up off the blanket and apologized to Keppler.

"Sorry Sir."

"You'll have to accept that," he pointed to the medal in Wagner's hand, "along with the other things you have to do as a soldier. They tell you where to go, what to do, and if you live through it, they hang decorations on you like you were some kind of damn Christmas tree. You know what happens to Christmas trees, don't you?" Keppler tried to sit up a little as he finished his sentence. "They dry out and get thrown away. So for now, you'll just have to wear you trimmings with patience and wait for the day you dry up and are freed from all of this." Keppler paused and looked down at the Iron Cross he held in his hand. Then he looked back up at the boy standing at the foot of the bed. "What about Aiken?" Keppler asked. Wagner just shook his head, unable to verbally say it. Keppler bowed his head again and looked at the small piece of tin in his hand.

"It makes you hate it even more doesn't it?" Keppler said softly before he looked up at Wagner.

"Yes Sir. That's why I was going to bring it back and give it too you. I'm ashamed to wear it." Keppler could see the child coming out in Wagner and he felt compassion for him. Wagner had hardened a lot since the train yards and that alone caused Keppler to feel despair. Wagner was a personification of the tragedy at work among the youth of Germany.

"Wagner, what are you doing out of bed?" It was Jeannie and she had come up behind him, taking him by the hand. "You'd better come back with me to your bed before some officer sees you and thinks you're fit for combat duty." She turned and glanced at Keppler who was half sitting, half lying on the bed. "See, I told you your friend was okay." She smiled at Keppler and for a moment he missed Gabi deeply. As they turned away, Keppler noticed she still held his hand and he smiled. 'Perhaps, given the right opportunities, there will be a future for Germany after all.' With that thought he tentatively drifted off to sleep again.

*****

Wagner allowed Jeannie to lead him back to his cot and put him back to bed. She leaned in close to him while she brought the blankets up around his neck and kissed him on the forehead.

"You have to be careful Wagner."

"Hyronimus, my name is Hyronimus." He interrupted, feeling dizzy at her presence. She smiled,

"Okay Hyronimus. You must be careful. If an officer sees you walking around, he will assume you're ready for combat duty and you'll be moved back up to the front."

"It sounds like you'd miss me." He could feel himself blush under the bandages as he said it. He could not believe he was being so forward. He had never had much luck with girls because he was so shy around them. Now it seemed he had the opposite problem and feared it would turn out just as badly. She leaned in and kissed him again on the forehead.

"Yes Hyronimus. I would miss you a lot." Then she gathered herself up and walked down the ward muttering something about finishing her duties.

Wagner's head swirled with feelings he had never considered before. He wanted to smile, but the attempt brought stabbing pain into his face.

Chapter 20

Battalion Aid Station, Murringen, Belgium

Christmas came and went with Jeannie's visits becoming more and more regular. She read to him in the evenings and would tell him stories of her hometown in Austria during the lulls in the day's activities. Wagner did not know what love was, but if he had to explain it to someone, he would have told him about Jeannie.

She was successful in keeping Wagner from being posted back on active duty until Keppler was ready to go back into the field. Finally, the news came. Wagner was to be transferred back to active duty the next day. He was being shipped out with Keppler in less than eight hours.

That night as Wagner lay in his bunk he felt her come and lay down beside him. Neither one said a word. He looked at her laying softly beside him in the moonlight. He wanted to kiss her, but he had never kissed a girl before. Even if he could have worked up the courage for such an act, he still had his bandages in the way.

A tear from Jeannie's eye escaped and melted into her cheek as she kissed him again softly on the forehead. Wagner wondered at the horrors her bright blue eyes must have seen in this place. She put her arm around his shoulders and pulled him into her bosom, the side of his face resting delicately on her chest as it slightly rose and fell with her breath. Wagner put his arm over her waist and pulled her in closer, reveling in her warmth. It was a magnificent experience. In the moonlight he could see her pulse as it beat out a rhythm on her neck and felt her breath tenderly caress a few of his stray hairs.

They both lay on the bed in the same position for a couple of hours, neither one of them speaking, just sharing the warmth of each other. Wagner could feel her heart beat lightly on the side of his head and hear its gentle rhythm in his ear. He closed his eyes and tried to keep her a part of him.

*****

Before the sun rose the next morning she was gone and he wondered for a moment if it had been a dream. An orderly came to take the bandages off his face and then left him to get dressed. He lifted his hand up to his recently un-bandaged nose and he could smell her perfume faintly on his palm.

Chapter 21

The doctor had come by and pronounced both Keppler and Wagner fit for duty. Wagner finally had a chance to look at himself in the mirror. He knew that in time there would be little evidence of the blows to his face, but for the moment he was black and blue all over, and his nose was still unusually large.

He was waiting outside the Divisional Hospital watching some of the Division's tanks and trucks going by on the road south. The Division had been reassigned to reinforce the Fifth Panzer Army. They were being ordered to take Bastogne. The Americans had put up a stubborn fight for two weeks straight in the city and even after being surrounded had held off attack after attack. The 12ᵗʰ Panzer was to break the siege once and for all.

They waited at the hospital all day. Their eight hour departure became sixteen as transportation was becoming scarce. They had to wait until nightfall for the main column to arrive. Nighttime was the only real safe time to travel now that the skies had cleared and the allies had been able to bring their air power into play.

"Sir." Wagner called out to the doctor as he passed by them in the growing darkness on the way back into the field hospital. The doctor stopped and swiveled to face Wagner, impatient as he was trying to ready the hospital to be moved with the rest of the Division.

"What is it?"

"I lost my Hitler Youth knife during my last engagement with the enemy and I wondering if you knew where the nearest quartermaster's truck was so I could get it replaced." The doctor looked at Wagner for a moment and then answered him.

"If you go around back of the hospital I'm sure you will be able to find a replacement there." With that the doctor turned and walked back into the hospital, calling for some of the orderlies to hurry their pace in preparing the patients for transfer.

Wagner shrugged his shoulders and walked through the trampled snow to the back of the hospital. When he came around the corner, he stopped in his tracks. There stacked almost as high as the hospital itself and stretched out for the length of the entire ward were dead bodies. The boots and belts were stripped off of the frozen cadavers, as were their helmets and other reusable materials. Some of them even had parts of their uniforms stripped leaving bare legs on some and bare torsos on others.

He did not know what to do. Before him over six hundred soldiers of the German army lay stacked like some discarded apparatus. There were several other soldiers there, packing away boxes of belts, boots, pants, and other stripped equipment from the dead.

"What do you need?" one of the men asked.

"I need a replacement for my Hitler Youth knife." Wagner stammered, trying to act calm at the site before him.

"Humph," the man grunted and disappeared behind some crates and came back with a knife for Wagner. "Here." He handed Wagner the knife handle first and then turned back to helping the others pack up three-ton trucks with the equipment. Wagner turned and walked back around to the front of the mobile hospital trying not to think of the white, frozen limbs and faces he had just seen.

"Wagner!" Wagner turned at the sound of the voice to see Corporal Adler Hearn striding up to him. He had a ghastly scar running down the side of his face where he had taken the shrapnel on the ridge.

"Hearn!" the two boys embraced for a moment. Wagner felt elated that Hearn was with him again. Until this very moment he had felt very alone in the world.

"I was told to report to you." Hearn said smiling, the scar on his cheek distracting to Wagner somewhat. "You are after all my truppen leader." Wagner felt embarrassed to be standing before Hearn as a superior NCO. "And might I add that your face looks good all puffed out." Wagner laughed despite the pain in his face at Hearn's teasing. Then he felt despair as he realized Hearn probably did not know about the fate of the truppen.

"I'm the truppen leader because I'm the only one left in the truppen." Wagner managed. He could tell by the look on Hearn's face that indeed he had not heard about the others. Hearn's face drained of color and he looked around for a place to sit down. He finally settled for the ground and fell to a sitting position, his mouth hanging open.

"You mean they're all gone like Bergin? Mapes, Aiken, Aalders, Saxton, Oney, even little Lubbert?" Hearn's voice dropped and he finished listing off the names to himself in a low reverenced utterance, as though he did not want to wake his dead friends from their sleep. He looked up at Wagner; tears welled up in the bottom of his eyes.

"I'm not too sure about Lubbert; he's missing in action. Saxton lost a leg and was sent home. The others as far as I know are all dead." Wagner tried to make it sound softer, but how could he soften the blow? It was then that Hearn noticed the Iron Cross hanging around Wagner's neck and Wagner became painfully aware of its presence there. He felt shame at the medal more now than before. It began to feel like a lead weight slowly strangling him. He wanted to tell Hearn it was not his idea and he would gladly give his life to have any of the others back, but all he could do was look away towards the road where the half-tracks of the 12th Division were speeding by on their way down South.

Hearn stood up and noticed that Keppler had arrived unannounced during the reunion of the boys. "Hello Sir," Hearn said, feeling awkward with the tears in his eyes.

"Corporal, it's good to see you again." Keppler turned to face Wagner. "I think someone wants to say goodbye to you." He slid to the side and there stood Jeannie. Wagner's heart sank. He was going away to the front again and chances were he would never see her again. It made her all the more beautiful. They embraced and Wagner ignored the nervous fluttering in his stomach and kissed her for the first time. The slight pain he still felt in his face washed away as his lips touched hers.

"I will think of you always," she said softly in his ear. She pulled away before Wagner could say anything and walked back inside the makeshift hospital to ready the wounded for their move with the Division. Wagner started after her, but Keppler caught him by the shoulder.

"It's better to remember her walking away from you," Keppler said as he gently held the boy in place. Wagner did not resist and soon turned back to see a half-track pulling into the snow and dirt churned courtyard. "It looks like our ride is here." Keppler put his other hand on Hearn's shoulder and they all three walked towards their transport. It was time to go back.

They traveled in the dark trying to make their way south to Bastogne. In the moonlight of the snow-covered countryside, the carnage of the past two weeks fighting could be clearly seen all along their trek. Destroyed Panzers, Shermans, artillery, anti-tank guns, and the dead were strewn around them as

133

they moved to their staging area twenty kilometers to the South.

The Division would have three days to regroup and then they were to attack the stubborn defenders of Bastogne. It was reported that the American airborne troops had been able to hold out against sixteen times their number for the last two weeks. Now the 12th SS Panzer Division had been dispatched to turn the tide and roll over the defenders.

Chapter 22

12th SS Panzer Divisional, four kilometers East from Bastogne

It took all night to coordinate the movement, but before the sun came up the next day the 12th SS Panzer Division had reached their staging area in the woods. They could hear the fierce fighting between the German and American forces clashing at Bastogne, the sounds of battle like a distant hymn behind closed church doors.

Wagner sat with Hearn and tried to eat. Despite their hunger, both felt little for the food before them. The division had been badly mauled over the last few weeks of fighting and they were taking three days to pull in replacements. It was no surprise when some showed up.

"Sergeant Wagner?" Wagner looked up from his meal to a small, smooth-faced boy in uniform. At first Wagner thought he was far too young to be here, but it was a ridiculous notion, because the boy was probably older than Wagner.

"Yes?" he asked still trying to take in the scene before him. There stood seven uniformed soldiers, all of them former Hitler Youth. Wagner looked at their new pea style camouflage and remembered that it was only a few weeks ago that his own clothing had been that crisp.

The youth called his truppen to attention and clicked his own heels together while raising his right hand.

"Heil Hitler!" The boy bellowed. He stood stiff before Wagner who allowed his spoon to drop back down into his stew. The boy continued, "Sergeant, we have been told to report to you for our assigned duties." Wagner leaned over to the side so he could see past the ridged spokesman and noticed that the others were all standing at attention as well. He turned back to his meal eating a few more bites before speaking to the group still at attention before him. "Do you want to get me killed?" He asked without looking up from his food. The youth did not know what to say for a moment and finally replied,

"No sergeant!"

"Then don't ever come to attention and salute me in the field again." Wagner looked up from his meal. "Is that clear?" The youth looked unsure of what to do as he loosened up and responded.

"Yes, sergeant." The others were slowly following suit relaxing their stance before him, but still standing motionless.

"That goes for the rest of you as well," Wagner said, raising his voice and pointing his spoon at them. He placed his now empty dish aside and dropped the spoon into its metal bottom with a clink, as he stood up. He walked around the loosely gathered group and looked them up and down. He noticed that they all were staring at the deep bruises around his eyes and nose from his wound and the Iron Cross around his neck.

Wagner did not feel shame the way he did when Hearn looked at his Iron Cross. He realized he felt nothing for these new replacements. They could not replace his friends. They did not know him and he did not want to know them.

"Show me how you would advance into battle," Wagner said turning and speaking to the youth that had declared himself their spokesman.

The youth smiled slightly at the chance to show what he was worth to his new sergeant. He turned and barked out the orders for the truppen to form up into a line and then turned them to the right and ordered them to march. Wagner looked at his boots and shook his head. Just a few weeks ago he had been the same as these replacements. Wagner called the group over to him.

"Come here all of you." They broke formation, came over to him and snapped to attention. "Are you all slow learners?" Slowly they relaxed their stances and stood in a semi circle around him. "This man behind me is Corporal Hearn." They all looked past Wagner to Hearn who was sitting on a log eating his chow. Hearn looked up at them briefly and then went back to his meal. Several of the new replacements noticed Hearn's black wound badge on his tunic and the massive red puffy scar on his cheek that made him look like a battle-hardened veteran.

"Corporal Hearn and myself are going to teach you how to stay alive for more than five minutes out here, which is how long you would live going into battle like that." Wagner paused and looked the group over. They all seemed so young to him, and Wagner had to keep reminding himself that some of these boys were older than he was. "Did you get something to eat?" he asked.

"No Sergeant," the spokesman said.

"Well you better go get it. It's a hot meal and you better take advantage because they only come along before a big fight." Wagner said.

"Why do we get a hot meal before a big fight?" one of the others asked.

Wagner looked at him and resisted the urge to smile before responding. "Because for some of you it will be your last meal." The youth hardened his face, not wanting to show any fear. Wagner turned his back on them and bent down to retrieve his mess kit. He picked up his bowl and began to wash it out with snow. The others realized they had been dismissed and made their way back to the field kitchen for their meal.

Once they were gone Hearn looked at Wagner. "Were we ever that foolish?" he asked. Wagner turned and looked at his scarred friend. "Yeah, and not too long ago either." he said, and then he paused, "Kind of nice, wasn't it?" Hearn smiled and nodded in response, trying to remember what innocence had felt like.

Keppler came into view walking through the trees the way the new replacements had retreated to eat. He walked up to Wagner and crouched down on his haunches before looking at him. "Are you going to be able to train them?"

"Yes Lieutenant," Wagner stated, putting his bowl away in his pack and turning to face his mentor.

"I figured as much," Keppler said with the hint of a smile. "I just thought I would ask." He looked at Hearn who had now finished his meal and was washing his bowl out with snow.

"You'll both learn to hate hot meals." Keppler said. Both of the boys nodded.

"We already do," Wagner replied.

"Good," Keppler said. "You're more experienced soldiers than you realize." Both of them smiled at Keppler. He stood and walked back the way he came, disappearing back into the trees. No sooner had he exited the scene than their new truppen emerged with their steaming meals.

"Sit and eat," Wagner said. "You have a heavy day ahead of you." Wagner pulled Hearn aside and they began to confer quietly with each other about the best way to train the new replacements. The truppen did as they were told, sitting and eating.

When they were done eating, Hearn and Wagner drilled the new truppen relentlessly throughout the day on their method of advance and their spacing when walking into a combat environment. Wagner mimicked Keppler's training as best he could and the new boys hung on every word he said. They worked hard on how to place their feet in the snow when they were advancing. He showed them how to advance on an enemy position when taking fire the way Keppler had done. He even gave them the same speech they had received on the hill from Keppler about dying for one's country. The speech made sense to Wagner more now than it did back then, but he could see that not all of these boys were believers. Hausser, one of the hardliners, rolled his eyes at the idea that it was better to live and fight another day if they could not win the battle than to die with supposed honor. Wagner wanted to push his point, but he did not want to make a scene that might eventually involve Manser.

Late in the day they broke for a quick bite to eat and then resumed the training by taking the new boys over to one of the Mark IV tanks. It sat under a tree with its engine turned off to keep it from becoming a target of enemy aircraft and to conserve the precious little fuel left in its tanks. They showed the boys a mock advance with armor. Wagner wanted to do more, but the sun was beginning to set and the truppen was beginning to tire.

Mealtime produced yet another warm stew.

"Geese," Hearn said after having the warm stew dumped into his bowl from the field kitchen staff, "they must expect a hard advance." Wagner nodded at Hearn's comment as stew fell into his bowl as well. Everyone knew they would be facing the American hundred and first airborne soon. It was an enemy division that demanded respect, and was no doubt the reason they were being fed so well.

The truppen ate in silence and after they were all done, Hearn and Wagner decided to try and find some bedding for their firing holes. The squad had complained at having to dig in when they were technically in the rear of the fighting, but Wagner carefully explained to them that they had to dig in just in case the Americans decided to shell their position. It was a familiar speech, having heard it from Keppler only a few weeks ago himself.

Wagner and Hearn chose two of the group to go with them to find some bedding for the bottoms of their cold holes. They decided to take the small wiry boy, named Henke, who had been elected the spokesman earlier that day and the hardliner Hausser. Wagner wanted to get Hausser away from the rest of the group for a little while since it seemed that he was the most rebellious of the lot, wanting to hold onto the old ideas of marching in battle and sing songs. Wagner had spent most of the day reeling him in and setting him straight.

"Okay, I want you to move like we are advancing on enemy positions. It will be good practice for you." Hausser rolled his eyes again, but he adopted a combative stance without any verbal complaining and moved out with Wagner and Hearn monitoring their progress.

Wagner and Hearn followed them pointing out their spacing and making sure they did not accidentally point their weapon at the other. They moved through the trees looking for pine bows or something to place in the bottom of their firing holes until they came upon a barn in a small clearing.

"Hey Wagner, you see what I see?" Hearn pointed to the outline of the barn in the moonlight.

"I sure do. I bet there is straw in there too." It seemed odd to think of the straw in the barn as a treasure, but Wagner felt it was nonetheless. "Okay you two show me how you would advance on that barn." There was an audible sigh from Hausser, but he moved off with Henke before Wagner could say anything.

Wagner and Hearn walked a few meters behind them to observe and were impressed by how much the two boys had learned during the day's activities, despite Hausser's grumbling.

"I think their life span has increased from five minutes to about an hour with some luck." Wagner muttered. Hearn only nodded in reply.

Henke and Hausser had reached the barn and were peering in through some of the slats on the wall that had separated. Wagner was just about to shout and tell them to get back on task when he heard a voice from inside the barn. It was not German and he instinctively crouched over and brought his weapon up to the ready. He had heard Lubbert speak English before so he knew it was not English that was being spoken. It sounded more like Polish, or something similar. Henke turned from his view, waving Wagner and Hearn over.

They trotted off through the snow for the last few meters making as little noise as possible and reached the opening in the slats. Wagner peered into the barn where a single lantern cast its light in shallow waves of orange light around the cramped room. Wagner could see four soldiers in the process of removing their Volksgrenadier uniforms and putting civilian clothes. Their shoulder patches were all from the 62nd Volksgrenadier Division. Wagner knew that meant all four of them were ethnic Germans. The 62nd Division had been made up of men taken from their homes in the Ukraine, Poland the Baltic States, and Russia. It was obvious they were changing so they could run away.

"They're running away." Wagner whispered to the others.

"What should we do Sergeant?" It was Hearn asking this time; glad he was not in command.

"We should kill them," Hausser said sliding the bolt on his rifle and chambering a round. The noise caused the four renegades inside the barn to pause for a moment and look around. Wagner motioned for the others to be quiet and the four men inside the barn soon resumed their clothing swap, one of them saying something in what Wagner thought was Polish, the others chuckling at whatever was said. Wagner stared hard at Hausser.

"If you ever do anything like that again, I'll shoot you myself." He whispered but his voice still had an edge to it that caused Hausser to lower his head and mumble an apology. "Wait until they come out of the barn into the open and then we'll arrest them." Wagner motioned for the others to spread out on either side of the barn doors. The small group moved off; Hearn and Henke taking one side while Wagner and Hausser took the other side.

Wagner wished they had come to the barn later or even earlier because he did not want to have to deal with this. He did not blame these men for wanting to escape, but he certainly would not allow it. He was still a soldier in the German army, no matter how much he wanted to go home. Duty was ingrained in him and he would do his duty as he had been taught.

The lantern that was burning inside the barn was extinguished and Wagner felt his heart rate increase. They were coming out. The door opened with a creak and the first one stuck his head out to make sure the coast was clear. He did not spot the group waiting for him so he waved the others out into the open. The rogue group snuck out and away from the barn heading for the distant tree line.

There were five of them now. One of the men must have remained out of sight in the barn. The deserters said nothing as they waded through the heavy snow, their desire to reach the tree line evident by the way they were already starting to hurry their pace. Wagner had been following the group with his rifle, waiting for them to get into the middle of the clearing before he spoke.

"Halt," Wagner said. He had not said it very loud, but it sounded like a thunderbolt to him in the silence.

The group seemed to panic at the word, and one of the renegades sprinted for the trees without looking back. Wagner looked at Hearn for a moment both of them shocked at the sudden burst of speed from the man. Wagner did not know what to do. He had counted on these men stopping when he told them too. The other four had turned to face them, but they looked like they were ready to run as well and Wagner knew he had to do something or all of them would just run off.

Pointing his rifle into the air he fired off a round and yelled, "Halt!" The four who remained standing and facing them sent their hands into the air and seemed to become rooted to their spots, but it only seemed to spur the man who was running for the trees on to greater strides through the hip deep snow. The man was going to be in the trees soon and Wagner had to make a decision.

"Can you wound him Hearn?" Wagner asked, knowing Hearn to be a better shot that he was.

"Not accurately in this fading light and not at this range, but I'm sure I can hit him." Hearn said, a pleading in his voice indicating that he would rather not shoot the man.

"Do it!" Wagner said. Wishing he could take the words back, but knowing if he could take them back he would just say them again.

Hearn paused for a painfully long time as the man fled closer and closer to the tree line until it seemed the man was going to make it. The rifle shot from Hearn's weapon seemed louder to Wagner than his own shot into the air. In the fading light the muzzle flash from Hearn's Mauser spewed four feet out from the barrel sending the 7.92mm round on its 755 meters per second trip into the fleeing renegade. The impact of the round sent the man crashing into the snow a couple of meters short of the trees where he had hoped to find safety.

"Wow, what a shot!" Hausser yelled as he jumped up and down in the snow excited to have been a witness to the deed. Wagner looked sideways at him and Hausser stopped, turning back to the four men with their hands up.

"Go check him Henke, and be careful. If he's only wounded and armed he may try to shoot you." Henke moved out and gave the group of four men a wide berth. "You men," Wagner tried to make his voice as authoritative as possible to maintain the deserter's cooperation, "kneel down and put your hands behind your heads so we can check you for weapons." The remaining four did as they were told.

"Hearn, cover us. They'll think twice about doing anything funny since they know how good a shot you are." He then turned to Hausser and stared hard at him as he spoke. "Don't do anything unless I tell you too, is that clear?" Hausser nodded and set his jaw, as if to keep himself from spurting off. "Good." Wagner stated.

He moved out with Hausser and they both approached the group carefully. Wagner searched them one at a time while Hausser stood pointing his rifle at them individually during each search. They all seemed to ignore Hausser however, keeping their eyes on Hearn who was covering the whole group from further out.

Wagner's search turned up a .45 handgun on one of the men and a map.

"Where did you get this?" Wagner asked the man holding the map up to his face. The man replied in English, and even though Wagner did not speak English, he had heard it enough that there was no mistaking it. He wished Lubbert were here to translate.

The thought of Lubbert crashed down upon his consciousness. He had not spent a day yet where he had not wondered about Lubbert's fate. He pushed the thought away, trying to focus on the task at hand. Wagner looked at one of the others in the group and pointed with the crumpled map in his hand at the English-speaking prisoner.

"Who is this man?" he asked.

The prisoner looked at Wagner and said in broken German "He is a pilot we captured. We convinced him to take us prisoner if we led him back to his own lines in return." Wagner looked at the three deserters and then at the pilot.

Henke came up to Wagner, having checked on the downed deserter. "He's dead," he said.

Wagner did not take his eyes of the prisoners. He was beginning to feel anger at these men for their treason.

"Good, it will save some time when it comes to the trial of these men." The color drained from the faces of the Ethnic Germans. They knew that once their case was brought to an officer their fate would be sealed.

"Please, I beg of you. This is not our fight." The man with broken German put his hands together as if in prayer. "Let us go. We just want to be able to go back to our families when this is all over." Wagner's anger burned up into his throat.

'What makes these men's lives any more important than mine?' He thought. 'I want to go home too, but you don't see me selling freedom to a captured pilot!' Before he knew what he was doing he had raised his rifle up and brought the butt of it crashing down into the man's face, dropping him in a heap in the snow. "Cowards!" Wagner yelled. The pilot and the other two men braced for the worst, but nothing happened.

"Hit him again! Hit him again!" Hausser vibrated with the desire to smash someone with his own rifle butt. A second glance from Wagner ended his excitement and Hausser choked on his outburst, regaining control of himself.

"Get to your feet." Wagner lowered his rifle pointing it at the man he had hit with his rifle butt. "The rest of you get up." They all struggled to their feet in the deep snow trying to keep their hands in the air. Wagner led them back towards the 12th Division's staging area. He noticed the pilot was looking with a calculating eye at all the tanks hidden in the trees. He could not have seen them from the air, but now that he was here it was obvious he wanted to note the location of each one.

Wagner took the captured party to Battalion head quarters. He turned the deserters and the American pilot over to Colonel Fagan personally.

"Good job Wagner." The Colonel said eyeing the captured pilot with interest. "We've had our trouble with this sort," he said indicating the three deserters. "We're glad you caught them, but this pilot is a real prize." He waved his hand at the three deserters and an armed escort took them away from in front of the Colonel's makeshift bunker. The headquarters had been set up in the basement of a partially collapsed house.

The Colonel spoke in English to the pilot for a moment, none of which Wagner understood, then he turned back to the youth. "Good work Wagner! I'm going to make sure you get some sort of credit for this." Fagan then pointed at the pilot and walked back into his bunker. Two of the Colonel's personal guards were holding the pilot by his arms and forced him to follow the Colonel.

"Let's go." Wagner said.

"Where too?" Hearn asked.

"To the barn," he replied. "We didn't get any straw for the bottom of our holes." As they were walking out of the command post area they heard the loud clap of a firing squad. The deserters had been 'dealt with' as Fagan promised. Wagner felt guilt welling up inside him. He might as well have pulled the trigger on those men himself. He knew what would happen to them when he turned them over, but what else could he have done? He tried not to think of the man kneeling before him in the snow with his hands clasped as if in prayer, begging to be let go. For a moment he pictured the man's family somewhere in the Ukraine, or Poland, or wherever he was from waiting for a father or husband to return home that would never come. Wagner clenched his hands into fists around his rifle driving the thought out of his mind. Guilt was getting too hard to carry around all the time. The group followed Wagner back to the barn. He noticed that Hearn would not look out towards the tree line despite the fact that you could not see the body of the man he had shot in the darkness anyway. Wagner knew how he felt. They gathered up armloads of straw for their holes and made it back to their Kompanie positions well into nightfall.

Chapter 23

01 January 1945 day 16 of Autumn Mist staging area for the 12th SS Panzer Division East of Bastogne

Keppler was on the way to Wagner's truppen to supervise some of their training when he heard a roar in the sky above him. It did not sound like any plane he had ever heard before and when he got a fix through the branches at the squadron he realized he was right. They were very fast and did not sound like they had propeller engines. They sounded more like V-2 rockets than planes, but they were piloted planes. There was no mistaking it by the way they moved.

He walked the rest of the way through the trees to Wagner's truppen trying to keep an ear out for any more of the strange craft he had seen, but he arrived at Wagner's position without any more sightings. When he arrived, he wished he could just turn around and head back. Unexpectedly Manser was there, but it was too late. Manser had already seen him. Manser was waving his arms about and relating information to Wagner's truppen as if he were the Fuhrer himself. He paused in his self-deception and called Keppler over.

"Keppler come, come I was just telling the men about the new fighter jets we are sending against the Americans and their weak allies." As much as Keppler wanted to hear about the new fighters he had seen streak overhead, he did not want to hear about it from Manser. The sound of plane engines drowned out anything else Manser was trying to say, saving Keppler the anguish of enduring Manser's exhortations of German supremacy and endurance.

Keppler, like everyone else, dove for cover expecting an allied bombardment, but it never came. After a few moments of relative peace, Keppler looked up to see the Luftwaffe flying overhead towards the American positions. He had never seen so many German planes in the sky at once in years. For two hours the Luftwaffe flew back and forth over their positions bombing and hitting their selected targets all over Belgium, Holland, and France. Manser pointed skyward and began to jump up and down, yelling that he had foreseen the Fuhrer's big strike and now it was underway.

Manser rushed off to the rear to make sure the Division was not needed sooner than their jump-off date. Keppler was glad to see him go and started working with Wagner and Hearn in the training of the new replacements to the truppen. Wagner had done a good job and praised him for the gains he had already made with the group. They were just getting ready to set up some more mock ambushes when Manser appeared running back through the trees, crashing through the branches without any regard for noise discipline as he came towards them. For a brief moment Keppler feared that Manser had actually convinced someone to approve an early attack.

"Keppler!" Manser yelled as he crashed through the last of the brush towards him. "You are to organize your platoon for a search of this sector!" He strode over to Keppler and shoved a map at him with a red box drawn on it. He was grinning like a schoolboy on his first day of classes as he thrust the map at him. "One of the pilots from the new Me 262 fighter jets went down in this area and command wants to retrieve him if possible. Since our Division is not committed to battle we are organizing search parties to comb the woods for him." Manser smiled. "I volunteered you naturally as you are the most capable in the kompanie!" Manser waited for a moment, hoping for a thank you from Keppler, but was forced to continue without any comment from his Lieutenant. "You can thank me later. Good luck Keppler!" Manser slapped him on the shoulder and strode off whistling, back the way he had come.

Keppler looked at the map and then up at Wagner who had stayed out of the way when Manser had shown up.

"Is your truppen ready for the field?" Keppler asked.

Wagner looked back at the new men in his truppen and then turned back to face Keppler before answering, "As ready as they'll ever be without combat experience."

"Well, I'm sure this area is going to be crawling with units from both sides, so they might just get some experience today." Keppler started back through the woods towards the rest of the platoon's positions. "Be ready to move out in twenty minutes, and pack light. We'll be back tonight so all you need is a bit of food, and water, but bring lots of ammunition."

*****

Wagner turned back to Hearn and looked at him before addressing the others and relaying Keppler's orders. He could see the same fear in Hearn's eyes that he felt himself. 'Will I be able to go back into combat?' It was a question Wagner could not answer until the time came. He had been wondering about being able to face bullets whipping through the air again since he left the hospital.

Wagner packed lightly as he instructed his truppen to do, but he made sure to bring his captured American .45 that he had recovered from the bottom of the American entrenchment two weeks ago. He held his Mauser at the ready as they moved through the thick trees, but was thankful for the handgun tucked in his belt. He had his plan to avoid torture at the hands of the American Indians. The Indian head patch he had seen on the dead American's shoulder haunted him during his waking hours and kept him from sleep most nights. 'Save the last bullet for myself.' It was not a popular plan, but it was better than the alternative of torture.

Keppler came over to Wagner during their trek through the trees and complimented him on the way his truppen moved through the snow. Wagner felt pride in the fact that Keppler approved. They searched for two hours before they heard their first sound of activity. Keppler waved them to cover and the platoon set up a quick ambush for the group coming through the trees towards them.

The group that emerged before them from the thick forest was a sorry looking lot and Wagner allowed himself to relax a little, as they were Germans. The truppen tromped through the snow without regard for sound discipline, as if they were out in the woods on a Sunday stroll. They were right among Keppler's platoon sized patrol before they noticed they had walked into another unit.

A Lieutenant leading the truppen that had come out of the woods looked dumfounded at the sight of the hidden men before him aiming their rifles in his direction.

"What are you men doing there?" he asked. "We're supposed to be looking for a downed pilot. Are you here to help or not?" The Lieutenant was the loudest of the bunch and was obviously flustered at having been caught unawares.

"Shut up and keep moving." It was Keppler who had appeared out of nowhere and was now standing next to the obnoxious officer.

"Well I'm sure you'll have some explaining to do when I report this to Battalion Head Quarters. What is you name?" The Lieutenant pulled out his notebook to record Keppler's answer.

Keppler, short of patience for the man reached up and grabbed him by the front of his tunic and pulled him in close. "Keppler. Johann Keppler. Now move your ass out of my area before you bring the whole American army down on us with your stupidity." The Lieutenant lowered his book and looked down at the Knights Cross with Oak Leaves, Swords, and Diamonds inside Keppler's collar.

"You're that Johann Keppler?" The dazed Lieutenant looked like he was going to ask Keppler for his autograph when Keppler pulled the Lieutenant past him and the man fell into the snow.

"Move your ass out of here." Keppler repeated with a hiss. The officer stood up and motioned for his men to follow him. They scampered out of the area. Keppler looked around at the rest of the platoon, some of whom were suppressing smiles at his treatment of another officer. Keppler kept his smile inward and motioned the platoon forward. They maintained their sound discipline as they moved, still able to hear the other truppen crashing about in the trees to their rear as they moved on to look for the pilot.

Keppler's party searched for the entire morning and turned up nothing. Just after they took a break and were eating their rations in the afternoon, Keppler motioned the platoon to ground. The platoon obeyed even though they could not hear anything. After a few minutes wait a small squad of American paratroopers appeared in the trees. They were moving carefully and they had in tow with them a German prisoner who was gagged and had his hands tied in front of him.

Keppler was letting them pass by, trying to determine if there were any other Americans with them when someone from the platoon fired and hit the lead American in the shoulder sending him to the snow covered forest floor. Then all hell broke loose. The platoon opened up and the Americans were riddled before them. The German prisoner had his hands in the air, tied together, and his eyes wide as bullets whipped past him into the riddled paratroopers.

Keppler was up and waving at the platoon to cease firing. The shooting slowly stopped and he advanced on the downed party of American paratroopers. The German prisoner rushed towards Keppler when he saw him stand up and almost knocked him over. Keppler grabbed the man and shoved him into the snow motioning for him to stay still.

Keppler moved down to the ambush site and looked over the riddled American bodies. They were all dead, that much was obvious, but he was more interested in the paratroopers being out here in the woods. He looked down at the screaming eagle patch on their shoulders and squatted down on his haunches beside one of the dead men. He took out his knife and cut the patch off the man's shoulder, then he returned to the recently liberated prisoner he had left sitting in the snow.

He pulled the man to his feet and cut the parachute cords used to tie his hands.

"Thank you," the man said in a shocked stupor. Keppler put his hand over the man's mouth and motioned for him to be quiet. He then led the man and the platoon out of the ambush site. Keppler made them move at a quick pace for half an hour away from the kill zone before he stopped the platoon. He set up skirmishers and a guard around the platoon's position before breaking silence. He called Wagner over to his position.

"Who fired at the Americans?" Keppler asked.

"It was one of the new guys. His name is Hausser." Wagner replied.

"Deal with him. Tell him that if he ever shoots before I give the order again I'll have him shot." Keppler was furious, but did not take his rage out on Wagner.

Wagner nodded and moved off towards his truppen's positions. Keppler then turned and faced the German pilot they had recovered.

"I take it you aren't a fighter pilot?" Keppler asked.

"No, I was flying a Junker 88 when I was shot down by a British Typhoon," he replied.

"Did you see anyone else?" Keppler asked.

"You mean other prisoners?" the bomber pilot asked. Keppler nodded an affirmative at the pilot's question. "No, I was the only one who managed to bail out of the Junker and the Americans picked me up as soon as I landed. They cut me down as my chute was caught up in the trees and took me prisoner, and then soon after you showed up." The pilot paused, "Thank you by the way."

"No problem," Keppler replied. He turned to his truppen leaders who were waiting and watching him for their orders. He motioned for them to move out and they started back through the trees towards the Division's area of operations. Keppler was calling off the search.

Chapter 24

01 January 1945 day 16 of Autumn Mist

Hearn moved out, keeping an eye on Hausser as he had been ordered. Hearn listened as Wagner bawled Hausser out, telling him he would be shot if he ever did that again and when they got back to the division he would be punished for his actions. Wagner had even taken Hausser's rifle away from him and now Hearn was carrying that with all the rest of his gear.

There was no denying that Hausser was a real hothead. Wagner wanted him to keep an eye on the kid, but it was a job Hearn really did not want. Besides having to lug the bastard's rifle around, he just knew Hausser was going to be more trouble than he was worth. Hausser persisted in smiling after Wagner left him. He was quietly bragging among the other replacements about his 'kill shot' on the American soldier and Hearn could smell trouble.

When they were almost back to the Division's area of operations, Keppler waved the platoon to a halt. Hearn took up a position behind a tree stump created by some previous shelling in the area and waited. Wagner motioned the truppen up and Hearn moved out with the rest of the truppen around the bulk of the platoon that had gone to ground. They were being sent on a sweep around the platoon's forward position.

Hearn moved through the trees at the ready, not sure what was going on, but keeping as quiet as possible. He even thought about giving Hausser back his rifle, just in case someone started shooting at them, but he restrained himself. Wagner had taken the rifle away, and only Wagner could give it back. He followed Wagner until they were in view of the platoon's hold up. Before them lay the slaughtered bodies from the previous truppen that had passed through their position. The loud, bumbling Lieutenant had led his men straight into an ambush and they had all been killed. The sight chilled Hearn to the bone. These men had been laughing and joking not more than three hours ago and now they were all dead because of poor leadership.

Wagner sent them around the perimeter, rifles at the ready to determine if the Americans were still in the area, but all Hearn found were empty shell casings in the trampled snow where the truppen had been attacked. Wagner moved back towards the platoon leaving Hearn in charge. Hausser wasted no time in coming up to Hearn after Wagner left.

"Did you see me take that American down back there?" he asked proudly.

"You should have waited for the command to fire." Hearn said sternly.

Hausser frowned. "I came here to kill Americans and free the Fatherland. Why should I have to wait to do it?" He was almost pouting as he finished his sentence. "Do you think I'll get in much trouble? When do you think I'll get my rifle back?" he asked.

Hearn looked into Hausser's eyes so his words might have more impact. "You'll get your rifle back when Lieutenant Keppler or Sergeant Wagner says you can have it back. If you ever shoot before ordered again, Lieutenant Keppler said he would shoot you himself and Lieutenant Keppler is a man of his word."

"What's his problem?" Hausser pouted. "You'd think I killed a German back there." He said jerking his thumb over his shoulder.

"You could have killed a lot of Germans back there." Hearn said with an obvious edge to his voice. Hausser lowered his eyes from Hearn's gaze and retreated back to his position without saying another word. The rest of the platoon was now coming forward and Hearn moved into a better position to cover their advance into the ambush site. They searched the dead for any survivors without luck.

'All this for a pilot?' Hearn thought to himself. Then he shrugged and moved out with the rest of the platoon back to their staging area.

They made it back without any further incidents and Hearn barely had time to set his gear down before Manser showed up and motioned him over. Hearn trotted over to Captain Manser and stood before him, waiting for him to say something. It was obvious Manser was angry about something.

"Well?"

"Well what Sir?"

"You are addressing a superior officer corporal, I expect you to salute me when you approach. Have you forgotten all I taught you already?" Hearn blushed with the berating and quickly saluted Manser as he was instructed to do. Manser returned the salute and then got down to business.

"Corporal, I would like you to gather a small group of men together and take out a patrol." Manser had his hands clasped behind his back.

"Yes Sir." Hearn paused for a moment then added "Where would you like me to go?"

Manser smiled as if he was going to give Hearn a present,

"I'd like you to scout into the American lines and determine if they are spaced to repel armor thrusts around Bastogne." He then leaned down so that his face was right in Hearn's. "Make me proud Corporal. I recommended you to the Colonel for this mission."

"Yes Sir," he said. Hearn felt sick and elated at the same time. He wanted to please Manser, but he did not want to take a patrol into the American lines.

Manser smiled, wheeled about, and started to stride away, "I knew I could count on you Hearn."

Hearn moved over to Wagner and told him about Manser's order.

"He's gone off his nut." Wagner stated. "Why doesn't he ask the Panzer Lehr division about the defenses around Bastogne? They've been fighting there for over two weeks!"

"Well, what am I to do?" Hearn felt like he should be defending Manser. "He gave me a direct order personally, and recommended me to the Colonel."

"Don't go all the way up to the lines." Wagner begged. "Just ask some of the men from the Panzer Lehr regiments that have been fighting there. They'll be able to tell you more than you could learn from a patrol anyway."

Hearn nodded and then asked, "Is there anyone in particular you would like me to take?"

"Well if you don't plan on going all the way I say take some of the new guys to give them some experience. Take Hausser and Henke for sure." Hearn winced as Wagner said the names.

"I think Hausser is crazy," Hearn protested.

"Well it's up to us to try and teach him some restraint before he gets us all killed and if you can expose him to some levels of responsibility like this patrol then perhaps he'll come around." Wagner explained. All of a sudden he felt uncomfortable giving direction and orders to Hearn. Hearn had always been his superior until the unfortunate shelling on the hill. "You'll figure it out." Wagner added trying to hand some of the decision making back to Hearn. The Sergeant turned and walked away.

153

Chapter 25

01 January 1945 day 16 of Autumn Mist

Hearn gathered up his gear again and made sure to pack light, taking just ammo and water. He collected Hausser, Henke, and another new soldier named Koch and told them to get their gear. He thrust Hausser's rifle out towards him. "Don't make me regret giving this back to you."

"We have to go out again?" Henke complained.

"Good," Hausser said grabbing his rifle.

"Make sure you follow orders this time Hausser," Hearn emphasized as he stepped close, "or I'll institute my own justice." Hausser shrank back a few inches and nodded.

"Do we have time to grab something to eat?" Koch asked.

"Just eat some of your sausage while we walk. We need to get to the Panzer Lehr Division area before it gets dark so we can properly identify ourselves without getting shot." The others grabbed their gear and followed Hearn down the road towards Bastogne.

As they walked, Hearn began to think about the explicit orders he had received from Manser on the duties of the patrol. 'All Manser has to do is ask any of the new guys with me and he'll know I disobeyed orders. Besides, Wagner is out of line. Who does he think he is, now that he's a big war hero? This is my big break. I have a responsibility to the division to inspect the American defenses myself. If I am successful I could earn my own squad!' Hearn's thoughts began to circulate in his head. He saw Wagner as a jealous Sergeant who wanted to keep a firm grip on his command of the truppen.

Before Hearn reached the Panzer Lehr Divisional rear he had made up his mind to go ahead with the patrol. Hearn reported to a Captain at the Divisional Head Quarters for the Panzer Lehr Division. Hearn was not impressed with the officer, as he seemed to be in on the conspiracy to keep him from following Manser's orders,

"You don't need to go up there. As I told your Captain Manser earlier, there isn't any need for him to send up a patrol. I can give you all the information you need. In fact I already told him all about the placement of the enemy positions." Hearn stiffened in his reserve to follow Manser's orders as he listened to the Captain. He had received a direct order and he was going to follow it.

"With all due respect Sir, I have received direct orders from my commanding officer to inspect the enemy lines before we move our armor up and that is exactly what I'm going to do." The Captain's eyes narrowed at Hearn's stubbornness.

"It's you funeral," he said in a monotone voice. The Captain handed Hearn a map and showed him the best rout to take to the front.

"Thank you Captain," Hearn said and waved his small patrol forward. The Captain shook his head and went back into his bunker mumbling something about stupidity and inexperience. Hearn narrowed his eyes and felt anger course through his veins. It seemed like everyone except for Manser doubted his ability to do his job.

Hearn led the squad through the heavily dug-in forward regiment of the Panzer Lehr division. The men in their holes looked blankly out at Hearn and his party as they passed by. They all looked like dead men waiting for someone to come along and fill in their holes.

As they neared the front, Hearn and the others found some firing holes to take refuge in until the sun went completely down. Hearn's group had to split up and Hearn found himself in a hole with two men from the Panzer Lehr Division. It was cold, like every other night, but this time Hearn did not think about the biting frost on his cheeks. He was focused on his mission.

"Why are you so anxious to go and get killed?" One of the men asked after Hearn explained the mission to them. "The Americans won't let you get too far before they kill all of you." He sounded almost hysterical.

"I'm following orders!" Hearn defended his decision to the two privates in the hole with him. He briefly thought of his friend Dieter Bergin and his last charge at the machinegun nest. He could see his arm hanging lame by his side as he clutched the grenade. Bergin had done it right.

"Orders? Ha!" the other man said, "Those orders are insane! Just like the orders to take Bastogne!" The first man nudged his friend with his elbow and shut him up.

"Never mind him," the first man said, "we've been fighting every day since the offensive began and the American paratroopers have killed a lot of our friends. He's not feeling too well." He then turned to his hushed companion and muttered something about Hearn being a hardliner that could get them in trouble. Hearn finally felt like he was earning some respect.

For the first time, Hearn took a hard look in the fading light at the two men in the hole with him. They both looked grizzled with two weeks growth of beards and their white camouflage tunics were spattered with bloodstains and torn.

"The only thing you'll find over there is death, boy." The second man hissed and then turned his head away from Hearn. An uncomfortable hush came over the hole and Hearn waited until the sun had completely set before moving out to retrieve his patrol from the various holes they were huddled in.

*****

Hearn cautioned the recruits to keep silence and they moved out through the scattered holes and defenses of the 43rd Regiment of the Panzer Lehr Division. Crawling through the trampled snow, Hearn paused behind some frozen bodies to let the patrol gather around him.

"If anyone gets lost, head straight back the way we came. The password is barstool. Does everyone understand?" Hearn whispered his words to them and they all whispered their affirmatives back.

"Okay. Do not shoot unless absolutely necessary or we're all dead men." Hearn looked in Hausser's direction as he said it and then he moved out. They had moved forward only about twenty-five meters towards the American lines when artillery shells started to land.

Hearn did not know which side was doing the shelling. The shells were falling among the German and the American lines and it was imperative that they find cover. He turned and started to belly crawl back towards the rest of the patrol in an attempt to gather them up and take them back to the 43rd's lines, but the only person he found was Hausser. Henke and Koch were nowhere to be found.

The shells were slamming down into the ground so hard around Hearn that some of the blasts sent him half a meter into the air before slamming him down amid frozen chunks of earth and snow. He had never been on the receiving end of artillery except for the stray shell on the hill, but that had been enough to spook Hearn.

"Follow me!" Hearn yelled into Hausser's ear trying to be heard over the crash of artillery shells. Wanting to escape the panic he felt, he crawled blindly along. Hearn tried to keep his eyes open, but they would not as he instinctively shut them tight with every blast, expecting to feel his cheek ripped from his face again. He did not see the hole in front of him until he fell into it. His descent came as a shock. Hearn landed hard on someone else who was curled up in the fetal position trying to gain as much cover as possible from the shelling.

His hands rested on the boots of the man in the bottom of the hole and in the darkness he could feel laces. Hearn knew that German jackboots did not have laces! He had just landed in a hole with an American paratrooper! The paratrooper was obviously as confused as Hearn as he started to swear in English at him for the intrusion. Hearn was struggling to get his knife out and defend himself when Hausser made the same mistake and plunged into the hole with them.

The American's foxhole was only big enough for one person, so three of them in the hole made it too cramped to move. The American was swearing at the top of his lungs, obviously mistaken as to the nationality of the two other people in the hole with him.

He put his hands out and started to shove on Hearn's chest trying to get him to leave the overcrowded hole. Hearn was in shock and did not know what to do, so he resisted being shoved out into the hailstorm of shrapnel raining down around the position by pushing the American back. It was Hausser who broke the shoving match up by drawing his Hitler Youth knife and stabbing the American.

The man had not expected the attack and howled in pain and shock at being skewered. A large blast from a shell near the hole sent both Hearn and Hausser crashing to the bottom of the hole. The American came down on top of them and all three of them lay still as the shelling continued.

The shelling ended as fast as it had begun and left silence in its wake. Overhead the cloud cover was starting to clear and the moon brought a bluish hue over the landscape of smoking shell holes, shattered bodies, and moaning wounded.

In the moonlight, both Hearn and Hausser could see the American's face mere millimeters away. The man was not dead yet, and he had tears running down his face, and some blood was frothing at the side of his mouth every time he exhaled, but the American did not make a sound. Hausser's knife handle was still protruding from the man's chest where he had been stabbed and Hausser was shaking beside Hearn at the sight of the mortally wounded American on top of him.

Hearn tried to shove the American up a little and make some room for him to move around and try to get some feeling back in his legs, but the shove caused the American to scream out in pain. Hearn looked over at Hausser, whose face was pale, even in the moonlight.

All three of them stayed motionless in the bottom of the hole: the American, in too much pain and too weak to move, and the boys, staying still to keep the American from screaming out. The American whimpered in a low chant for about two hours straight and it had a terrible effect on Hearn's nerves. He wanted to take the knife Hausser had left there in his chest and finish the man off to shut him up, but he just could not bear to do it. He wished Hausser would do the job and finish what he started, but one look at him and Hearn knew Hausser could not do it either. The cold was terrible and added to the misery of the cramped hole.

After two hours, the American started to mumble something in Latin and Hearn recognized it as a prayer his mother used to say to him. The American was struggling against the pain, bringing his right hand up towards his chest. Both boys were immobilized with fear when the American moved for the first time in hours. Hearn thought for a moment the man was going to pull Hausser's knife out and attack him with it, but the paratrooper put his hand inside the collar of his jacket instead. The American pulled out a cross and with his blood stained lips he kissed it and let out his last breath with a hiss. His hand flopped back down to his side and was silent.

Hearn felt Hausser next to him start to sob quietly, but he did not look at him. He wanted to give Hausser a moment to compose himself because Hearn felt like he might cry too. He knew if he looked at Hausser it would set off his own tears.

Hausser got control of himself after a few minutes and after Hearn had stuffed the feelings down far enough, he shoved the dead American off of his legs that had been pinned underneath with Hausser's for several hours. The hole was tight and there was nowhere for the American to go but out, onto the ground above them.

Hearn's legs were numb from being cramped up under the dying American and it made the pushing more difficult. Hausser was helping him and they barely were able to push the corpse out of the hole. Hearn gripped the knife by the handle and pulled hard on it, but it was stuck tight. He pulled harder and harder, finally bracing his back against one side of the hole and his boot soles on the steaming chest of the dead soldier and pulled. The knife came out with a sucking sound and Hearn crashed to the bottom of the crowded hole again. He offered the knife back to Hausser, but Hausser turned his head away and refused to take it. Hearn placed it outside the hole next to the dead American.

He tried to straighten his legs out as best he could and rubbed them to get the circulation back. They felt like pins and needles and he could not feel his toes at all. He was not sure if it was due to the extreme cold or having been cramped up for so long, but not all the feeling returned to his legs as he rubbed. They were quite numb. After a few minutes of rubbing Hearn pulled Hausser down to the bottom of the hole.

"Careful or someone will see you." Hearn whispered. The sun was coming up and Hearn and Hausser were stuck in enemy lines. Hearn retrieved the knife from the edge of the hole and offered it back to Hausser, but he turned away from it, trying not to look at it. "Hausser, take the knife!" Hearn whispered as sternly as he could, not wanting to hold it any longer himself. Hausser took it and put it back into its sheath without wiping it off.

Hearn sat silently in the bottom of the hole, its contents becoming more apparent as the sun came up. He grabbed the American's pack and searched it for food. He found some canned rations to share with Hausser. Hearn wondered how the other two had managed.

Chapter 26

02 January 1945 day 17 or Autumn Mist

Henke and Koch reported back to Wagner first thing in the morning about the botched patrol into American lines. Wagner was furious at the attempt, but held his temper, not wanting to bring Manser's own rage down upon him.

"So you don't know what happened to the others?" Wagner asked, his voice on the edge of yelling.

"No Sergeant, as soon as the shelling started we did as Hearn told us too and made our way back. We barely made it." Henke looked at the ground and brushed some snow in a fan shape with the toe of his boot.

"There was nothing you could have done." Wagner reassured him. He patted him on the shoulder and turned to go look for Keppler to give him the news.

*****

Lieutenant Keppler stood silently in Colonel Fagan's command post, the shoulder patch of the 101st American Division called Screaming Eagles lay on the desk and the Colonel was looking at it through narrowed eyes.

"It means nothing," Manser said finally breaking the silence.

"I beg to differ Sir," Keppler said, keeping his attention focused on Fagan. "We ambushed and killed an entire patrol of American paratroopers in the woods North East of here when we recovered the pilot. They were well supplied with ammunition and rations, and they even had full winter gear on. They were hardly the ragged, hard-pressed defenders we are supposed to be up against."

Manser sighed. The pilot Keppler recovered was still a sore spot. Manser wanted his men to be the ones who found the downed He262 pilot, not a common bomber pilot. No one ever got a medal for rescuing a bomber pilot. The only fortunate news Manser had was that no one found the missing

He262 pilot.

"I tend to agree with Captain Manser on this Lieutenant." Fagan stated, finally looking up from the patch on his table. "Just because the American airborne is extending well supplied patrols that far north from Bastogne doesn't mean they have received major reinforcements. These paratroopers your men killed yesterday could have been lost or separated from their division. Did you encounter any more of them?" Fagan asked.

"We came upon a truppen from the 2nd Panzer Division that had been ambushed and killed." Keppler said halfheartedly, knowing now that command was going to ignore the evidence before them.

"Well, did you see any American paratroopers at the site?" Manser asked accusingly.

"No, there were no American bodies," the fight gone from Keppler's voice now that he knew Fagan had made up his mind on the matter.

Fagan looked sternly at Manser and Manser clamped his mouth shut.

"Keppler, I value your experience as a soldier and I will take this report under advisement. However having said that, I can't just ring up General Model and tell him that we think the 101st airborne at Bastogne has been significantly reinforced and that it might be a mistake to attack in full tomorrow." Fagan looked quickly at Manser to make sure he was not thinking of interrupting. Then he looked back at Keppler who stood quietly before him. "The division will be back up to strength today and will be able to handle whatever the Americans have managed to put into Bastogne."

"Yes Sir," Keppler said.

"Good luck tomorrow Lieutenant," Fagan said. "You may go," Keppler nodded and turned and left the command bunker.

Once he stepped outside Keppler could see Wagner standing over in the trees waiting for him. Keppler could tell by the look on Wagner's face that whatever he had to say was not good news. He walked over to him and Wagner started immediately,

"Hearn and Hausser are missing," Keppler's mind reeled with possibilities. It reminded him of Lubbert, who had now been missing for two weeks. Possibly, they would never know what happened to the boy.

"What happened?" Keppler asked.

Wagner told Keppler all about the patrol order Manser gave Hearn and about his own order to stay out of the American lines.

"But they went anyway?" Keppler asked, angry at the waste.

"I guess he felt like he had to obey Manser's orders." Wagner looked around to see if anyone was listening to them, then he said in a softer voice. "It was a stupid order." Keppler looked around after Wagner said it to make sure no one heard the comment.

"Yes it was, but you need to be careful or you'll find yourself going on a patrol up to the front as well. Manser doesn't take criticism lightly." Keppler could not keep the cutting tone from his voice no matter how much he tried. Something had to be done about Manser.

Manser wanted so badly to be recognized and get a medal for his unit's action that he was willing to pay with the lives of everyone in the Kompanie. He moved closer to Wagner and lowered his voice to a whisper. "Steer clear of Manser if you can. He'll take the whole Kompanie down with him if he gets the chance."

"Yes Sir," Wagner retreated through the trees to gather the truppen together and finish preparing them for the attack tomorrow.

Keppler stood in the snow where Wagner had left him and started to think of the best way to deal with Manser before he killed any more of Germany's youth. Someone had to stop him; that much was clear. Even so, Keppler did not know how he was going to do it. Something out of the corner of his eye caught his attention and he turned. There leaning up against a tree a few meters away was Heini. He had his arms folded across his blood stained chest and he was looking sternly at Keppler.

"How can I protect them?" Keppler asked the apparition. Heini did not answer, he just turned and walked away into the trees until Keppler could no longer see him.

Chapter 27

02 January 1945 day 17 or Autumn Mist

Corporal Hearn and Private Hausser crouched in the hole for the better part of the day. They ate all of the American's rations and the canned bacon was not sitting well with either one of them, but they managed to keep it down. Both boys believed that at any moment they could be discovered and the fear coupled with the cold played on their nerves. It had been the longest day in Hearn's life.

After searching the contents of the American's hole, Hearn had found a broken piece of mirror attached to a stick that the American had used to look around the perimeter of the hole without sticking his head up. Hearn had been using the mirror trying to get a better idea of the predicament they were in and looking for a way out of their situation. It did not look good. Their own lines seemed like a world away and the Americans were all around them. The enemy paratroopers stayed low which was the only reason the boys had not been discovered, but they could hear talking and low voices all around them in English confirming to them the need to stay absolutely quiet.

"Do you see anyone?" Hausser whispered into Hearn's ear.

"No," Hearn said, trying to concentrate on the terrain around them. The paratroopers were spread pretty thin, some of the foxholes being as far apart as eight to ten meters, but there was no way they would survive a mad dash back to their own lines before being spotted.

There was a foxhole about seven meters away from their position. Hearn had almost given up watching it, thinking it might be empty when he saw the top hump of an American helmet for a brief moment as it broke the surface of the ground before disappearing back below the level of the earth.

"There are Americans seven meters away to the South West of our position." He reported to Hausser, his voice barely audible.

"Do you think they'll notice the body?" Hausser sounded scared and motioned to the now frozen body of the American they had ejected from the foxhole.

"No." Hearn whispered. "There are bodies all over the place from both sides. They'll think he fell victim to the shelling."

"So what's the plan?" Hausser asked, trying to keep his voice down to a whisper, but fear casing it to crack a little. "Do we wait until nightfall and then crawl back to our own lines?"

Hearn dropped the mirror down so he could look into Hausser's eyes. "No."

Hausser looked too shocked to speak at Hearn's answer.

"They'll shoot us for sure if we try to get back through." Hearn stated in a matter of fact manner. He lifted the mirror back up and resumed scanning the area around them. "They will have changed the password by now, so we won't be able to answer the sentry's call," he chanced a glance over at Hausser and the boy was white with fear.

"So we're stuck here?" he whispered, looking like he was going to make a run for their lines that were thirty-five meters away.

"We'll have to wait until the division attacks tomorrow, and hope we don't get killed by friendly fire." Hearn pulled the mirror back down again and put his hand on Hausser's shoulder to steady him as he was shaking. "Just relax Hausser, no one knows we're here." As if in challenge to his statement someone yelled out in English.

Hausser gripped his rifle so hard Hearn thought for a moment he might actually snap it in half. Hearn brought the mirror back up to see if anyone was coming, but the ground was barren accept for the dead and the churned up earth from the constant artillery shelling the area had received.

Then he noticed someone else had a mirror sticking up above the earth from the American foxhole seven meters away. The mirror was set up at an angle that made it obvious the occupants were looking in Hearn's direction. Again the English voice called out. Hearn was sure they were calling a person's name.

"Oh crap," Hearn said, feeling his heart start to beat harder in his chest.

"What!" Hausser had lost control and said the word too loud. The mirror in the far hole disappeared and all was quiet for a moment. Hausser was shaking and looked like he might wet himself. "If they capture us, they'll torture us!" Hausser practically yelled his statement and pulled a grenade from his belt.

Hearn remembered the stories Manser had told him about the American torturers and how they made even the strongest of German men talk after a time. 'Always fight to the death.' Manser had told them time and time again, impressing upon them the honor gained in being killed in combat rather than being tortured into submission.

Again someone from the far hole yelled out, but this time the voice was in broken German with an English accent. "Come out with your hands up."

Hearn's head was reeling. What should he do? He knew the odds of surviving a fight were not even worth the time it would take to calculate them. He also refused to be captured and tortured!

As if to answer his question, Hausser unscrewed the cap on his grenade, pulled on the fuse activating it, and stood up in the hole. It was the last conscious act Hausser made. One of the Americans watching in his mirror jumped up and shot Hausser right between the eyes before he could throw his grenade.

Hearn watched as Hausser's dead body and the live grenade came crashing back down into the hole on top of him. He reached around for the grenade, his face smashed into the bottom of the hole under Hausser's twitching corpse. He was sure that the grenade would go off at any moment. He thought of the smoking hole into which Dieter Bergin had plunged and what the shattered remains looked like. He was sure the grenade would go off any moment and turn him into a replica of Bergin. Finally his hand found the grenade and tossed it up and over the edge of the pit where it exploded near the brim with a loud thump.

The dead American they had tossed up and out of the hole came careening back down into the hole in the wake of the explosion and added itself to the weight of Hausser's body on top of him. To make matters worse, the explosion also loosened some of the earth on the side of the foxhole and it too came down upon him.

Hearn found himself pinned in the bottom of the foxhole just as the German lines thirty-five meters away opened up in response to the explosion and the shooting. It took the entire course of the firefight for Hearn to get himself free of the bodies and earth that had almost buried him alive. He looked down at Hausser's lifeless face. It had stiffened up in death into the shape of a scream, the eyes staring wide. Hearn knew then he was not going to make it home.

After the shooting stopped, there was smoke covering the ground all around him from newly exploded shells. In his new environment Hearn now found himself standing exposed from the waist up trying to retrieve his rifle. He thought if he could get his weapon free from the ruins of the hole he would stand a better chance at making a break for his own lines rather than staying here with two dead bodies. He was concentrating so hard on pulling his rifle free he did not see the American that had crawled up behind him.

Hearn tried to jump up and run as something poked him in the back. All he managed to do was fall onto his face, his boots having slid back down into the hole under Hausser's lifeless legs. "Don't move," the broken German voice said, "or I'll shoot you."

Hearn was frantic; he could not fight to the death as Manser had told them to do. He was captured! He was going to be prisoner! He had to try and escape!

Hearn drew his knife and turned on his captor, but the big burly American had plenty of time to react and smashed Hearn in the face with the butt of his rifle. Spots began to swim in front of his eyes and Hearn could feel his Hitler Youth knife slip from his fingers. He heard it thump onto the frozen ground as he tried to stay conscious.

When he finally came around, he was vaguely aware of snow building up inside his collar at the back of his shirt as the American dragged him along the ground. He tried to struggle and get free, but his head pounded with the effort to the point that he almost passed out again. His hands had been tied behind his back. Hearn closed his eyes and tried to will away the tears. He did not want the Americans to see any weakness. The spots closed in again and when Hearn came to he was tied to a chair in one of Bastogne's shelled out houses. The big American was sitting in front of him when he opened his eyes.

"How old are you?" he asked in his broken German.

"Hearn, Adler, 2nd Kompanie, 12th Panzer Division," he answered, blinking hard, trying to focus on the man in front of him.

The big American moved closer and lowered his voice a little so it would not sound so gruff. "I just wanted to know how old you were, kid." He drew back and looked at Hearn for a moment.

'He's probably wondering what part of me to cut off first.' Hearn thought to himself, trying to keep from shaking harder than he already was. He was captured and there was nothing he could do about it but try to be brave until they finished him off. He noticed his Hitler youth knife sitting on the table beside the American and fear gripped his insides and twisted them until Hearn lost bladder control, wetting his pants. He was shaking so hard he could not concentrate on what was going on. Someone else in the room spoke something in English, to which the man replied and turned back to Hearn,

"How did a boy like you end up in the SS?" Hearn barely heard the question.

He was paralyzed with fear. The warm urine spread into a dark stain over the front of his trousers and ran down his legs into his boots.

'My duty is to escape.' He remembered back to Manser's assertion that their only chance to survive would be escape since the Americans killed all their prisoners of war.

The big American removed his helmet in an attempt to look less intimidating, revealing a Mohawk haircut that some of the hundred and first airborne sported. At the sight of the hair Hearn gasped, his heart seizing up with horror. The American was an Indian torturer! He had seen haircuts like that in the pictures Manser had shown him. The torturing was about to begin!

Hearn jumped up; his hands still tied behind his back and searched around for the door. 'I must get free!' He legs felt like rubber and it was hard to make them work, but he managed to start running for a broken down door that had sandbags in front of its base. He was only able to take about three strides towards freedom before the big American came crashing down on him, tackling him to the floor.

"Let me go!" Hearn screamed his voice crackling in adolescence. He could smell the urine from his pants and it was the last straw. He had been broken before the man could even cut him up. Hearn started to cry in huge sobs as he was wrestled back into the chair.

"Easy boy!" The big American said holding Hearn tight like a vice. "Just take it easy!" The broken German was anything but reassuring.

Hearn tried to stop crying but he could not hold it back. He continued to sob uncontrollably. 'I have failed! I have let Germany down! I have let my friends down! Bergin had given the ultimate sacrifice, and all I have accomplished is getting captured. Even Hausser had done better!' Hearn looked down at the front of his pants that had a large dark stain on them and felt his distress deepen. In his mind, he was not only proving to be a failure, but worse, a coward.

The American paratrooper put his helmet back on and went to the back of the room to confer with another man. Hearn was overcome with dread. They were probably deciding how to make him talk; the best way to cut him up. Hearn lost track of how long he was sitting in the chair. Eventually one of the Americans left only to return moments later with another German prisoner. The captured German was wearing the uniform of a tanker and came into the room in front of his American escort.

"Are you okay?" the tanker asked. Hearn did not know what to make of this event. The man was a fellow prisoner but Hearn was leery. This was not how things were supposed to happen. It could be a trick. Hearn did not answer him. "You will come with me. These Americans will not harm you. They have treated us well." Hearn narrowed his eyes in suspicion and then focused on his Hitler youth knife on the table. The Americans seemed to be going to a lot of trouble to get him to let down his guard. "My name is Hans, what is yours?"

"Adler Hearn." He was surprised that his voice even worked amid his shaking and panic-induced delirium. He focused on the tanker again and saw genuine concern in the man's face.

"Well Adler, the war is over for you. Come with me, you will stay with the rest of us." The man held out his arm and Hearn's suspicions melted away with the hope that his deliverance might actually be at hand. He stood shakily to his feet and crossed the room. The tanker put his arm around Hearn's shoulders and pulled him in close. "It is okay to be afraid. I am afraid too." The words chased away some of Hearn's inadequacy. "You will find some comfort with the rest of us." The man's voice was reassuring and Hearn allowed himself to be herded out of the room and across the street under guard into a makeshift prisoner collection point.

In the small crowded house, Hearn saw some men from the 3rd parachute division and a few of the Panzer Lehr division men. He was the only Hitler youth in the room and the others greeted him with nods and smiles. It was the first time since his capture that Hearn felt like he might actually be okay. One of the men offered him some food, but Hearn turned it down. He did not feel up to eating. The war for Adler Hearn was indeed over.

Chapter 28

03 January 1945 day 18 of Autumn Mist

During the early morning hours, Keppler moved with the rest of the Division to their jump off point. The remnants of the 42nd Regiment looked happy to be giving up their position in the front line to the newly outfitted 12th Division.

Keppler noticed that only half the tanks had come up with the Division. When he got a chance, he asked one of the tank commanders why they only had half their armor with them. The answer made Keppler shake his head in disbelief.

"They told us that they are holding them in reserve in case we break through, but I've been told by some of the supply men that the other tanks are staying back because we don't have the fuel to move them."

Keppler's heart sank. He knew that no matter how successful the attack was today, it would be a waste of time. Their supplies had come to an end and the momentum of the attack was going to die out. He went in search of Wagner and found him near the front in a firing pit with Henke and Koch. He waved him out of the hole and pulled him aside.

"No hero stuff today okay?" Keppler said, realizing that Wagner was the last one left of the truppen he had originally come here to train and lead.

"No hero stuff," Wagner repeated.

They both watched as the 88 flak gun crews set up their large weaponry just inside the tree line and brought their elevation down to 30 degrees. Keppler smiled and patted Wagner's shoulder. Wagner went back to his hole to await the signal for the attack. Keppler crouched into a firing pit near Manser's command post, waiting for the opening salvo to begin.

About a kilometer back in the trees a couple of sIG33's and six 15cm guns opened up. The incoming shells screamed their arrival as they crashed down into the outskirts of Bastogne. Geysers of earth and snow were sent careening skyward and the ground under Keppler's feet shook. The artillery continued to blast into the American lines and the 88's that had been moved up into the tree line started to fire flak bursts above the dug-in American defenders. The exploding black clouds rained down shrapnel from above the defender's heads. Large pieces of flak designed to rip planes apart peppered the ground all across the attack zone.

One 88 shell burst through the side of a home that was still partly standing and exploded in the house, shredding the remaining walls from inside. Above the din of exploding shells and bursting flak rounds, Keppler could hear the nebelwerfer rocket launchers firing their strings of rocket fire deeper into the shattered city. It did not look like anything could survive such a scouring of gunfire.

The return artillery fire from the distant American batteries seemed to be directed into the trees behind the Kompanie to quiet the 88's and further into the trees to try and reduce the incoming fire from the artillery batteries. For the most part, the Kompanie remained in the ready position, unharmed.

After a thirty-five minute pounding from the flak guns, artillery, and rockets everything fell silent and the whistles started to blow. Keppler was up and running with the rest of the Kompanie. Their entire regiment was thrown into the attack as well as two platoons of Panther tanks and two platoons of Mark IV's. Three of the Panthers did not make it all the way out of the tree line before incoming anti-tank rounds took them out.

The armor had their engines cranked full out, trying to cover the distance and close with the enemy. Black diesel smoke poured from their exhausts, displaying the waste of precious fuel being used in a futile effort. A Mark IV near Keppler took three hits in the side simultaneously, one from a bazooka and two from 35mm anti-tank rounds. The impact sent the 23-ton tank skidding sideways where its tread ground over one of the supporting infantrymen's legs and sat still amid the man's screams. The other tanks were almost up to their top speed of 40km per hour by the time the American artillery began to fall.

The artillery rounds pounded down like rain, but Keppler urged his platoon to continue their charge. They needed to get closer to the Americans to escape the barrage. The tanks fired their machineguns and their 75mm main guns as they advanced, trying to reach the outskirts of the city before they lost any more of their number to incoming fire.

A Panther G took a direct hit from an artillery round, right on the front of its chassis. The impact caused the 45-ton Panther to shudder to a halt as its engine stalled. A large crater was carved out of the front of the armor, but the hull was not compromised. The impact of the round had disabled the machinegun, but its 75mm gun continued to fire and after a moment's pause the tank's engine started up again, black diesel pouring out as it rejoined the advance again.

The American small arms were not as fast in reacting to the attack as the anti-tank units, but their fire was damaging when it started. Four .30cal machineguns opened up from inside the rubble and spewed fire into the charging ranks of the Kompanie. Several men went down and the attack began to falter. Keppler watched as his attacking Kompanie started to fall into American foxholes to seek cover from the incoming fire.

Some of the holes still held living American soldiers and hand-to-hand combat were needed to secure places of refuge from the growing intensity of incoming American fire. Keppler continued to charge, not caring for his own safety, feeling the suffocating numbness close in on him similar to earlier at the crossroads.

Colonel Faust saw that the attack was faltering and sent in the second wave of tanks and infantry to try and push into the ruined city. As another regiment left the tree line, the American observers shifted the artillery fire to meet the emergence of this new threat and gave Keppler's Kompanie the reprieve they needed to continue on.

A Panther's 75mm round took out one of the machinegun emplacements that had been set up inside the shattered remains of a house. All four walls exploded outward and the roof collapsed on the American defenders inside, silencing the .30 machinegun. A second machinegun emplacement became worthless as a Mark IV tank moved into its field of fire and was taken out by a bazooka round. The machinegun crew, forced to disperse and relocate, was quickly gunned down by the charging forward elements of the attack.

Keppler continued to run and noticed that Wagner's truppen was with him as he came to a partially collapsed wall. The forward elements of the regiment had reached the city limits. Keppler looked back into the attacking waves of German infantry and noticed a couple hundred gray-green and white camouflaged humps lying in the pinkish snow. The regiment had already sustained heavy losses and the attack had just begun.

Keppler could see Manser emerge from one of the captured American foxholes, his lugar in hand. He waved to the men charging up behind him as if he were the only one who could lead them to victory. Keppler thought about bringing his Mauser 98k on line and shooting him in the head. No one would know if he shot Manser in all this madness.

An American Thompson sub-machinegun pulled him from his murderous thought as .45cal slugs chewed into the concrete wall beside him. Keppler flopped to the ground instinctively firing back at his attacker. The American was shooting from inside a riddled house across the rubble-strewn street. Keppler's un-aimed shot was a reflex action and hit the American soldier in the forehead to send him crashing back through the open doorway.

Chambering another round, Keppler turned back to see if Manser was still charging across the open ground. The Captain was nowhere to be seen. He looked at the truppen crouched down beside the building with Wagner and decided that he had better things to do than start shooting their own officers. He had to get these boys moving or they would become sitting targets of opportunity.

"Let's go!" Keppler had to yell to be heard over the gunfire. He waved the truppen to their feet and ran across the rubble-strewn street to the house where he had just shot the American. Rounds zipped by them as they ran and Keppler crashed into the house through the open doorway. Inside a group of three American paratroopers was busy setting up another .30cal machinegun. He shot the closest paratrooper in the chest and then stepped in closer, hitting a second one in the jaw with the walnut butt of his weapon, spraying the third man with blood and teeth.

The third American lunged at Keppler, trying to knock him to the ground. The American was much smaller than Keppler and did not manage to knock him over. The paratrooper had managed to get a knife out and rammed it into Keppler's rib cage. The American was obviously inexperienced in Combat and did not turn the blade sideways so it could slide through the ribs. The knife struck bone and slid off to the side giving Keppler a gash down the side of his chest but leaving him alive and able to fight back.

Keppler knocked the knife away and butted his helmeted head into the American's face. The man fought for his life, lunging at Keppler and biting him hard on the neck. Keppler had the American flipped around before they hit the ground. He landed hard on the paratrooper and the man's bite slacked off as air came rushing out of his lungs in a "humph" sound. Keppler took the moment to gain the initiative and drove his fist into the paratrooper's throat, hitting him in the windpipe. The American's hands dropped down for a moment as he was out of breath and struggling to take in air. Keppler started to beat him in the face with his fists and then grabbed a brick from off of the floor and delivered a final blow. The entire event had not taken more than a minute and was over by the time Wagner arrived with the truppen through the door.

As soon as the truppen came bursting into the house, Wagner raised his rifle and shot the second paratrooper as he was rising to his elbows after taking the hit to his jaw from Keppler's rifle butt. Keppler reached over and retrieved his rifle, ejecting the spent cartridge and chambering a new one. The rest of the truppen looked on with pale faces at Keppler covered in blood splatters from the man he had bludgeoned to death.

"You've been hit." Wagner stated, looking at Keppler's chest where the American paratrooper had tried to stab him through.

"It's just a scratch." Keppler lied. The blow had probably fractured a rib and the cut was deep; but the bleeding made it look worse than it really was. His ribs did not hurt near as much as his neck where the American had bit him, but Keppler had suffered worse than this before. He knew he would be okay. He took his tunic and shirt off for a moment and wadded some field dressing onto the cut, then tied it into place. He dressed promptly after the hasty patch job trying to block out the cold.

"Wagner, take Koch with you and make sure the basement is empty." Wagner nodded at Keppler and started towards the open doorway that led to the basement. "Sergeant," Wagner turned, as Keppler called him, "make sure you toss down a grenade before you check it out." Wagner nodded and pulled a grenade from his belt.

Keppler turned to the rest of the truppen. "What are you waiting for? Search the house and make sure it's clear before we move onto the next one." The truppen moved off in pairs and threes to search the house just as Wagner's grenade exploded down the basement stairs. Wagner and Koch ran down into the dust filled cellar with their rifles at the ready and returned coughing from the thick air giving Keppler the thumbs up.

The house proved to be empty and Keppler gathered the squad around him. "Okay, the first rule of clearing out houses is you throw in a grenade first. Make sure that you stay in groups in case it turns into hand to hand combat, but don't get too bunched together or a grenade could take the whole works of you out at once." The boys looked scared and Keppler remembered for a moment that they were just kids sent here to kill and be killed. He almost ordered them out of the house and back to the jump off point, but he knew that would be pointless.

"Let's go." He led them back out into the street that was alive with rounds zipping by and scattered bodies from both sides as the fighting raged in and out of doors. The truppen moved up to the next house on the block and stayed crouched behind Keppler who had taken a grenade out of his belt and unscrewed the cap. He pulled the fuse and let it smoke in his hand for a few seconds before throwing it through the blown out window. As his grenade was going in, an American pineapple grenade came out.

The boys all dove for cover as they saw the American fragmentation grenade come arcing out, but Keppler jumped up and caught it in the air and threw it back through the window right behind his own grenade. Both of the grenades went off almost simultaneously inside the house. Keppler jumped up immediately following the blast and ran through the door. Wagner and the others were a little slower in following his lead, but managed to get to their feet and start running by the time Keppler entered the house. Rounds from a machinegun across the street pelted into the side of the house and zipped all around the boys as they charged up the stairs and into the carnage inside. The truppen managed make it into the house unscathed.

The grenades had done their work for them. The main floor was littered dead defenders and the air was thick with gunpowder. Keppler moved to the bottom of the stairs just as an English voice from upstairs called out in challenge to the sound of boots clomping downstairs. Keppler drew another grenade from his belt and pulled the string activating the fuse. He waited until almost the last moment before throwing it. He had held it long enough that the grenade burst at the peak of its arc through the air just inside the doorway of the attic. Keppler charged up the narrow stairs with his rifle at the ready and Wagner was right behind him with another youth following him. All three of them charged into the room to discover a paratrooper lying on the floor with his leg blown off. Keppler made the mistake of assuming the enemy soldier was dead and turned his back to take the boys back downstairs.

Machinegun fire shot through the small room pelting the walls all around them. Rounds zipped by Keppler and Wagner so close they could feel the air currents behind the bullets, but miraculously none of the rounds hit either of them. The other boy was not so lucky. .45cal slugs chewed into his chest and he fell to the wooden floor in a crumpled heap. Keppler spun around and shot the American at point blank range, silencing the machinegun. Wagner looked at Keppler and then bent down to examine the fallen youth.

"He's dead." Wagner reported the obvious. Keppler cursed himself for being so careless and then felt guilt because he could not remember the boy's name.

Both Keppler and Wagner moved back down the stairs. The rest of the truppen seemed frozen into place, looking at the stairway and waiting for the other youth to come down the stairs. Keppler broke their trance telling them to watch for enemy soldiers.

"Did you check the basement?" Wagner asked Koch.

"No one there." His face was drained of color.

More machinegun fire from across the street pelted into the front of the house sending the truppen to the rubble-strewn floor for cover. Keppler unfazed by the incoming rounds moved over to the doorway to assess the situation. He could see several bodies in the street where they had been gunned down by the enemy machinegun.

The enemy machinegun was set up with a good field of fire and well protected against small arms. Keppler was trying to figure out a way to attack the position when a Panther G appeared rumbling down the street towards the stronghold. The bricks and mortar in the street were crushed under the 45-ton monster as it approached the house. The machinegun fired in vain at the Panther, its rounds flailing off of the front armor plating of the Panther as it advanced.

As the tank approached the basement stronghold it lowered its 75mm main gun and shoved it right through one of the windows. Keppler opened his bolt to make sure he had a fresh round in the chamber and then slammed it shut again.

"Get ready to fire." The truppen all moved into good fields of fire and lifted their rifles up into the ready position. The tank blasted its main gun into the basement of the house. The recoil from the shot made the tank rock back on its treads and sent its barrel cutting up through the masonry wall into the main floor of the house briefly before it settled back down into place. Dust and smoke poured out of every window, door, and hole in the house. Not long after, a few stragglers came running out of the front door to make a break for the houses further down the street.

Keppler fired first; his target careened to the bottom of the stairs and was still. The rest of the truppen followed suit. Wagner hit one of them before he even got all the way through the door. The shooting continued sporadically, as enemy soldiers would appear from time to time running out of the dust choked house until there were eight crumpled forms strewn at various points along the stairway.

"That's what happens when you lose your head." Keppler said, trying to impress upon the young boys the importance of keeping their composure. "You have to keep it together or you'll end up running like a bunch of damn lemmings off a cliff." Keppler opened his bolt and took out a fresh clip of ammunition. He slammed it into the magazine and slapped the bolt shut. He then chambered a round. He stood near the doorframe and glanced quickly down the street before running out into the open to proceed to the next house.

The tank that had taken out the American machinegun emplacement had pulled away from the shattered house and was moving on down the street, firing its machineguns and main gun into the opposing houses. The amount of fire coming down the street was stunted and Keppler waved the truppen forward to the next house on the street.

He was just getting ready to lob another grenade through the doorway when he saw the tube of a bazooka come out of the top floor window, aimed at the Panther. Keppler dropped to one knee and sighted in on the enemy soldier's arm, as that was all he could see of the American. He fired and hit the soldier with the bazooka in the elbow, shattering the joint. The bazooka went off, but the round missed the Panther and smashed into a house. The feeble walls came crashing down out into the street and overtop of the Panther, burying it for a moment.

A grenade came flying out of the house into the street near Keppler and he dove into the rubble to escape the blast of the pineapple. The explosion came but was muffled, and it was not until Keppler looked up from his position that he saw why. One of Wagner's truppen, again he could not remember the boy's name, had flopped himself down on top of the grenade before it went off. His riddled body lay still in the cold frozen rubble of the street. His boot had blown off in the explosion, leaving one torn, socked foot exposed. Keppler was stunned for a moment at how small the boy's foot was. Then he came to his senses and pulled the fuse on his own grenade and lobbed it into the window above him. He heard a scurrying in the house just before the explosion of his stick grenade.

There was cold numbness coursing through his veins. He ascended the stairs holding his Mauser like it was a pistol in his right hand. He walked into the carnage that his grenade had created. Two dead Americans lay twisted into odd angles and the third was dragging a shattered leg behind him, trying to crawl into the kitchen. Keppler raised his rifle up in one hand and shot the man in the back of the head.

Chambering another round, he turned as the rest of the truppen entered the house and split up, throwing grenades and checking the upstairs and the downstairs for enemy soldiers. Just as it had other times before, Keppler could feel the numbness close up on his breath.

Wagner barked out orders to the rest of the truppen as Keppler just stood there inside the doorway, trying to take in air. Keppler thought he was going to pass out. Spots swam in front of his face and he was vaguely aware of the truppen securing the house with grenades. A bullet slapped into the wooden doorframe he was leaning against. He willed himself into action as a group of American paratroopers were charging from across the road.

The Panther had pulled itself free of the toppled wall just in time to take a bazooka round into one of its treads, immobilizing it. The tank spewed fire into the houses across the street trying to keep enemy sappers at bay. The Panther had its hands full and did not engage the charging group of Americans bent on retaking the house occupied by Keppler and the truppen.

Keppler jumped to the side as carbine rounds from the Americans came whizzing through the door in earnest. Koch did not move fast enough and was hit in the stomach, hurling him to the ground. Keppler came up at the window and shot the lead paratrooper in the face, sending his body back into the man behind him. A hailstorm of rounds poured out of the house as the rest of the truppen opened up amid the wailing. Koch clutched at his stomach and kicked his boots on the floor in pain. Outside all of the Americans went down, some of them hit and the rest seeking cover. A grenade came through the door, and then another and another.

Keppler kicked one of them back out through the doorway. Wagner grabbed one and threw it out the window, and the third one skidded across the floor and began to bounce down the stairs to the cellar. All three of the grenades went off at once. The grenade that bounced down the stairs exploded harmlessly in the cellar. The other two grenades cracked outside in black clouds of shrapnel, boomeranging shards back in through the door and the window. A small piece of burning metal hit Keppler in the upper thigh right through the muscle.

The impact of the fragment sent Keppler to the floor beside Koch who was still twisting around and kicking with his boots as he screamed. Keppler rolled back over below the window before the carbine rounds chewing into the doorframe could find him. Wagner tossed one of his own grenades out the door and it exploded among the rubble with a thump. Some of the incoming rounds petered out, but there were still shots coming through the window and the door impacting on the far wall in small clouds of plaster and concrete.

Keppler got to his knees and shot one of the attackers in the chest, sending him careening backwards into the rubble. He chambered another round and hit a second American in the shoulder, spinning the man around and depositing him on top of one of his fallen comrades. The paratrooper gripped his shoulder and screamed for a medic. Keppler quickly ejected his spent round and fired another bullet into the top of the American's helmet, silencing the screams from outside. More rounds pounded into the American attackers from the truppen and the paratroopers pulled back the way they came, dragging a couple of their wounded behind them.

Keppler turned from the window and sat down on the floor. The squad waited, pale and wide eyed, scattered around the interior of the house. Henke had moved into the doorway and was trying to comfort Koch as he screamed for his mother and clutched at his stomach with blood soaked hands. The rest of the boys were terrified. Their faces were white with fear and Koch's screaming added to the terror.

"We have to move Koch away from the doorway." Wagner stated in a monotone voice. Keppler looked up at the youth who was becoming more and more a hard-boiled veteran. He felt as much sorrow over Wagner's transformation as he did about Koch who was gut shot and howling in pain.

"You're right." Keppler replied. He got to his feet and they both helped Henke move Koch further into the interior of the house.

Koch was squirming so hard and was so slippery with blood that Keppler almost dropped him.

"Koch!" he yelled over Koch's screaming, "You'll have to relax! All your screaming is going to make the pain worse!" Keppler had seen many soldiers gut shot and knew it was one of the most painful wounds you could receive. The thought of this boy having to endure it wrenched Keppler's own stomach.

"It hurts!" He screamed into Keppler's face as if Keppler had done the deed himself. Tears streamed down Koch's face. "I need my mother!" He shook with pain and sobbing. "Take me home to my mother!" Blood drooled out from the corner of his mouth. The scene was having a terrible effect on the nerves of the other boys.

Keppler heard plenty of soldiers cry out for people, especially when they were dying, but to see this boy in pain, wounded in battle, and calling for his mother was almost more than he could bear. He had to turn and walk away from the youth. Keppler tried to tune out the cries behind him as Henke attempted in vain to sooth his wounded friend.

Keppler crossed to the front of the house and looked out into the street. The fighting was still fierce, but it had moved down the block as a new wave of men from the second regiment came into the city and carried the attack a little further into Bastogne. They were only on the outskirts of the city and the resistance was fierce. The previously buried Panther was now sitting in the middle of the street with thick black smoke pouring out of its hatch, a victim of American sappers. Keppler did not know when the tank got hit.

He watched the burning tank, trying to think of what he should do with Koch. The tank shuddered and detonated, sending shards of steel outwards and a thick black mushroom cloud of smoke into the cold air. The tank's magazine had exploded. Keppler turned back into the house and moved over to Wagner.

"Move the truppen out and down the street. The other regiment is carrying the attack and we need to move up with them. Make sure to watch for enemy soldiers that were passed by. I'm going to stay here with Koch for a little while." Wagner waved the others out of the house and into the street. The boys passed by Keppler one by one, their faces white as sheets. They looked like a procession of ghosts. Henke was the last to leave and as he walked by he looked pleadingly into Keppler's eyes and gripped Keppler's arm.

"Please help him Sir." He looked back in agony at his friend, "You'll be okay Koch!" and then, with a final pleading look at Keppler, he followed Wagner out into the rubble. Keppler looked at his arm where Henke had gripped; there was a bloody handprint on the camouflage and Keppler was amazed at how small Henke's hand was.

When the truppen had moved down the block Keppler walked over to Koch, kneeled down, and lifted the boy up into his arms. He was surprised at how light he was. The pain in Keppler's leg where he had taken the piece of shrapnel, his aching ribs, and the burning bite on his neck all melted away as his mind became occupied with the boy.

"Help me Lieutenant." The boy pleaded, his jaw quivering. "I can't take the pain any more! It hurts so bad!" His words were lost in a quivering voice as he started to cry again. His face was pale white from the pain and loss of blood; he, like the other boys who had just left the house, looked like an apparition. Keppler reached around behind the Koch and felt an exit wound from the bullet the size of his fist.

"Hold on boy," Keppler said, rocking the wounded youth back and forth in his lap. "It will all be over soon." There was no hope for Koch. Nothing could save him. He would be dead from loss of blood before he could be evacuated and operated on. The Division could not evacuate him until the area was secured and Keppler's duty demanded that he push on with the rest of the regiment. He fought his feelings. He wanted to take the boy up in his arms and carry him back to the battalion field hospital despite the futility of the notion.

Keppler looked down at Koch as he clutched his stomach and cried and screamed in pain. Keppler felt warm tears spring to his eyes and course down his cheeks as he clamped his hand over Koch's mouth and nose. The cries for mother stifled into a muffled scream. The boy's eyes flew open wide as he fought for breath. He was too weak to fight and his eyes locked with Keppler's until the life left them. Koch's hands finally relaxed and flopped to the ground, leaving his stomach wound open to the air.

"I'm sorry Koch." Keppler sobbed. "I'm so sorry." He finally relaxed his grip over Koch's mouth and nose and gently laid him on the floor. Then he took Koch's hands and folded them over his small chest trying to make the boy look peaceful. Keppler let his head fall down to the boy's small hands and his whole body shook as he wept.

Chapter 29

Bastogne, Belgium

Wagner took the truppen out of the house and down the street cautiously. This was a different kind of environment than the woods he had left behind. Wagner did not like it at all. Enemy soldiers could pop up anywhere in these surroundings. He moved the truppen down the side of the street where dead bodies from both sides marked the swath made by the Division's reserve regiment.

The Division had pushed hard but had yet only taken a small portion of the city. The cost had been heavy. 12th Division casualties were generously scattered around the rubble and houses. Smoking hulls of tanks and support vehicles littered the roads and lay sprinkled about like discarded toys.

Wagner waved his truppen apart trying to impress upon them the necessity of maintaining their spacing as they came closer to the shooting. Despite his efforts to keep them separated they instinctively drifted closer together from time to time, scared in their surroundings and seeking security from each other. Ahead of them the battle raged. The bodies in the street and surrounding area were getting more plentiful as they moved on, an indication that the attack was slowing down and grinding to a halt.

A form jumped up in front of him and Wagner almost shot the man before he released his grip on his trigger at the last moment. He almost sent a bullet into Captain Manser.

"Wagner!" Manser yelled, his eyes wild. "Come over here!" Wagner waved the truppen to the ground and moved over to his superior officer.

"Yes Sir?" he asked, noting that Manser was alone and had been crouching in a hole.

"I have been looking for you!" It was obvious Manser was lying. It was clear he had been hiding, trying to stay out of the line of fire.

"What would you like Sir?" For the first time in his life, Wagner felt liberated from Manser. He looked upon his Captain as a coward, shrinking from enemy fire in a shell hole. Wagner knew at that moment he was twice the man

Manser would ever be.

"I am taking charge of your truppen. We're going to flank the Americans and punch a hole in their lines." He thrust his lugar out to the side and pointed towards the firing. "We'll move out that way!"

As much as Wagner hated the thought of Manser leading the truppen he had to bite down on his lip to keep from laughing at the spectacle before him. As a Hitler Youth he had always thought Manser to be a brilliant military leader and strategist. Now that Wagner was a soldier and a veteran of combat, Manser was magically transformed before his eyes into a comical idiot.

"Yes Sir." Wagner replied.

Manser started to walk off through the rubble, stumbling for a moment and almost falling on his face, his lugar still held high in the air. "Forward!" He yelled.

Wagner turned to the truppen. None of them moved, staying in their positions waiting for Wagner's orders. He let Manser take a few more steps and then waved the truppen forward, motioning for them to maintain their spacing.

Manser led them, stumbling from time to time up to the front where the shooting was a constant barrage of noise. They came to the corner of a house and Manser waved Wagner up to him. Wagner slid along the wall until he was near Manser, motioning the rest of the squad into cover.

Machinegun fire raged across the street into the opposing houses as German and American troops took turns rushing their enemy trying to gain an upper hand. In the middle of the intersection, near enough to Wagner that he could feel the heat from the flames, two Mark IV tanks sat burning. The German 12th SS Panzer Division's attack had come to a halt. The strategic gains in Bastongne were minimal. The American Paratroopers had stopped the entire weight of the 12th SS Panzer Division.

Manser rolled back down the wall and past Wagner motioning for him to follow. Wagner turned and walked back down the side of the house towards the place where Manser slunk down. Wagner stood above him, disgusted at the sight of his cowardly captain.

Manser's face drained of color. "After a careful assessment of the situation, I think we need to reinforce this side of the line." Manser said jerking his thumb to the house beside them.

"Yes Sir," Wagner said. The humor he felt towards the idiocy of Manser had given way to disdain.

"I'll leave you to take up position as I know the Colonel needs me back at the mobile headquarters to help him plan the next attack." And with that Manser retreated down the street the way they had come. Wagner watched him go and felt himself hoping an American bullet might get him. Unfortunately, Manser trotted off unharmed.

Wagner rejoined the truppen and led them to the rear of the house they were currently using for cover. As soon as he entered the back of the structure he found himself face to barrel with the business end of a Mauser 98k. On the other end an alert sentry from the reserve regiment looked Wagner up and down and then waved him and his truppen into the building. Wagner brought his scared squad into the house and placed them among the current defenders of the house.

The inexperienced youth took up positions beside the older soldiers in the house and began firing their weapons through cracks and holes at the Americans across the street. A corporal came up to Wagner and looked at his shoulder boards.

"Good timing Sergeant." The corporal was old enough to be Wagner's father. "The Americans have reinforced with some armor and are counterattacking. I don't suppose you've brought any panzerfausts with you?"

Wagner shook his head in the negative having a hard time hearing the man for the noise.

"Well we're happy to have you just the same!" The corporal yelled. "What are your orders?" Wagner looked at the man and tried to think of what to say. He would actually be happier if this guy stayed in charge, but he could see that it was not going to happen so he leaned in close so his adolescent voice could be heard.

"We hold the house!" He yelled.

The man leaned back and smiled, slapping Wagner on the shoulder. Then the corporal scurried off and re-joined the defenders shooting into the house across the street.

Wagner made his way upstairs where two machinegun crews were laying down fire from the windows. Across the room a small hole had been blown in the wall and Wagner decided it was a good a place as any to make a stand. Empty brass casings littered the floor to the point where it was difficult to walk without losing his balance. The fallschirmjagergewehr 42 light machineguns were busy pouring out fire as fast as the loaders could feed belts into the units. As he took up his position at the hole in the wall he could see more of the street below him. Smashed tanks from both sides clogged the roads and the bullets were so thick passing between the buildings that it almost looked like one might be able to walk across them to the other side.

'Keppler had been right.' Wagner thought to himself. 'The Americans have pushed a lot of reinforcements into Bastogne.' Wagner could see that the weight of the 12th Division's attack had not only been halted, they were now fighting just to hang onto what they had.

He brought his Mauser up and sighted down the barrel looking for a target. It took him a while, but he finally found one.

Chapter 30

Bastogne Belgium

Keppler stood up in the destroyed remains of the house. Dead American troops lay scattered throughout the main floor and Koch lay at Keppler's feet. He bent down and closed Koch's eyes. Walking out the front door he looked down at the other boy who had thrown himself on the grenade, his small foot now lightly covered in dust from the explosions and skirmishes outside the house. Keppler cursed himself for not remembering the small boy's name. He went down the stairs, picked the boy's boot up off the ground and put it back on his exposed foot.

To his right, large pillars of smoke drifted up into the crisp air. The steady chatter of machineguns and popping of small arms rolled through the streets around him that he now shared with the dead. Keppler turned from the shredded boy and leaned down over one of the American casualties, unclasping two grenades from his lifeless chest. He hooked the grenades to his belt and hefted his Mauser 98k up into the ready position.

Keppler moved out down the road towards the fighting. He could tell by the sound of the battle that the attack had been halted and all of the Division's regiments were engaged with a large blocking force. He hoped Wagner had managed to move up with the rest of the regiment. He could not bare the thought of seeing the truppen right now. He was not sure if he could ever face Wagner and his truppen again.

Keppler stumbled over some strewn rubble just as a bullet whipped over his head and added an extra pockmark to the wall beside him. His clumsiness had just saved his life.

'Sniper!' Keppler dove headlong into the rubble-strewn street. Instead of correcting his fall, he plunged forward and rolled on the ground. A second round whizzed by him and broke a brick in half where his head was a moment earlier.

Keppler was up and running, zigzagging across the open ground. Two more shots whipped by, missing him by mere millimeters before he reached the house across the street. Without stopping, Keppler charged up the stairs and into the house. He moved to the back of the shattered dwelling trying to do the math in his head as to the direction and distance of the sniper.

'The sound of the bullet came with the round itself, so the sniper is close.' Keppler was sure about the direction and when he peeked through a large hole made by a tank shell he was sure he knew where the sniper was. He could not see the sniper, but it was the only logical place for the man to be.

The sniper had let Wagner and the others go by, waiting for an officer to appear and make his shot worth something. A Lieutenant was always a better target than a sergeant. Keppler made up his mind. He would hunt the sniper. Killing a sniper was not an easy chore Keppler knew, but he needed to release his mind from the burden of having murdered Koch. A sniper was a soldier's predator and it seemed like the perfect penance to go after him.

Keppler left the remains of the house he had sought shelter in and moved towards the snipers position. He was careful in his approach to the large building. The sniper had chosen the fourth floor of what used to be an apartment building. It was a wise choice. The sniper had an excellent view of the surrounding rubble. Keppler moved slowly, blending in with the destroyed surroundings, not wanting to attract the attention of the sniper in any way.

Instead of going straight for the house, as a novice would do, Keppler eased his way around in a wide sweep. His leg was aching from the shrapnel he had taken. The deep gash in his side bled through the bandages. His neck burned from the bite he had received. Keppler reveled in it. The pain became another part of his penance. He endured it as he had learned to endure all things.

Reaching the twisted wreckage of an American tank destroyer near the four-story apartment, Keppler crawled around the front of it, careful not to make any noise. On the other side laying prone in a small depression he saw the first American. It was one of the sniper's security team carefully concealed to guard the approach to the house. The enemy soldier was facing the other way and did not notice Keppler behind him.

Keppler looked away from the man. He had learned that if you stare at an enemy soldier he would become aware of danger. Men whose senses were attuned to combat could feel your stare. He focused on the rubble beside the man and slowly drew out his knife. He moved up behind the paratrooper without a sound and grabbed the American with his free hand, clamping over the enemy soldier's mouth and nose. He drove the knife up under the jaw and into the American's brain killing him instantly.

Keppler was careful to prop the American back up with his rifle as if nothing had happened. He melted back into the rubble and moved on to where he knew he would find the other member of the sniper's security team.

He made his way up and over a large pile of rubble that used to be the front of a house. Once on the other side he saw a brief flash of movement to his left. Keppler's heart was pounding hard in his chest as he waited for the enemy bullet to pierce his body, but nothing came. The movement turned out to be a tattered piece of cloth flapping gently in the cold air, caught on a piece of re-bar in the rubble.

Just as Keppler was about to breath out a sigh of relief, he heard the clicking of a magazine being replaced on a rifle. He whirled to his right, the direction of the noise, but still he could see nothing. Moving slowly, careful not to disturb the rubble too much under his boots, Keppler crept towards the inner ruins of the house, his blood thumping in his ears so hard it drowned out the gunfire in the distance. The walls of the home were so decimated that they were only about waist high on him, their ruins strewn around on the ground and making even the simple task of walking a chore. He moved to the closest wall and was careful to stay low. The wall had yellow flowered wallpaper on it and Keppler noted how it stuck out in the midst of all the destruction.

Another sound came to his ears, this time the scrape of a boot sole on brick. It was on the other side of the wall! He gripped his rifle until his knuckles were white, wondering what he would find on the other side of the yellow flowered wall. He jumped up swinging his rifle around. An American soldier looked up just in time to get the butt of Keppler's rifle in his face. He rolled over the wall and with his knife slit the unconscious man's throat.

The sharp crack of the sniper's rifle caused Keppler to jump. Fortunately, the shot had been fired out towards the street. The sniper did not know his security team had been killed. Now it was just the sniper and Keppler.

The buildings around Keppler seemed like a ghost town and made the hunt more personal. Another rifle crack pulled Keppler's gaze up. The sniper was exactly where Keppler had thought he would be. A small wisp of smoke from a fourth floor window betrayed the sniper's position. A third shot cracked the air. The sniper was after someone. Keppler slowly opened the chamber of his rifle to make sure there was a live round there and then he latched it shut again.

When he went into the remains of the apartment building, Keppler discovered the staircase was blown apart and that there was no way to the top floor except for a rope hanging down through a hole in the roof. Cautiously, Keppler moved up to the rope and looked through the three-meter hole in the ceiling of the room. The rope carried on up to the fourth floor, strung up through the succeeding holes in the other levels of the building.

Keppler thought about climbing the rope, but he noticed a can tied to the top. He knew it would be filled with rocks that would rattle and warn the sniper of someone's approach and earn Keppler a bullet in the head for his stupidity.

Looking around he quickly formulated another plan. He moved back outside and over to the neighboring building that stood two stories above the ground. He made his way carefully up the partial staircase painfully aware that he might not have found all of the sniper's security team.

At the top of the rickety stairs, Keppler had to jump over a large hole in the floor that dropped all the way down into the basement of the shattered building. He moved out into the open floor space of the building. He felt exposed with one of the walls crumbled away, leaving the whole side of the room open to the outside. He carefully walked up to the edge of the floor and looked up to see if he could get a shot off from this angle.

He could see the sniper's window clearly now. He watched for another telltale sign the sniper was still there, something like a wisp of smoke or steam from the man's warm exhale in the cold, but there was nothing. His gut twisted with fear as he waited to see any sign of the sniper.

'He could have noticed his dead security team by now and climbed down the rope. He could have me sighted in from the ground below and I wouldn't even know it.' The image of crosshairs being sighted in on his chest or his head played over and over in his mind until he was almost ready to retreat back into the building. He fought the urge and stood his ground. It was all part of the penance. He was seeking absolution and if it earned him a sniper's bullet in the head, then he would accept it.

It was difficult not to breathe out hard with a sigh of relief when the sniper's rifle barrel again appeared at the window and he saw the sniper leaning out slightly trying to get a good angle on a target back on the main road. Keppler brought his rifle all the way up and took careful aim.

The sniper was fast, sensing the danger he brought his rifle down quickly towards Keppler. Keppler relaxed, exhaled, and squeezed the trigger. The sniper's round ripped at Keppler's coat sleeve tearing out a large chunk of fabric at the same time Keppler's bullet impacted into the neck of the sniper.

The man's throat exploded in a red spray all over the side of the window as he flew back into the building from whence he came.

Dropping his rifle down Keppler did not bother to look at his sleeve. He ran for the decrepit staircase and leapt over the hole that plunged to the basement. If the sniper had more security they would be all over him soon. He reached the bottom of the stairs in the house and waited to hear the sound of a boot scrape or the rattle of equipment or the clicking of a weapon, but there was nothing. Moving to the side of the building, Keppler's wounded leg began to seize up. It was getting difficult to walk. He hoped he did not have to fight his way back to the main road.

The distraction of hunting the sniper was over and the memory of Koch's eyes boring into him as he suffocated the child came crashing back into his memory. Keppler tried to hold it back, but he could not keep it from replaying in his mind. He had not only failed to protect these boys, he had resorted to killing them himself with his bare hands. Keppler knew he could never forgive himself, and there was no penance he could do to erase his deed.

Chapter 31

Bastogne Belgium

Captain Manser walked down the road towards the Division's rear. He could not keep his hands from shaking and felt some shame in his competence as a combat officer. When Wagner and the other men had appeared he had been cowering in the rubble, unable to move. He was glad that they did not suspect him of being a coward and he was happier still to be able to walk away from the fighting.

The attack had not gone as he had planned and he was tempted to ask for a transfer, as Colonel Faust did not seem to take him seriously enough. Manser believed his talents as an officer were wasted in the line and put to better use in the command bunker going over the maps and battle plans.

Manser looked up and blinked hard. He could not believe his eyes. There walking towards him with a small armed guard was Colonel Faust.

"Manser!" the Colonel bellowed. "What are you doing back here?" His face was turning red with anger at the sight of the Captain walking towards him. "Why aren't you up with your Kompanie?"

Manser wished he could shrink back into the rubble and hide, but it was too late. "I was coming back for reinforcements!" he lied. "I sent two runners and neither one of them returned so I decided to come myself!" He hoped he was not shaking too much and giving his deception away.

The Colonel was quiet for a moment staring into Manser's eyes as he walked closer trying to see if the lie was there. Then before he could say anything to refute Manser's answer, the side of the Colonel's head exploded. The sound of the sniper's shot traveled right behind the bullet, which meant the sniper close.

Manser dove behind a pile of rubble and tried to cover himself with some of the loose bricks. The Colonel's security force scattered for the building beside them, leaving the Colonel's dead body laying in the street with the countless others who were steaming on the ground to eventually freeze solid.

A second round impacted into the bricks Manser had sought cover behind and he started to shake harder. The sniper was aiming at him now and there was nothing he could do about it! A third shot claimed one of the Colonel's men as he ran up some stairs for shelter.

He tried to look behind himself at his outstretched legs to see if any part of him was exposed, but Manser did not want to move around too much in case he exposed any part of his head. The distant sound of battle was the only noise Manser could hear above his own labored breathing and the thumping of his heart in his chest.

He lay there waiting for the sniper to end his life, but nothing happened. He chanced a glance over to where the Colonel's body lay in the street and he began to feel some elation. 'With the Colonel gone, I am the next one in line to be promoted! I will finally be made a Colonel!' He reveled in the thought for a long time. He did not know how long he had been laying in the rubble, but Manser started to believe that the sniper moved on. He started to move around. 'I am now the commanding officer of the regiment! I can't afford to stay hiding any longer. There is a battle to be won!'

Manser, lost in his thoughts for personal glory, got to his feet and called out for the security team to come out of their hiding places as he needed to get back up to the regiment. Two rifle shots almost in succession of each other echoed above the distant fighting and sent Manser diving back down into the rubble pile from where he had just emerged. He stayed there for a moment until he realized that no bullets had come near him. He felt foolish for diving into the rubble and called for the security team to come out immediately. The team did not appear.

Manser got to his feet; angry at the lack of respect he was receiving. He marched to the doorway where he had seen the security team flee for cover. Standing in the doorway, Manser looked down at the cowering men inside,

"Get to your feet!" he commanded. The small team leapt up at his order. "I am assuming command of the Battalion in Colonel Faust's recent demise. I need to get up to the front." The team looked at each other and then moved out of the house without saying anything to each other, or to Manser.

Chapter 32

Bastogne Belgium

Wagner pressed a fresh clip into his magazine. The Americans had brought up two more tanks and were sending 35mm rounds into some of the houses. He was not sure how much longer they could hold the line. He brought his rifle back up to the hole he had been shooting through and watched as a stream of liquid fire shot out and engulfed one of the American Sherman tanks.

Someone had gotten close enough to use a flame-thrower. The American tank was covered in flames, the liquid fire pouring into the interior of the tank through cracks and seams around the hatches. It did not take long for the top of the tank to open and give birth to a human torch. The tanker emerged trying to escape from the flames. He was shot before his torso cleared the hatch.

Down in the rubble a huge fireball emerged, the sound of the explosion reaching Wagner a second after he saw the flames. One of the Americans had hit the flame-thrower. Wagner came out of his trance and shot a round off at an American helmet that had popped up in a window across the street, but his bullet missed impacting on the concrete wall and sending the helmet back below the windowsill.

He had just chambered another round when the floor underneath him heaved upwards and then collapsed angling to the floor below. A tank had fired a round into the house and the floor under him gave way. He slid down the collapsed floor as if it were a slide and landed hard amid bricks and dust on the first floor of the house.

Wagner had the wind knocked out of him. He struggled for breath in the dust-choked interior. There was a huge hole in the wall on the main floor where the tank shell had hit. There was no more firing from inside the house and Wagner searched around in the thick dust for his rifle.

A couple of the original defenders from the corporal's truppen made their way past him in the swirling smoke and dust, coughing, to the back door and left the house. Wagner got shakily to his knees still feeling around the rubble for his rifle but could not find it. Unsteadily standing on his rubbery legs, he looked around for any signs of his truppen.

Movement in the rubble caught his eye and Wagner walked over to discover Henke half-buried under bricks. He pulled the youth clear and stood him on his feet.

"Are you okay?" Wagner asked. Henke looked blankly at Wagner and then nodded an affirmative. "Where is everyone else?" Wagner asked looking around the dusty room. As the powder cleared a little through the massive hole in the wall he could see dust covered humps all around him. He bent over several of them checking the boys from his truppen. They were twisted into strange angles and some of them had blood trickling out of their ears or mouths. The house had become a tomb. His entire truppen had been wiped out with the exception of Henke. Wagner did not know what to do. He dropped to the dust-covered floor and hugged his legs, rocking back and forth. He fought the tears that welled up in his burning eyes.

"What are we going to do Sergeant?" Henke was scared. Wagner looked sternly at Henke and then softened. He still had a responsibility to Henke. He realized that Henke was shaking him slightly trying to get Wagner to stand up.

"We get the hell out of here," Wagner said. He knew it was hopeless to try and hold the house now. He chanced a quick glance out of the massive hole and could see the Americans advancing all along their line through the rubble. "It looks like the whole regiment is retreating."

He bent down and picked up an Mp40 machinegun from one of the corpses and a couple of grenades out of the man's belt. He realized the body he was pilfering was that of the corporal who had greeted him. "Get a weapon Henke and let's get out of here!"

Henke bent down and picked up a rifle from the lifeless fingers of another defender and they both made for the back door. They had just exited from the house when grenades started to go off behind them. The Americans had come knocking. The guilt and feeling of failure Wagner felt at loosing his men was replaced by a fear that gripped him at the very core. He had never retreated before and as he ran through the rubble strewn streets with Henke he hoped he never had to do it again. Grown men and other Hitler Youth were running all around him, trying to keep ahead of the American advance. It looked to Wagner like the whole world was coming apart.

The regiment's retreat was more like a rout; the hard-pressed soldiers had reached their breaking point. The 12th Panzer Division had advanced farther than any other unit into the American fortress of Bastogne, only a few hundred feet into the city before being thrown back. Their timing had been poor, as the 7th Armored Division had reinforced the 101st Airborne.

Wagner and Henke ran down the rubble-strewn road towards the rear, keeping pace with the others around them. Hundreds of retreating SS moved through the yards and houses to put some space between them and the attacking Americans. Wagner's panic started to subside at the sight of so many German soldiers running away. It was a weird feeling, but Wagner suddenly began to feel strangely numb to it all. The feeling helped, as he was able to concentrate on keeping his footing in the debris that covered the ground instead of how hard his heart was pumping in his chest.

He came around a corner, Henke in tow, and almost knocked Captain Manser over who was making his way up to the front with the security squad.

"Wagner! Where are you going?" Manser asked, half-annoyed at being run into and half terrified at the sight of the running soldiers all around him.

"The regiment's line broke. The entire battalion is retreating." Wagner said, regaining all his composure in sight of the coward before him.

"But I am now the regimental commander and I order them to hold!" Manser actually stamped his foot on the ground in protest of the retreat going on around him.

"Good luck telling them that," Wagner said waving his hand around him. It was then he realized that he spoke to Manser as if he were an equal. He had not called him Sir or answered him with Sir, but Manser was too flustered to notice.

Manser turned to the security team with him and ordered them to withdraw. Manser then turned and joined the platoons and Kompanies in their retreat. Wagner trotted with Henke behind Manser, wondering what would become of them. They had failed. That much was clear. The American lines had held and pushed the weight of the panzer division back.

The Division's withdrawal came to a halt near the outskirts of Bastogne where the badly mauled regiments took up defensive positions in the rubble ruins they had fought so hard to clear of the enemy. The battalion's Kompanies dug in and waited for their orders.

Manser set up his headquarters in a basement and started to beg XLVII Panzer Corps over the radio for reinforcements. He was told that there were none to give him. Manser was ordered to hold onto his piece of Bastogne at all costs and if possible retake the ground lost. After receiving his orders Manser put in a good accounting for himself. He spared no words to describe how he personally stopped the retreat of the Battalion after the death of Colonel Faust. He continued to explain how he also stabilized the lines despite the determined American attacks.

The truth of the matter was the soldiers had turned to face the enemy on their own, having nowhere else to go except back across an open field. Manser was promoted over the radio and told that a commendation was sure to follow.

Wagner dug in with the rest of the Kompanie's remains to await the renewed American attacks, but they never came. It seemed the Americans were taking a breather from the fighting as well.

"I see you managed to stay alive." Wagner whirled around at the sound of the voice to see Keppler leaning on his rifle, his leg bandaged up.

"Lieutenant!" Wagner jumped up and embraced Keppler before he got control of himself and dropped his arms, backing away. "I'm glad to see you made it out okay Sir. I was worried about you." Wagner felt a rush of relief wave over him at the sight of Keppler. With Keppler back in charge Wagner felt that their chances for survival were being increased.

"What about the rest of the truppen?" Keppler asked avoiding eye contact with Henke.

"Henke is my truppen." Wagner replied. Keppler looked at Henke and then averted his guilt-ridden glance. He thought of Henke's pleas for him to help Koch and the boy's smothered face oozed into Keppler's consciousness.

"Is the Kompanie in similar shape?" Keppler asked trying to keep from breaking down in front of these boys.

"Right now, it's more like the size of a platoon instead of a Kompanie." Wagner replied, looking down at his boots.

"Did Koch make it? Is he going to be okay Lieutenant?" Henke was looking around Keppler as if Koch might waiting behind him.

Keppler hung his head. The frantic look in Koch's eyes plagued him. He could feel Koch squirming under his hand as he fought for breath. Shame continued to wave over him. The retribution of hunting the sniper seemed even more ridiculous now as he forced himself to look into Henke's eyes.

"He didn't make it." Keppler choked and flopped to the ground in a sitting position to stare at his boots. Henke fell into Wagner's shoulder and cried. After a few minutes Henke regained control of himself and wiped his frozen cheeks with the back of his hand.

"All my friends are dead." Henke whimpered.

Keppler and Wagner let the comment go unanswered. After a long uncomfortable silence, Wagner opened his pack and pulled out some rations. Soon all three of them, happy for something to occupy their minds, devoured the rations of sausage and black bread. They all ate in silence, as if it was their last supper.

Nighttime came and in the dark, bitter cold sporadic fighting resumed. The Americans probed the lines with patrols trying to determine the strength and position of the Battalion. Wagner was too tired to be scared and spent his time counting the rounds of ammunition he had left. It was not much; he was short of rounds like everyone else.

He had traded his Mp40 as soon as he could for a Mauser 98k. He had more ammo for the Mauser than the machinegun, but it was not going to last long in a firefight.

Chapter 33

Bastogne Belgium

When morning came, word spread among the Kompanie that the military police had found Lubbert. He was discovered hiding in a coal shed several kilometers in the rear and was being transferred for punishment to the regiment. They were bringing him back this very moment at Manser's request. He had insisted that he be the one to do the honors of punishing Lubbert personally. Manser was beside himself with rage, pacing back and forth in his basement bunker, muttering something about his disbelief that one of his own had become a deserter. Keppler knew that Manser's justice would be swift and merciless. Wagner also knew this and Keppler was not surprised that Wagner sought him out as soon as he heard the news.

"What are they going to do with him?" Wagner had moved next to Keppler so he could talk quietly with the Lieutenant. They stood outside the command bunker as ordered to await the arrival of Lubbert.

"The standing orders are to shoot deserters." Keppler muttered, his mind racing to think of a way to save Lubbert.

"They're going to shoot little Lubbert?" Wagner was horrified. "He's only ten years old! Can't they take that into account?"

"Manser doesn't care," Keppler said.

Just then a truck drove up with some supplies for the battalion and two military police jumped out of the back. Lubbert was with them. As they pushed him forward, Keppler noticed how small Lubbert really was.

'He's just a child,' Keppler thought, 'like the rest of them.'

Lubbert had already been stripped of his equipment. He was wearing his camouflage tunic and pants. He was just a small boy, playing soldier. Keppler looked around at the remnants of the Kompanie gathered here at Manser's order to witness Lubbert's execution. Many of them were just young boys.

"Bring him here." Manser commanded as he emerged from his bunker.

The military police shoved Lubbert towards Manser and he gave Lubbert

201

a backhand across the face, knocking him to the ground. "You are a grave disappointment to me. I will ensure that your family suffers the same fate as you do." Manser turned to Keppler and pointed to Wagner and Henke.

"Lieutenant, form a firing squad out of Lubbert's truppen. I want this deserter shot." Keppler stood there with his mouth locked shut, unsure of what he should do. He knew he could not obey the order, and would rather be shot with Lubbert than have to endure the agony of carrying out the command. Manser noted Keppler's hesitation and became enraged.

"Did you hear me Lieutenant! I said gather the men and have this traitor shot!" Manser had pulled his lugar out of its holster and was waving it around in the air to add emphasis to his words. Manser gripped Lubbert by the front of his tunic and pulled him to his feet. Lubbert's eyes were full of fear and some blood trickled from his nose where Manser had struck him.

Keppler felt the memory resurfacing like an incoming shell. It hit with the force of a bullet and the rubble landscape around him melted away. He was there again, standing on the train platform with his companions. The Russian boy was looking right into his eyes. The SS Captain waded through the crowd to the boy and picked him up. Keppler did not try to fight the memory this time; he let it run its course. The lugar went off and the small Russian's body fell to the wooden platform with a loud thump. The massed civilians broke out into a riot fearing for their lives. They attacked the Captain who had foolishly placed himself in the middle of a mob. Keppler and the others received their orders to open fire and they all raised their weapons and began to shoot the women and children on the platform, most of them had only been trying to flee the massacre. None of them made it. Georg looked down at the slaughtered people at their feet when the ordeal was over. "We don't deserve to win this war." Georg said quietly, and Keppler nodded his head in agreement.

The waking dream came to an end and Keppler realized that Manser was now standing right in front of him yelling at the top of his lungs. "Keppler what are you doing! I told you to shoot this man!" In a rage Manser turned and still holding Lubbert by the front of his tunic raised his own lugar up and to Lubbert's head.

Keppler could restrain himself no longer. With amazing speed he drew the Hitler Youth knife Manser had given him five years ago and rammed it to the hilt into Manser's neck. Manser's eyes flew wide at the blow and lost his grip on Lubbert who fell to the ground. The lugar in Manser's hand went off as he jerked the round careening harmlessly off into the ruins.

The military police stood frozen in shock at what they had just witnessed, as did the rest of the Kompanie. Manser shook, trying to form words with his mouth, but nothing came out, his mouth managing only to make popping sounds. Time slowed down for Keppler and Manser dropped at a snail's pace. One of the military police opened his mouth and started to bring his weapon up. Keppler could not make out the man's words, as they were lost in the slowing of time. He watched Manser hit the ground, snow lifting up and away from his point of impact.

The military policeman that was bringing his weapon up suddenly went down, shot in the chest by Wagner. Before anyone else could react to the killing of Manser and the military policeman, all hell broke loose.

Rounds whipped by Keppler, one of them claiming the second military policeman who had started to dive for cover. Keppler turned to face the incoming rounds as time resumed its natural speed. The Americans were attacking in force. He felt no desire to fight any more. He slacked the grip on his rifle that hung in his left hand and he let it fall to the ground.

Keppler lifted his arms up and out towards the attacking Americans as if to embrace them. He would finally be released. Looking to his right he saw Georg leaning up against a crumbling wall. His old friend looked young and fresh like the early days. Georg smiled, "You know we never did deserve to win this war," he mouthed to Keppler.

Keppler did not feel the impact of the bullet that hit him until after he spun around from its force onto the snow-covered ground. He landed beside Manser's dead body. Keppler felt joy as he watched blood run out of his own mouth onto the white snow. It was a serious wound, he could tell.

"You did it." Keppler knew the voice. He used all of his energy to turn his head to the side to face Heini. Heini sat cross-legged and smiling on the ground beside him. His blood soaked tunic fluttered slightly in the breeze as he reached out and touched Keppler's forehead. "You did it Keppler, you did your duty." Heini brushed one of the hairs back from Keppler's face. "I'm so very proud of you." Keppler gasped for breath but it would not come. Keppler could feel a wave of peace wash over him as Heini watched him die.

Chapter 34

Bastogne Belgium

After shooting the Military Policeman, Wagner was forced to turn and meet the charging Americans. Out of the corner of his eye he had seen Keppler go down but he dare not look to see if he was okay. He chambered another round and aimed at one of the attacking paratroopers. Wagner fired again and again, his target finally going down.

Wagner refilled his magazine and was about to chamber another round just as a bullet smashed into his chest. His helmet was knocked down over his eyes, and his breath caught in his throat. He felt constricted lying on his back and tried to get up. Someone jumped onto him and straddled his legs. The man grabbed him by the brim of his helmet, jerking his head back. It was the moment Wagner had feared since he was ten! There above him, knife raised up to start the torture Manser had promised them all, was an American Indian!

'Oh no!' Wagner thought, 'here comes the torture!' Despite the lack of breath and the black spots that were now floating before his eyes, Wagner flailed his fists against the chest of his attacker and tried to get away from him. The American Indian kneeled over him and stared. The knife wavered in the air above him, ready to begin the horrible art of torture, but it did not fall. Instead, the knife stayed poised.

Wagner felt himself losing consciousness and somehow he knew he was dying. He always thought he would fear death, but now, facing the horrors of torture, he saw death as an escape. 'I have cheated him.' He smiled and closed his eyes.

Chapter 35

Bastogne Belgium

Lubbert was the only one in the Kompanie who was not shot or engaged in hand-to-hand combat. He stood there frozen with fear; his hands were in the air waiting for the enemy to shoot him, but nothing happen. Everything had materialized so quickly: Keppler killing Manser, Wagner shooting the policeman, then the attack. Now SS soldiers from the regiment were breaking and running. Lubbert did not know what to do. He just stood there with his hands still in the air.

One of the Americans came over to little Lubbert as the fighting diminished. The noise of warfare faded out towards the tree line. The strain was too much and the SS battalion had been routed. Lubbert was now a prisoner of war. The American grabbed Lubbert's hands and tied them behind his back. He then led Lubbert away from the distant sounds of fighting.

Then Lubbert saw him. There before him sat an American Indian! He was sitting down beside Wagner and Lubbert's legs went limp with fear. Strong hands on his arms kept him from falling to the ground. 'He's tortured Wagner to death and now he's going to torture me!'

The American Indian beside Wagner's body sadly returned his knife, unused to his belt.

'He wanted Wagner to last longer!' Lubbert thought. 'He's sad he couldn't torture him some more!'

It was then that the Indian looked up and his fixed his eyes on Lubbert. The Indian torturer stood up and walked over to him. The killer fumbled in his pocket and pulled out some chocolate, offering it to Lubbert.

'The chocolate! He knows I shot that American soldier on the ridge and then ate his chocolate with Wagner! How could he know about that?' Lubbert's fear waved over him until he thought he might actually drown in it. He was shaking uncontrollably. He wanted to run, but his legs were paralyzed by fright and all he managed was to jerk a little. He felt faint and started to cry.

Two Americans, one holding each arm, kept Lubbert on his feet and he felt shame wave over him as he looked down at Wagner's dead eyes and then over to Keppler who was lying in a growing puddle of blood, his eyes also empty of life. They had given the ultimate sacrifice, just like Manser said they all should do. Keppler and Wagner had saved him and died in the process.

He had run from his friends and now they were all dead! Everyone was dead! All the faces of Lubbert's friends started to flash across his mind. The faces accompanied by laughing and songs all flooded in from his memory like a chant to haunt him. The American Indian had mercifully disappeared from Lubbert's sight and he allowed himself to be dragged further and further behind enemy lines, his legs useless with fright.

"Watch him close Jim, he may be small but I've seen these kids kill if they get the chance. They are bred and trained for killing." Lubbert felt both of the hands holding his arms tighten at the comment. He tried to look around him and see what was going on, but his eyes were too blurry with tears to see anything. He wanted to wipe his eyes but his hands were tied securely behind his back.

"Just take it easy kid and you won't get hurt." It was the same voice that had warned 'Jim' to be wary. Lubbert stayed limp, not wanting to make things any worse than they already were.

Chapter 36

London England

A month later Lubbert found himself in a prisoner of war camp just outside of London. The British had, in Lubbert's mind, mercifully delivered him from the American Indians that Manser promised would torture him. The German prisoners in the camp assured Lubbert that he would get to go home when the war was over and they all fussed over him, making sure he brushed his teeth and combed his hair. He was one of a few Hitler Youth transferred here after the fighting in Belgium. Most of the others ended up in camps throughout France.

Lubbert had been sent to London because he had lived there with his family before the war. There was hope among his British captors that they might be able to educate him and save him from the terrible brainwashing he had received. Lubbert had no idea what brainwashing was, but he went along anyway. He was willing to do anything to keep from getting tortured.

He was in a camp with men who had become accustomed to being prisoners of war. Some of these men he now found himself with had been prisoners of war since the allies had invaded in Normandy. They seemed to know what they were talking about when they told Lubbert that everything would be okay.

Because he was the smallest and youngest, the men in the camp had nicknamed Lubbert, "Little Soldier". Lubbert detested the title. He was not a soldier; he had failed his friends and his family. He had run away. Lubbert had thought many times of writing to his parents, but he could not bring himself to put pen to paper. They may have been relocated, or perhaps even killed. Lubbert was not even sure that the British would mail a letter for him. The Germany that once held so many childhood dreams for Lubbert now only came to him in nightmares. He ached to somehow apologize for his failure, but he did not know how.

Manser had said his parents would be killed for Lubbert's cowardice, but Keppler had saved him and finished Manser off before the orders to execute

209

Lubbert's family could be given. There was a chance they could still be alive. Lubbert choked back tears as he pictured them. They would set a place at the table every night as his mother had promised, with the hope that their son would make it home for dinner. They did not know where he was, or when he was coming home. In fact, Lubbert was uncertain whether he would ever see home again.

The British commander of the camp wanted Lubbert to be placed with a British family because of his age and his ability to speak English, but Lubbert resisted the idea with all his might. He had to stay here with his fellow prisoners because they were his only chance to get home. What if he left and the others were suddenly sent back to Germany? There was no way he would allow himself to be tricked into staying behind. The camp commander had found out where Lubbert's father used to work in London and sent people who used to work with his father to try and talk him into living with them. Lubbert had refused. Lubbert had been quite young when his family had left London to return to Germany, so he did not remember any of the people anyway.

An organization called the Red Cross sent volunteers every day to help out with the prisoners. These people had insisted that if Lubbert was to stay in the camp, he had to spend his days doing schoolwork. Due to his time as a soldier, they said he was far behind in his education. His last schoolteacher in Germany said there was no practical use in mastering reading, writing and mathematics at this time in history. They needed children like Lubbert to understand the superiority of the German race and the glorious battles that had been won by the highly developed German soldiers. Lubbert was taught all he needed to know about defending the Reich. He had been told that those would be the most important lessons he would ever learn. Now the Red Cross was telling him that he needed more education.

The most frustrating thing for Lubbert was the math. The only math he had taken in the last few years was regarding numbers of infantry in a truppen, a platoon, and a kompanie; how many rounds did a Mauser 98k hold in the magazine; how many artillery pieces constituted a battery. If the Red Cross schoolteacher had asked him any of these questions, he was sure she would have been impressed with the answers. Lubbert had learned however, not to volunteer any answers. The only time he had volunteered an answer was when he wrote a paragraph explaining the inferiority of the Jewish race. He had remembered it from one of his textbooks and thought the teacher would be very impressed with his sentence structure and grammar. He could not understand why the lady had turned red and ripped the page out of his notebook. After that, Lubbert never volunteered an answer again. He would count their pigs and sheep, and copy pages from a dictionary, trying to make sense of their practical value. He had been at the top of his class at home. Now, these studies seemed difficult, confusing, and a waste of time. He was sure it was supposed to make him feel inferior somehow.

Frustrated by his studies and lonely for home, Lubbert spent as much time by himself as he could. Today, the lessons seemed harder than usual and he needed some air to clear his head. He asked to be excused and walked outside to the fence at the end of the yard. He hooked his fingers into the wire as he watched a group of British children playing a few meters away on the other side. The small group, as many others had, came with curiosity to watch the German prisoners. These ones had quickly become bored with what they saw. They had joined hands and were dancing around in a circle singing a song Lubbert was not familiar with. Lubbert was intrigued by the game, until he saw how it ended. These children were falling; just as he had seen his friends fall on the battlefields of Belgium. The difference was that these children fell for fun. There was no blood, no vacant expression, and they could get up again. They fell laughing and Lubbert hated them for it. A tear rolled down his cheek, as they started up again. He could not bear to watch, but the sickening melody of their jolly game followed him back into the classroom.

"Ring around the rosy, pocket full of poesy, husha, husha, they all fall down!"

Printed in the United States
1396800005B/34-36